CATASTROPHE IN LE TOUQUET

PETER CHILD

Benbow Publications

Published in 2006 by Benbow Publications

British Library
Cataloguing in Publication Data.

ISBN: 0–9540910–5–1

Printed by Lightning Source UK Limited,
6 Precedent Drive, Rooksley,
Milton Keynes, MK13 8PR

First Edition

THE MICHEL RONAY TRILOGY

MARSEILLE TAXI

AUGUST IN GRAMBOIS

CHRISTMAS IN MARSEILLE

OTHER TITLES BY THE AUTHOR

VEHICLE PAINTER'S NOTES

VEHICLE FINE FINISHING

VEHICLE FABRICATIONS IN G.R.P.

NOTES FOR GOOD DRIVERS

NOTES FOR COMPANY DRIVERS

ACKNOWLEDGEMENTS

Once again, I wish to gratefully acknowledge the help and assistance given to me by Sue Gresham, who edited and set out the book, and Wendy Tobitt for the splendid cover presentation. Without these talented and patient ladies this book would not have been possible.

Peter Child

INTRODUCTION

Le Touquet is a beautiful and stylish French coastal town which has developed and flourished since 1837 when a notary called Alphonse Daloz bought the land in the hope that it was arable. He planted an assortment of vegetables and cereals, pine and other trees in an attempt to create a business. Unfortunately only the trees survived but by the turn of the century they had matured into a beautiful pine forest by the sea. In 1903 two Englishmen bought the forest and commenced the building of luxury villas and hotels. After advertising in London, the English became aware of Le Touquet and it soon became very fashionable for the wealthy to spend time and money in this idyllic place.

By the 1920's it had become the place to be for 'le weekend'. Now mostly rich Parisians own the expensive villas in the forest and some say it represents a little Paris by the sea and is reflected in the name Le Touquet Paris-Plage.

The chic and best shopping is at Rue St. Jean, which stretches from the seafront to the Casino and is the ideal place for Michel Ronay, a taxi driver, and his cousin, Henri to set up a business catering for the many tourists who visit each year. With Michel's mistress, Josette, Henri and his wife, Jackie, her mother, Josephine, and Uncle Pascal along with all the other members of the family there to lend a hand, what could possibly go wrong?

CHAPTER 1

Michel Ronay awoke; face down in the luxurious bed he had bought just before Christmas, to find his fiancé, Josette, snuggled underneath his left side, her thick black hair caught up around his face and the scent of her delicate perfume invading his senses. He kissed her gently on the lips and murmured "I'll always be with you, ma petite, now and for evermore."

Michel had made up his mind and there was no going back. Yesterday he had left Monique, his second wife, her son Frederik and all her family at the villa in Grambois.

The run up to Christmas had been more than eventful and he had realised in the most desperate moments that the only thing that mattered to him was the love he felt for Josette. All his mistresses paled into a dim glow of insignificance when compared with the incomparable Josette. Naturally he would miss the fortune to be inherited in cash and property that would have come from Monique's relations, but he knew that to be true to himself and the love of his life, he would have to forgo a fortune. Not easy at any time of life and certainly harder to bear the older one became. On the positive side, however, there was the great business opportunity before him with cousin Henri in Le Touquet. They were going into the tourist industry, offering all manner of tours and amenities to attract the British and Americans who ventured into France on holiday. No stone would be left unturned, no opportunity missed to provide whatever the discerning holiday maker wished for, at the right price of course. Michel and Henri had mutually agreed what the right price would be. It was any amount possible that ensured they were millionaires within a year. 'A good, positive financial plan to start any business' thought Michel, as he lay comfortably in the warm bed with Josette. In an instant he would be transformed from a harassed Marseille taxi driver to a millionaire with all the luxuries that go with such financial status.

Michel thought about the two weeks up to Christmas; Edward Salvator, a crook of the very worst kind, had been killed in a car crash and his evil son, Claude, had been arrested by Cyril Gerrard and his stout band of gendarmes, aided by Michel, and was now in custody much to his relief. All of Michel's mistresses had been attended to in the nicest way possible and kissed goodbye. There had been a few tears but he had braved each situation. It is a problem when you are so popular. Finally, he had told Monique that he was leaving her and he wanted a divorce. She had cried a little, but deep in her heart she did not believe that he would divorce her and she was sure that he would be back in time. Monique knew her husband too well and the lure of a comfortable home life and a wife who tolerated all his mistresses with the added financial bonus of her inheritance would ensure his safe return in due course.

"Ma petite" murmured Josette as she stirred from a deep sleep. Michel kissed her again and whispered "I'll make us some coffee."

"Oh, Michel, I do love you." He smiled and kissed her again before slipping from the bed and making his way to the kitchen.

An hour later the lovers had showered, dressed and were seated at the kitchen table eating warm croissants with honey as they sipped more coffee.

"We're going to Le Touquet?" queried Josette.

"Oui, ma petite, Le Touquet, I'm going into the tourist business with my cousin Henri."

"But you're a taxi driver, here in Marseille" she replied.

"Not any more, ma petite, we have a new and exciting life ahead of us."

"I'm not sure I want to go to Le Touquet" she said ruefully.

"Why not?"

"Michel, it's right up north, near Calais, its cold up there all year round and you know what the northerners are like."

"Non, I don't."

"Precisely, you're planning to start a business that you know nothing about in a place you've never been to with a relative, who up until Christmas, you hadn't seen for years and didn't like!"

"I know, but I've discussed the whole thing thoroughly with Henri and I'm sure it will work."

"When did you discuss this great business venture?"

"On the way to Orange, when we went to collect Alexis and Hélène after their car accident."

"Michel, I don't think you've thought this through and you're using this misguided opportunity to run away from Marseille."

"I'm not running away, I'm starting a new life with you, ma

petite, I know we'll be successful and happy in Le Touquet."

"I'm not convinced."

"Josette, I promise you that….."

"Michel, we've only just moved into this flat" she interrupted.

"I know."

"I want to stay here in Marseille; can't you start the business here?"

"Non, ma petite, look Henri has got everything arranged, we have a house to move into straight away…."

"A house?"

"Oui, our own house, Henri inherited it and has given it to us for the time being, that is until we buy something luxurious for ourselves in the country."

"Oh" she said quietly and Michel felt that he was at last winning her round.

"And we'll certainly need some extra room if we start a family after we're married in the spring."

She warmed a little at that.

"Oui" she replied.

"It's a great opportunity for both of us; to start a new life together, that's what you want, isn't it?"

"Oui" she replied "but I wanted a new life here in Marseille, not up north."

"Listen, ma chérie, if Henri and I work together, we'll be well off, better than we've ever been or ever could be here in Marseille" Michel said firmly.

"Do you really think so?" she asked plaintively.

"Oui, I do think so" replied Michel emphatically, unsure whether he had convinced her or not.

"If you're so sure, I guess I'd better start packing" she replied half heartedly.

"Bon, the sooner we get everything tied up here the sooner we can start the business in Le Touquet" he said with a smile.

Josette nodded and replied "I'm certainly going to miss being here."

"Ma chérie, we'll soon make friends and settle in, believe me."

"Bon" she replied quietly and without enthusiasm as she stood up from the table.

"Whilst you do that I'll sort the car out and get some fuel, it's a long way to Le Touquet" he said with a grin.

"Don't remind me" she mumbled under her breathe.

Michel stood up and gave his fiancé a light kiss on the cheek and after slipping into his warm jacket, left the flat. It was cold and bright in the street and Michel breathed deeply, he felt free at last.

Clearing the dusting of snow from the Mercedes windscreen Michele then slid quickly in behind the wheel. He was both excited and uncertain of what lay ahead and decided to pop into Ricky's bar first of all, to see if Antone was about. He felt that he needed to discuss his intended move with an intelligent and understanding person. The Mercedes eventually started up and with a puff of thick black diesel exhaust, Michel pulled out into the Rue du Camas and headed for le Vieux Port and Ricky's bar.

The traffic was light and he made good progress down la Canebiére, the main thoroughfare in Marseille, before swinging round into Rue Bonneterie and parking outside Ricky's. He entered his favourite bar, with its warm, snug interior and creaking wicker chairs. Jacques, the barman, looked up and smiled broadly.

"Bonjour, Michel, bonjour" he said excitedly.

"Bonjour, Jacques, ça va?"

"Oui, ça va, I didn't expect to see you so soon after Christmas, I thought you were up at Grambois with all the family" said a wide eyed Jacques.

"I was, but I'm here now, and they're still up there, thank heavens."

"So you're in Marseille with your fiancé then?" enquired Jacques as he poured a brandy for one of his best customers.

"Oui, but just for today" replied Michel as he picked up the glass and sipped at the golden liquid.

"Off somewhere nice then?"

"Le Touquet."

"Le Touquet! But that's up north, near Calais!" exclaimed Jacques.

"Correct" replied Michel.

"How long are you going for?" asked Jacques in a pained voice.

"For ever" came the reply.

"Oh, mon Dieu, mon Dieu, are you sure you know what you're doing?"

"Oui."

"Does your wife know?" asked Jacques as he poured a brandy for himself.

"Oui."

"And what did she say when you told her?"

"Nothing, she just cried" replied Michel slightly crestfallen.

"I think I'm going to cry too" whispered the gay barman.

"Oh, please don't cry, Jacques, I can't bear to see grown men cry" said Michel gently.

"You wait until Antone hears about this, he'll be shocked" whispered Jacques indignantly, as his eyes began to water.

"I know, and I hope to see him before I go" said Michel.

"He'll be in soon and he'll try to talk you out of it" said Jacques firmly with little tears running down his cheeks.

"Perhaps" replied Michel.

"I know he will" replied the tearful Jacques as he wiped his eyes on the cloth that he had taken from over his shoulder before using it to wipe the bar like a fussy mother hen.

They fell silent and Michel stared into his brandy. The bar was quiet with only a few of the very regulars sitting at the glass topped wicker tables reading, smoking and sipping at their drinks. Michel was glad, he did not want too many of his acquaintances close to him at this sensitive time. He began to realise the enormity of what he planned to do.

Jacques moved to the other end of the bar to serve one of the other customers who had struggled up from a table, coughing slightly, whilst Michel finished his brandy. Within moments of putting down the empty glass the corpulent form of Antone appeared at the door and with a flourish the great man entered, beaming as usual. He spotted Michel immediately.

"Michel, Michel, ça va?"

"Oui, bien sûr" replied Michel with a broad smile.

"Bon" replied Antone as he approached the bar.

Jacques poured his lover a brandy as Antone greeted him and then turning to Michel asked "What are you doing here; I thought you were in Grambois with your extended family?"

"I was, but I've left them there."

"Why, dear boy?"

"He's leaving!" interrupted Jacques.

Antone looked at Jacques and asked "have you been crying again?"

"Oui" mumbled the tearful Jacques.

"Why this time?" enquired Antone.

"Because he's leaving" replied Jacques as he dabbed his eyes with the bar cloth before wiping it once again over the bar top.

"Well I'm sure Michel will be back again this evening as usual" replied Antone in a genial tone.

"Non, you don't understand, he's leaving us for ever!" exclaimed Jacques.

Antone looked at Michel with amazement, took a large sip at his brandy and said "you're not going to commit suicide are you?"

"Non, I'm going to start a new life in Le Touquet" replied Michel.

"That's almost as bad" said Antone at which point Jacques cried a little more.

"Oh, do stop crying, dear, you know how it upsets me to see you cry, I mean, I can stand it when grown men cry, but not you."

Michel had to smile.

"Now, bring us more brandy and you'd better have a double for yourself, whilst I talk seriously to Michel about his future" said Antone with authority. He then led Michel to his favourite table at the rear of the premises. As they lowered themselves into the creaking chairs Michel said "I'm glad we've met today, I didn't want to go before seeing you."

"I arrived just in time, eh?"

"Oui."

"Do you really intend to go to Le Touquet?" asked Antone seriously.

"Oui."

"When?"

"Today."

"Today!" exclaimed Antone as Jacques arrived with double brandies for the two of them.

"Oui."

"You can't possibly go today" replied Antone as he sipped his brandy.

"Josette is back at the flat packing everything right now" replied Michel as he lifted the glass to his lips.

"Michel, you are in imminent danger of making a complete fool of yourself" said Antone seriously.

"Why, because I've made the decision to start a new life with Josette, away from here, away from Gerrard and Salvator and his cronies, away from Marseille and it's overcrowded streets, I'm fed up to the back teeth with driving a taxi all day and all night long, I need a change, I want a change and I'm going to have one" replied Michel with just a little anger in his voice.

"Michel, you are blinded by love to the realities of your situation, I promise you."

"I don't think so."

"I think you are infatuated with Josette and hiding behind that is your wish to run away from everything" replied Antone calmly.

"Non."

"And who can blame you?"

Michel sipped his brandy and slowly shook his head.

There was a short silence before Antone said gently "No one is the answer, you have had a difficult time over the last few months and this is your understandable reaction to it all."

"I'm going to start a business with cousin Henri in le Touquet, and he and I believe it will be a great success" said Michel firmly.

"Ah, cousin Henri, he and his wife are the couple that you dreaded coming to Marseille before Christmas as I remember" replied Antone with a curious smile.

"Well that was then."

"And what changed your mind in such a short time, pray?"

"I realised that Henri is a successful business man, well respected, and he sees in me a person who is ambitious and has lots of potential……"

"He's not risking much but you are risking everything" interrupted Antone.

"You obviously think I shouldn't go" replied Michel.

"I know you shouldn't go, Michel, it will be a catastrophe, a catastrophe in Le Touquet" said Antone as he finished his brandy.

"Well, it's my life" replied Michel.

"Indeed it is, all yours, but that fact must not deter your friends from trying to stop you ruining it" and with that Antone waved to Jacques for more brandy.

"Well I'm committed to it now" replied Michel half heartedly.

"Non my friend, you are not, just think it through and then tell

Henri."

"I've given my word."

"Ah, but given in the heat of burning, blinding passion, and now, after cool reflection, well, I'm sure Henri will understand" said Antone.

"He's from Le Touquet."

"Ah, oui, perhaps not then" replied Antone as Jacques arrived with two more double brandies.

"I shouldn't be drinking like this, I've got a long drive ahead of me today" said Michel.

"Take my advice and go tomorrow if you must, I mean one more day in Marseille with your friends is not going to make any difference to the rest of your life" said Antone in a reassuring tone.

"True" replied Michel as he sipped the brandy.

"Marseille" said Antone wistfully "the place where you were born, Michel, and everybody knows you and you know everybody. Have you considered how it will be to start afresh, as if you were just born in Le Touquet, why it'll take another lifetime before you are known as well as you are here. All those new friends and mistresses to meet, and will you be able to forget all those you have left behind?" Michel felt a little uncomfortable and sipped his brandy.

"I think I'd better have one of Jacques special baguettes to soak up some of this alcohol" said Michel.

"Good idea, I'll join you" and Antone waved to Jacques.

The bar was becoming both busy and noisy but in the midst of this Michel heard a voice he recognised. He turned slightly and saw René at the bar with Jacques nodding and then pointing in his direction. Antone saw Michel's friend at the same time.

"There's René" he chortled.

"So it is" replied Michel and smiled as his best friend approached.

"Michel, ça va?" beamed René.

"René" replied Michel.

"Come and join us" said Antone as he gestured towards a chair.

"Bonjour Antone and merci" replied René as he sat down opposite Michel.

"Well, this is a surprise, I thought you'd be heading up the autoroute to the cold north by now" said René before sipping his brandy.

"You knew this silly boy was going to leave Marseille?" asked Antone.

"Oui, he told me before Christmas."

"And, as his best friend, didn't you try to stop him?" demanded Antone.

"Well, non……"

"You're a fine friend then" interrupted Antone.

"Yvonne and I were too upset at the time to say much, really…."

"How do you think we feel? Jacques and I have only just found out, he's crying and I can't stop drinking, we're both in a terrible mess over it all, I put some of it down to shock, the rest to sadness" said Antone before he took a large gulp of brandy. Then Jacques arrived and said "I expect you all need one of my special baguettes" and he nodded.

"Bless you, dear, you're a positive mind reader" replied Antone and then, with a smile, Jacques rushed off to prepare his specials of mixed cheeses and Parma ham encased within crisp, warm, fluffy bread.

"When are you going?" asked René.

"This afternoon" replied Michel.

"Don't think so" said René and then continued "it's a long way to Le Touquet, a two day trip, and you've been drinking."

"I'm alright" replied Michel.

"I've already told him, another day here won't hurt" said Antone.

"It makes sense, Michel" said René gently.

"Josette is at the flat, packing, I've told her we're going today" replied Michel.

"Does she really want to go?" asked René.

"Well, it's a bit of an adventure, but I'm sure she'll be fine once we're there" said Michel.

"So she doesn't want to go then" said Antone with certainty.

"Oh, Antone, of course she wants to go, she wants to be with me" replied Michel testily.

"Oui, but she wants to be with you here in Marseille, not in some little tourist spot up north, cold and buffeted by the Atlantic ocean!"

"You don't understand" replied Michel and he took another sip of brandy and then peered down into the glass after he had replaced it on the table. He was now becoming more concerned with the situation, with doubts creeping in at the edges of his grand plan for a new life with Josette. They remained silent for a few moments, each deep in thought. Suddenly a voice they all knew broke the silence with "bonjour, Michel and mes amis." Michel raised his head quickly and saw the smiling face of Jean Gambetta.

"Bonjour, Jean" they all chorused.

"What are you doing here?" asked Michel.

"Taking a break after the Christmas rush" Jean grinned, and the picture of his dim and dusty little garage, full of old cars, in the Rue de Verdun off the Rue du Camas, sprang into Michel's mind.

"Michel is leaving" said René.

"Already? He hasn't bought me a drink yet!" exclaimed Jean as he eased himself into the chair next to Michel.

"Non he's leaving Marseille" said René.

"What for?" asked Jean.

"He's going to Le Touquet" said Antone.

"Why?" asked Jean.

"To start a business" replied René quietly.

"A business! Michel?" and with that Jean burst out laughing.

"It's true" said Michel.

"What sort of business? Car repairs, by any chance? You'll be your own best customer, Michel" and Jean laughed again.

"He's never coming back" said René sadly.

"Of course he's coming back, that's if he ever goes" replied Jean as Jacques arrived with the baguettes.

"They look good, I think I'll have one of those, Jacques, and a beer, s'il vous plait" said Jean.

"Oui, Jean" replied Jacques and he disappeared back into the crowded bar.

"I'm serious, Jean" said Michel.

"Really?" replied Jean in an unconcerned tone.

"I'm going to start a new life with Josette….."

"I knew there'd be a woman involved" interrupted Jean.

"And with Monique's cousin, Henri………"

"Does Monique know all about this?" interrupted Jean.

"Oui" replied Michel.

"And what did she say when you told her?" asked Jean as he looked Michel in the eye.

"She cried" said Michel.

"What, with relief that you're going, or sadness because she loves you and knows you're making a fool of yourself?" asked Jean with a smile. That went in deep and Michel felt even more uncomfortable hearing that from his late father's best friend. Jean Gambetta had been like a second father to Michel. The smiling, grey haired old man sitting next to Michel, knew him too well.

"Sadness, I think" replied Michel.

"Oui, of course" said Jean.

"But I'm determined to go, you only have one life, and I intend to change mine for the better" said Michel firmly.

"Bon" replied Jean with a twinkle in his eye. At that moment Jacques arrived with Jean's beer and baguette.

"Merci."

"Better have another round of drinks, Jacques, everybody, the same again?" asked Antone. They all nodded and Antone said "put it all on my bill, s'il vous plait."

They all remained quiet as they began to consume the delicious baguettes that Jacques had prepared and had just finished eating when he appeared with another round of drinks. They all drank to Michel, Josette and the new business venture with cousin Henri in Le Touquet. They had hardly finished the toasting to success when Jacques arrived with an anxious expression and said "Michel, Josette is on the 'phone for you." Michel went a little pale.

"Bon" he replied nervously.

"Bon chance, mon ami" said Antone with a smile as Michel left the table and headed for the little private corridor behind the bar. He picked up the 'phone slowly and held it to his ear.

"Oui, ma petite" he said quietly.

"Michel" she began in a firm tone "you went out ages ago to see to the car and get some fuel…."

"Oui, ma petite" he interrupted "but…….."

"You got held up in Ricky's bar!"

"I can explain everything……."

"When did Ricky's start selling fuel?"

"Ma petite……….."

"Better come home quick, Michel, or the trip to Le Touquet is off!" and with that she put the 'phone down.

"Mon Dieu" he whispered to himself.

"Well how is the little lady?" enquired Jean with a grin as Michel returned and slumped down in the creaking chair next to him.

"She's fine, all packed and ready to go" Michel lied.

"Better get you home then" said René.

"Oui" replied Michel.

"I'll drive you" said René.

"Oh, non" protested Michel.

"Listen, Michel, you've had far too much to drink, and it's too late to set off now" said René firmly.

"And it'll probably take you all evening to pacify Josette" smiled Antone. As good friends, none of them were fooled by Michel and his situation.

"OK" replied Michel as he finished his drink and then stood up to leave. They all looked at him for a moment before Jean left his seat and embraced Michel, kissing him on both cheeks, whilst whispering "au revoir, ma petite enfant." Michel felt he was welling up slightly. Then Antone stood and embraced him, clasping him hard to his portly frame.

"Bon chance, mon ami, bon chance" he said with feeling.

"Merci, Antone" Michel replied.

"Come on then, let's get you home" said René.

Michel followed his friend through the crowded bar and as they neared the door, Jacques rushed out from behind the bar and embraced Michel, kissing him on both cheeks several times. With tears running down his face he whispered "au, revoir, au revoir, mon ami, au revoir, I shall miss you so much." Michel felt quite moved by the re-action of all his life long friends to the news that he was leaving Marseille. He just nodded and left the warmth of the bar for the cold, bright Rue Bonneterie and René's taxi.

René was silent as they drove up la Canebiére in the busy afternoon traffic and only spoke as they turned into Rue du Camas.

"Michel, please come in and see Yvonne."

"What now?"

"Oui, she'll be so disappointed if you don't say au revoir."

"OK, I'm so late now I'm sure another few minutes won't

hurt."

"Merci, and I'll run you down in the morning to collect your car, just ring me when you're ready."

"Merci, René." There was a parking space just passed René's flat and as he pulled into it Michel hoped that Josette could not see them from her flat almost opposite. They hurried into the building and Michel followed his friend upstairs to his spacious apartment. Yvonne, René's statuesque wife, greeted her lover with a broad smile and twinkling eyes.

"Michel, ma petite" she cooed as she kissed him on both cheeks.

"Yvonne, ça va?"

"Oui, come in and sit down, I didn't expect to see you again for quite a while" she said as she waved Michel to the comfortable settee.

"A drink, Michel?"

"Non, chérie, black coffee for both of us" said René.

"Stayed too long at Ricky's perhaps?"

"Oui" mumbled Michel.

"You naughty boys" she laughed as she went out into the kitchen.

After two cups of sweet, black coffee, Michel felt a little more sober and his confidence began to return as he explained his business ideas to his friends. They were pleased for him but also anxious for its success. Michel painted a robust picture of the opportunities that lay ahead in Le Touquet and with grand gestures he invited them both to come and stay in August and witness for themselves the great success of the Michel and Henri partnership. All their little objections and cautions were swept aside by Michel's enthusiasm for the new life he had chosen for himself and his beloved Josette. Then he remembered, Josette was packed and still waiting for his return. He suddenly felt anxious and glanced at his watch. It was almost four o'clock and he had been gone for hours, had too much to drink and his Mercedes was still low on fuel and parked outside Ricky's in the Rue Bonneterie. It would all need some careful explaining to his fiancé.

"I must leave you now, ma petites" he said.

"So soon?" queried Yvonne.

"Oui."

"Will we see you before August?" she asked.

"I'm not sure, Henri and I are bound to be very busy, getting everything going, you understand, but if I can slip away for a day or two, I will" Michel replied.

"Well 'phone us and let us know how you're getting on" said René.

"I will, I promise" replied Michel, and then with hugs, embraces and many kisses he left his friends and made his way across the street to Josette's flat. He felt little pangs of anxiety as he turned the key in the door and let himself in.

"I'm back, ma chérie" he called gently. There was no reply and he found his beloved sitting on the settee looking decidedly annoyed.

"Well?" she asked.

"I'm back at last, chérie" he said as he went to kiss her.

"I can see that, Michel" she replied as she turned her head away.

"I'm sorry I've been so long, but…….."

"But; there's always a 'but', Michel, and I'm getting tired of it" she interrupted.

"But………"

"There you go again!" she exclaimed loudly.

"Will you listen to me or are you going to interrupt me every time I try to explain?" he shouted.

Suddenly he saw another side of Josette that he had never seen before. Was this the demure, petite, Princess of love who he had held a hundred times in his arms and often hurriedly made love to? He thought she sounded a little too much like Monique, his second wife, now staying at his villa in Grambois with the rest of her family. A touch of anxiety crept into his mind.

"I went down to le Vieux Port to get some fuel and I decided to pop into Ricky's to see if Antone was there……"

"Why did you want to see Antone?" she demanded.

"Because I wanted his advice on some aspects of the business" he replied.

"You mean, you wanted his advice on whether you're doing the right thing or not!" She began to sound horribly like Monique and just a touch too perceptive for Michel's liking.

"Antone has so much experience of the world and it is always good to get his opinion, on everything" Michel replied.

"I bet you went to Ricky's before you got the fuel" she said.

"Well, actually……."

"So you did?"

"The car is still outside Ricky's………"

"Why?"

"They thought….."

"They? Who's 'they'?" she asked, her eyes gleaming.

"Well, Antone, and Jacques of course and, err, René and, err, Jean" he half whispered.

"So you and your mates are having a final drink up and au revoir party, whilst I'm stuck here on my own doing all the packing for both of us!" she exploded.

"It wasn't like that" he protested.

"Sounds like it to me!" she replied.

"Look….." he started.

"And why has the car been left outside Ricky's as if I couldn't guess?" she interrupted.

"They felt that as we had all had just a little too much to drink……"

"How did you get home then?"

"René brought me."

"In his taxi?"

"Oui."

"He hadn't had too much then, had he?"

"Non, ma petite…" he said gently, attempting to pacify the love of his life.

"Just you!"

"Well, Antone as well….."

"I don't want to hear it, not any of it" and with that she burst into tears. Michel immediately sat beside her and put his arm around her delicate shoulders.

"Ma petite" he whispered "please don't cry, please, I'm very sorry, really I am." Josette continued to cry and Michel just held his head gently against hers until she had finished and wiped her eyes with his handkerchief.

"I think we're making a terrible mistake going to Le Touquet, and we'll regret it" she said, sniffing gently.

"Non, ma petite, it'll be wonderful, a new life for both of us with plenty of money" he replied.

"I doubt it" she said.

"You're just a little nervous and excited about it, I am as well, but once we're there we'll both be very happy, I promise" he smiled into her tear stained face.

"Oh, Michel, I do hope so" she replied.

"Look, it'll be alright, we'll be with Henri and Jackie, and all their family and we'll soon make new friends, you'll see, in a year we won't know ourselves, I promise." She brightened up a little at that and gave him a faint smile.

"That's better, now, suppose you make us a nice cup of coffee and we can sit here and talk about our future and then we'll get René to run us down to le Vieux Port to La Galleot for dinner, and after that I'll be alright to drive the car back here. Then we can have an early night and set off tomorrow to Le Touquet."

"There's still loads to do" she said plaintively.

"I'm sure, but we can see to it tomorrow" he replied.

It was almost seven when Michel 'phoned René and asked him to take the lovers to La Galleot. Without hesitation he agreed and they were soon on their way to one of Michel's favourite restaurants overlooking le Vieux Port and within walking distance of Ricky's bar.

"You know, Josette, we're all going to miss you" said René as he negotiated the early evening traffic in la Canebiére.

"I'm going to miss everybody too" replied Josette from the back seat as she gazed wistfully out of the side window at the busy thoroughfare that she knew so well. Michel felt uncomfortable and tried to change the subject.

"La Canebiére is always busy, isn't it?" he commented.

"Oui" replied René and then added "it'll be a lot quieter in Le Touquet, I'm sure."

"Possibly" mumbled Michel in reply.

"Still, you said you wanted a quiet life" said René.

"Non, I said I wanted to start a new life" replied Michel a little testily.

"Whatever" said René as he swung his taxi into le Vieux Port and headed towards La Galleot.

Michel was glad when René stopped outside the restaurant because he felt that any more talk of people 'missing people' would bring on floods of tears from Josette and make their departure to a new life even more difficult. Michel was truly beginning to feel the strain.

"Bon chance, mes amis" said René with a smile.

"Au revoir, René" replied Josette with moist eyes.

"Au revoir" said Michel as he gave a little wave to his best friend.

They entered the sparkling, romantically lit restaurant and were greeted by Madame Charnay, the charismatic owner.

"Ah, monsieur Michel and Mademoiselle Josette" she purred.

"Madame Charnay, ça va?" replied Michel.

"Oui, monsieur, a discreet table for two?" she enquired.

"Oui, madame, overlooking the port, s'il vous plait" said Michel.

"Of course, this way" she replied and then led them to a table in the far corner of the restaurant, by the picture window, that allowed them a romantic and unobstructed view of the harbour, with its myriad of sailing yachts and luxury motor cruisers all bobbing gently at anchor.

They sat and looked at the view until Madame Charnay brought the menus and wine list. Michel thanked her and began to peruse the menu when Josette said, wistfully "this is the last time we'll have dinner here."

"Oui, ma petite, but only for a while, we're bound to come back now and then, and I promise we'll always come here for dinner." She tried to smile at her fiancé and then glanced down at the menu with a sad expression. It was all becoming hard work for Michel.

After lengthy consideration they both ordered bouillabaisse to start followed by Scampi Provençal for Josette and Tournedos Rossini for Michel. To Madame's surprise they only ordered sparkling water to drink.

"I have a long way to drive tomorrow" said Michel giving that as a reason for his abstinence.

"Oh?" said Madame.

"We're going to Le Touquet" said Josette.

"For a short vacation?" enquired Madame.

"Non, for good" replied Josette.

"Mon Dieu! Whatever for?" asked Madame.

"To start a business" said Michel proudly.

"Can't you start it here?" persisted Madame.

"Non, I'm going into the tourist business with my cousin Henri, and he lives there, in fact he's already got a successful shop quite near the beach."

"Bon, what does he sell in his shop?"

"Ladies shoes" replied Michel and he noticed that Madame seemed unimpressed.

"Bon, well, I shall miss you" replied Madame before she hurried away to attend to other customers.

They finished their meal in comparative silence and Michel felt relieved when he at last called Madame for l'addition. After he had paid and they had bade farewell to Madame Charnay the lovers made their way to Ricky's and without even looking in at the bar, Michel unlocked the Mercedes and slipped behind the wheel. They drove home to Rue du Camas, parked the car and went silently in to the flat.

Over more coffee they talked for a while, keeping off the subject of their new life in Le Touquet, before going to bed. Cuddling in the warmth of the bed that they had bought for Christmas, neither of them had wanted to make love. Michel hoped he was not making a dreadful mistake and Antone's words kept ringing in his ears 'a catastrophe in Le Touquet', as he fell into an uneasy sleep.

CHAPTER 2

It was lunch time the next day before Michel and Josette had finished packing, loaded the Mercedes and handed the keys of the flat back to the agents. Michel had tried to recover the three months rent in advance that Josette had paid before Christmas but it was all to no avail. The hardnosed secretary was adamant and it all seemed very unfair. After struggling with the agent from hell, Michel drove to the Bourse and collected a large amount of cash from his bank safe deposit box. He considered his financial position for a few moments before deciding to leave a very useful amount in the box, just in case he made an early return to Marseille.

The Mercedes swung onto the autoroute and Michel looked up at the blue signs that read 'Lyon' and 'Paris' he felt excited and relieved that they were at last on their way and at the beginning of their new life. He felt confident that he would be able to put the past behind him and in time, forget everything that had troubled him in Marseille.

Josette seemed to be in a better mood and she chatted happily about an aunt who lived at Macon and as it was en route she asked if they might call in and see the dear lady. Michel readily agreed, hoping that would keep his fiancé in her present happy frame of mind.

"It'll be quite late before we reach Macon" said Michel "will that be alright?"

"Oui, Aunt Eloise never goes to bed early" replied Josette.

"Bon, she won't mind us just dropping in then?"

"Non, it'll be alright" smiled Josette.

"Bon."

"She's a widow but she's got a lot of energy, in fact she never stops" said Josette fondly.

"Never stops what?"

"Never stops enjoying herself" replied Josette.

"A woman after my own heart" replied Michel.

"She's good fun."

"When did you last see her?"

"Oh, it must have been in the spring, last year, when I went to

Paris with my parents" replied Josette. Although calling on Eloise was a stop that Michel had not planned he felt the inconvenience was worth it to keep Josette happy. His fiancé was a delight when she was in a good mood and not so jolly when she was unhappy, in fact, very difficult, and it was a side of her nature that had only just been revealed to Michel, and he felt slightly concerned.

The Mercedes swept on up the A6, the autoroute du soleil, for hours, first passing Avignon and then Orange before reaching Valence. Michel pulled into a service area just north of the town for a break and something to eat. They were both getting tired and hungry. As they sat drinking coffee and munching baguettes Michel said "I had hoped we'd get as far as Nemours tonight, but I think that by the time we've got round Lyon and stopped to see Aunt, that'll be it for today."

"Well we were a bit late leaving Marseille" replied Josette.

"So much to do" mumbled Michel."

"Perhaps we can stay the night with Aunt" said Josette brightly.

"Think she'd mind?"

"Non, she'll be glad of the company."

"Bon, but if not, she'll know somewhere to stay."

"I'm sure we can stay with her" smiled Josette.

Refreshed and feeling better the lovers settled into the Mercedes and prepared for the last part of the journey. It seemed an age before they reached Vienne and Michel knew that Lyon just lay ahead; soon they passed through the Peage at the end of the autoroute. The traffic became very heavy as they reached the outskirts of the city where the local drivers were joining the autoroute traffic from every conceivable direction and adding to the most dreadful congestion.

They crept slowly forward in the jam with time against them. It seemed an eternity before they were at last free of the traffic and Michel breathed a sigh of relief as they rejoined the A6 autoroute and accelerated north towards Macon.

"It's going to be very late before we get to your Aunt's home" said Michel with concern.

"I've told you, it's OK" Josette replied.

"If you say so"

"I just hope I can remember where she lives" said Josette

lightly.

"What?" shouted Michel.

"Well it was almost a year ago, my Dad was driving and I didn't pay much attention…."

"Do you ever?" he questioned and then instantly regretted it.

"Oui, I do pay attention, I do!" she exclaimed before bursting into tears.

"I'm sorry, ma petite, I didn't mean to say that, I'm just a bit tired and….."

"You should be sorry" she interrupted as she sniffled back her tears.

"I'm sure we'll find Aunt's house, it's just that it's dark and late…."

"Don't worry, I'll remember the way when we get to Macon and she's bound to be up, watching television or something" she whimpered. They continued the last part of the journey in silence and only when Michel swung off the autoroute to the Peage on the slip road to Macon centre ville did they speak.

"Well, here we are" he said.

"Oui, just drive to the centre and I'm sure I'll remember something" Josette replied.

They drove on until they reached what appeared to be the middle of the town and then the signpost that said 'toutes directions' and underneath the name 'Bourg-en-Bresse' prompted Josette.

"There, that way, the road to Bourg-en-Bresse, and we'll turn off soon into Rue Montrevel, that's where she lives" she said excitedly.

"Bon" replied a relieved Michel and he drove the car slowly to ensure he did not drive past the turning.

"It's not far now" she said.

"Bon."

"It's on the left, near here." Suddenly, there it was, at a small cross road on the outskirts of Macon. Michel swung the car to the left and proceeded down the poorly lit street.

"Where's her house?" asked Michel.

"Further down on the left, it's a large house on a corner, I'll recognise it as soon as I see it" she replied. He drove slowly until Josette exclaimed "there it is!" Michel noticed that the house looked neat and well cared for in the dim street light as he pulled up and switched off the engine whilst sighing "at last."

Josette was out of the car and at the front door before Michel could struggle out of his seat after the long drive from Marseille.

The door opened and Josette said "Aunt!"

"Josette, ma petite, what a surprise!" replied Aunt Eloise. Michel had joined them and followed his fiancé into the warm interior of the house.

"Aunt, this is Michel, my fiancé" beamed Josette.

"Michel, bon, welcome" said Eloise with a big smile as she held out her hand. She was not what Michel expected and she certainly did not fit into his idea of what an 'old Aunt' normally looked like. A quick mental flash of Monique's Aunts, Alexis and Hélène, came into view and then disappeared. Eloise was about forty five, quite tall with thick black hair, cut in a page boy style, big brown eyes and a large, firm bust line with a slim waist. Michel could see the family likeness, Eloise being a mature version of Josette, and deliciously bigger.

"Aunt Eloise, enchanted" replied Michel as he took her hand and gently squeezed it.

"Oh, call me Eloise, si'l vous plait" she said with a smile that came from her eyes as well as her lips. She made Michel feel very sexy.

"Now then, come and sit down and tell me all your news, whilst I pour the drinks" said Eloise as she ushered them into her spacious lounge. They sat on the settee opposite an open fire whilst Eloise went to the substantial array of drinks assembled on a large silver tray situated on an occasional table.

"What will you have?" she enquired. They both asked for brandy and Michel noticed that Eloise poured out a very large measure for each of them. As she handed them their drinks she asked "what are you doing in Macon?"

"We're on our way to Le Touquet" replied Josette as Eloise sat in an armchair near Michel and crossed her long legs with a flourish.

"For a vacation?"

"Non, we're going to live there."

"Why?" asked Eloise.

"My cousin, Henri, has a business there and I'm going to join him" said Michel.

“Bon, what sort of business?”

“He has a ladies shoe shop.”

“You’re going to sell ladies shoes?” Eloise asked.

“Non, we’re going into the tourist industry” said Michel proudly.

“Bon, so you’re the one who understands the tourist business?” asked Eloise.

“Non, Michel is a taxi driver in Marseille” beamed Josette.

“I deal with a lot of tourists” said Michel trying to regain some dignity and importance.

“Well, it’s a start” replied Eloise as she sipped at her brandy.

“Oui, it’s a great opportunity” said Michel.

”Oui, and you’re engaged, when did that happen?” asked Eloise neatly changing the subject.

“Just before Christmas” smiled Josette.

“Congratulations to both of you, I hope you’ll be as happy as I was with Roger.”

“Merci, Eloise” replied Josette.

“Oui, he was such an understanding person” said Eloise wistfully as she spoke of her late husband.

“We all loved him” said Josette.

“Oui, he was much older than me you know, and all the family, especially your father, didn’t want me to marry him.”

“Really?”

“Oui, but he just swept me off my feet, he was charming, good looking and had plenty of money” said Eloise and added “always a winning combination.”

“Bon” said Josette.

“How could I resist him?”

“You couldn’t” agreed Josette.

“And he was so tolerant, especially as he got older, you know, when he was too frail to travel, he used to get his best friend, Pierré, to take me away to Monaco for a holiday twice a year.”

“Bon” said Josette and Michel smiled as he pictured Pierré on top of Eloise every night making her vacation complete in every way.

“A woman’s happiness is guaranteed if she marries an older man” said Eloise with conviction.

“Really?” smiled Josette.

"Oui, and you're doing the right thing, marrying Michel" said Eloise with a smile.

"Michel's not old" replied Josette a little taken aback.

"Non, not 'old' but more mature and I'm sure that comes with age and arrives once you've been round the block a few times" she said with deadly accuracy. Michel laughed out loud.

"He laughs like an old married man" said Eloise.

"Oui, he's been married before" said Josette.

"And you're just waiting for the divorce to come through?" asked Eloise.

"Oui" replied Josette.

"I thought so" smiled Eloise.

"We're very happy" said Michel.

"I'm sure you are, and I really do wish you the very best. The most important things in life are love, happiness and your health. It doesn't matter what anybody thinks, just enjoy every day as if it's your last" said Eloise with conviction.

"I agree" said Michel before taking a generous sip of brandy.

"Now, ma petites, have you eaten?" demanded Eloise.

"Oui, at Valence" replied Michel.

"Coffee and baguettes" added Josette..

"Mon Dieu! You must be starving!" exclaimed Eloise.

"Non, merci…." began Josette politely but Eloise shook her head and picked up the telephone from a side table close by and dialled quickly.

"Jules, c'est moi,….. oui,…. I've got two starving enfants with me, oui,…….. my niece and her fiancé from Marseille, oui,….. in fifteen minutes then…..au revoir." Eloise replaced the receiver and said "there, it's all arranged, my friend Jules owns the best restaurant in Macon, and we have to be there in fifteen minutes otherwise he'll close for the night, so hurry ma petites!"

Michel and Josette followed Eloise out into the dark street and down the side of the house to a garage. Eloise opened the door with a flourish and Michel could see a large black BMW saloon in the dim light. Eloise was behind the wheel in a flash and within moments the engine burst into life. Michel slipped into the front whilst Josette sat behind. With a roar the BMW reversed out and without stopping to close the garage door, Eloise accelerated the big car at full throttle down the street. She drove at high speed with panache and accuracy and Michel was most impressed and quite relaxed as Eloise cornered the car effortlessly through Macon. At last they pulled up outside an elegant and attractively lit restaurant.

"Here we are, ma petites, in ten minutes flat" she said as she glanced at the dashboard clock.

"Bravo" said Michel. Eloise smiled and they followed her into the restaurant. It was warm and welcoming with a delicious smell of cooked food and spices. Jules appeared and kissed Eloise on both cheeks as he held her close, a bit too close thought Michel for just a friend. They were introduced and then escorted to a table close to a large open fire. Jules produced menus for all three and a wine list for Michel and said "let me recommend the boeuf bourguignon tonight, the meat is particularly tender."

"Merci, Jules" said Eloise with a smile and Michel noticed how Jules smiled back, it was a touch too intimate. Jules was quite tall and well built with dark wavy hair swept back with a touch of grey at the temples. He had bright blue eyes and his smiling, generous mouth made him quite attractive.

"Have you known Jules long?" enquired Michel after Jules had left them to attend to another table.

"Long enough to be very close friends" Eloise replied with a smile before returning to the menu.

"He's very good looking" said Josette.

"Isn't he just" replied Eloise and she smiled again before adding "and he's very athletic." Michel hid behind the menu to conceal his knowing smile.

"I'll have the pate followed by the boeuf bourguignon" said Michel.

"I'll join you" said Josette.

"And I'll have melon and then the boeuf" said Eloise. Michel chose a local red wine and their order was then taken by a very attentive Jules.

"Well, your new business is going to be quite an adventure for you, have you spent much time in Le Touquet?" asked Eloise.

"We've never been there" replied Josette.

"Never?" enquired Eloise in a surprised tone.

"Non."

"Well, I hope you like it" said Eloise.

"I'm sure we will" said Michel.
"When we eventually get there" added Josette.
"Tomorrow, surely?" enquired Eloise.
"Oui, but before then we've got to find somewhere to stay tonight" replied Josette.
"Oh, Josette, you silly thing, you'll stay with me tonight" said Eloise in a surprised tone.
"Are you sure, Aunt?"
"But of course, I have three spare bedrooms, plenty of room for you two" she smiled and Michel breathed a sigh of relief as Jules placed the starters in front of the diners. With a 'bon appetite' and a smile he left them to enjoy the meal. The pate was delicious, the bourguignon was to die for, the red wine blended perfectly and only Michel could manage an ice cream after the main course.
"There" said Eloise as she finished her coffee "have you had enough, ma petites?"
"Oui, merci, Eloise" replied Michel."
"Bon, let's go then, Jules will want to close up now." Michel waved to Jules and called for l'addition.
"It's taken care of" said Eloise "so come on, let's go."
"Merci, Eloise" said a surprised and grateful Michel.
As they left the restaurant Eloise said to Jules "don't be long, chérie." Michel pretended he did not hear and just thanked Jules and then complimented him on his cuisine. Eloise drove home sedately and in a relaxed manner, when Michel, half asleep with a mixture of tiredness, brandy, red wine and a very good dinner, was brought to his senses by Eloise announcing "Jules will be coming back later."
"Bon" he mumbled, not totally surprised.
"Oui, he normally stays one or two nights a week" said Eloise in a matter of fact tone.
"Bon" said Michel feeling tired and hoping that Jules would not make too much noise as he met the widow's needs.
"I thought I should tell you both" she said.
"The new man in your life, Aunt?" enquired Josette.
"Not the newest, but certainly one of the best" she replied and Michel grinned. Josette was right, her Aunt enjoyed herself.
Back in the warmth of the spacious lounge, Michel and his fiancé lingered over large brandies and relaxed as Eloise chatted

on about the family members scattered throughout France. Observing Michel slowly closing his eyes Eloise remarked “you must be tired, ma petites.”

“Oui” replied Michel as there was a knock at the door.

“That’ll be Jules” said Eloise with a smile. Within moments the good looking restaurant owner was in and wishing the lovers ‘bon nuit’, and promising to see them in the morning.

Eloise led them to a cosy bedroom, comfortable and well furnished.

“You’ll get a good nights sleep here, it’s very quiet and Jules and I are right next door if you need anything” she said and then wished them ‘bon nuit.’ They tumbled into the soft bed, kissed gently and fell into a deep sleep almost immediately, entwined in each others arms.

A steady ‘thump, thump’ on the wall behind the bed invaded Michel’s sleep. He gradually came to and listened. Was it a machine? The central heating pipes? It was so regular, it had to be something mechanical. The noise continued, never varying in speed or volume. He felt Josette stir and he whispered “are you awake, chérie?”

“Oui” she whispered back in the darkness and then asked “what’s that noise?”

“I don’t know” he replied and then suddenly they heard “Oh, oui, oui, oui, oui, Jules!”

“I know now” said Michel and Josette laughed.

They heard Jules say “you’re gorgeous, just gorgeous, I could fuck you from now ‘til eternity!”

“Oh, no, Jules, not that long, please, we need to sleep, we’ve got to drive all the way to Le Touquet tomorrow!” whispered Michel and Josette laughed out loud.

“Remember what Eloise said, he’s athletic which means this could go on all night” whispered Michel.

“Oh, non” whispered Josette.

“I think Eloise is working off l’addition” said Michel.

“Probably, but he can’t go on for ever, surely?” she replied.

“He looked fit to me and not that tired when he came here after work” he whispered. The steady ‘thump’ continued, never changing in rhythm or speed.

“Oh, Jules, Jules, harder now, much harder…. harder” shouted

Eloise.

"This could be it" said Michel and Josette giggled. The 'thump' slowed a little and became more measured.

"How's that, ma chérie?" gasped Jules.

"Oh, mon Dieu, mon Dieu! Oui!... Oui!, oh, Jules this is too good, never stop, never stop!" cried Eloise.

"Oh, oui, please stop" said Michel and Josette giggled again.

"Oh, Jules, you're so big, you fill me right up……." Eloise gasped and the 'thump' began to speed up.

"This is it" said Michel with confidence as the rhythm intensified.

"Oh, chérie, ma petite! Ma petite!" shouted Jules as the 'thump' suddenly became both faster and much louder.

"Mon Dieu! He'll push her through the wall in a minute!" exclaimed Michel.

"Mon Dieu! Mon Dieu!" screamed Eloise. The 'thump' increased in speed for just a few moments before coming to an abrupt halt.

"Thank heavens, he's finished, perhaps we can get some rest now" said Michel with relief and the lovers cuddled up and were soon fast asleep.

When Michel next awoke he could see daylight peeping through the curtains and could hardly believe his ears as the sound of the steady 'thump' invaded his senses.

"Mon Dieu! He's at it again!" he exclaimed as Josette stirred.

"What is it, chérie?" she asked.

"Listen,………. Jules is making an early start" he replied.

"Oh, non" said Josette.

"Come on, petite, let's get up now, we've a long way to go today" said Michel.

"Non, Michel, it wouldn't be polite to get up before they've finished" replied Josette.

"Why?"

"We might disturb them" she replied.

"Disturb them! They've kept us awake half the night!"

"Oh, non, you exaggerate, petite, besides, they're in love, like us" smiled Josette.

"Nonsense" he replied and climbed out of the bed and made his way to the bathroom.

It was some time later that Jules and Eloise surfaced and joined the lovers in the spacious kitchen. Josette poured several cups of coffee for Eloise and her lover before the over sexed pair said anything sensible. The conversation was slow and uninteresting and Michel realised that Eloise and the man in her life were very much night birds and mornings were not their best time. He was impatient to leave and Josette sensing his mood hurried along and collected their belongings. Eloise spent some moments alone with Josette when Michel went to the Mercedes. Then, after many embraces and kisses, the lovers said their 'goodbyes' and set off to drive back through Macon towards the autoroute. As Michel swung onto the A6 Josette said "Eloise has given us some money."

"Really, how much?"

"I don't know."

"Well count it, chérie." Josette opened her handbag and took out a wad of 500 Franc notes.

"Mon Dieu!" exclaimed Michel as he glanced at the money in her hand.

"Exactly" said Josette "she's been very generous."

"She certainly has" replied Michel.

"She gave it to me just as we were leaving and said it was her little contribution to our future happiness, wasn't that sweet?"

"Very."

"She really is very special" said Josette as she counted the big red notes.

"How much?" enquired Michel, just as Josette turned the last note.

"Ten thousand Francs" she replied and Michel whistled.

"That's a good start to the day" said Michel.

"Certainly is and let's hope it stays that way" said Josette. Michel smiled and nodded as he accelerated the Mercedes to a higher speed, feeling confident and relaxed.

They swept on past Chalon heading for Auxerre and Paris, the everlasting autoroute stretching out before them. They stopped at a service area close to Auxerre for fuel and a much needed break. Michel was quite happy for them to linger over chicken salads and nondescript gateaux's, as he believed that they had made good progress over the last few hours. Soon they would reach Paris and

Le Touquet did not look that much further on the map. They relaxed over coffee and chatted about their new home and Josette had plenty of ideas for improving the house that Henri had inherited.

"You haven't even seen it yet" Michel laughed.

"I know, but I can imagine how it will be and I am sure I can make it nice for us" she replied. Michel lent over and kissed his fiancé very tenderly.

"I love you very much, ma chérie" he whispered.

"I love you too" she replied.

"I know."

"When are we going to get married then?" she whispered. The question went into Michel like a high voltage electric shock. How could she manage to spoil a romantic moment in an autoroute café like that? He gathered his composure and whispered back "soon."

"How soon is soon?" she persisted.

"As soon as we get to Le Touquet and I get divorced" he whispered back.

"How soon is that going to be, chérie?" her emphasis on 'that' slightly alarmed him.

"Well, we have to move into our new home, start up the business with Henri and……"

"Michel" she interrupted "I want to get married because I want a baby!"

"I know, ma petite, I know" he repeated, struggling for time to think. 'She wants a baby, for heavens sake! Right in the middle of a new business venture, is she mad?' he thought.

"I promise, I'll contact a solicitor tomorrow, in fact it'll be the very first thing I do in Le Touquet" he said. She brightened up at that and smiled.

"I do love you, chérie" she whispered.

"I know" he replied somewhat shaken.

The Mercedes raced smoothly towards Paris with Michel wondering whether he could cope with a new home, new business, new wife and a baby. It seemed as if there now too many 'new' things in his life. Already he was missing the 'old' things, like Ricky's bar and Yvonne and Nicole and…. he stopped there, they all belonged to yesterday and yesterday was gone, but then he thought that yesterday had been pretty good. They say you never realise what you have until it has gone. He fell into a reflective mood as they passed Sens and headed for Melun.

"You're very quiet, chérie" remarked Josette.

"Oui, I'm just concentrating on the driving, petite" he replied.

"Bon, you need to, the Parisien drivers are a dangerous nightmare and we'll be there soon" she said with feeling as she looked at the map.

"Oui."

It was now becoming darker and a few drivers had already put their lights on. The journey was taking longer than Michel had imagined and he wondered what time they would eventually reach Le Touquet. It seemed to take an age after they had passed Melun before they reached the Paris périphérique, that infamous high speed ring road around the most sensual city in the world. By the time the lovers reached it, however, it was moving at the pace of a large French snail. The rush hour in Paris is the same as any other European city as the workers hurry home to their wives, lovers, husbands or mistresses.

"Mon Dieu, just look at it, I'm beginning to think we'll never get to Le Touquet tonight" said Michel as he waved at the columns of traffic around them.

"Of course we will, petite, once we're round this bit, we'll take the autoroute to Amiens and we're nearly there" replied Josette tapping the map.

"I know, it doesn't look far on the map but it seems to take a long time to get anywhere" replied Michel regretting the time spent at the café at Auxerre.

"Never mind, chérie, we're in no rush and we're together" she smiled.

"Oui" he replied but he was beginning to feel the strain.

They moved forward metre by metre and soon they were able to speed up to a fast walking pace which slowly developed until they were at last making headway as the traffic volume eased.

"I'm glad we don't live in Paris, I'd go mad driving in this traffic every day" he said.

"You'd get used to it" she replied.

They followed the périphérique round to the exit sign which read Amiens, autoroute A16 and Michel sighed with relief as he swung the Mercedes off the congested ring road. Within two hours they had reached the outskirts of Amiens and they both were feeling a little more relaxed.

"Not long now, chérie" said Michel.

"Bon, can we stop soon for something to eat, I'm getting hungry" she replied.

"Oui, let's just get past Amiens and then we'll find somewhere" he said.

They stopped at Abbeville and enjoyed pizza, gateaux and coffee. On the autoroute they had seen the sign which read 'Le Touquet-Paris-Plage' and Michel felt relieved that they were almost there.

It was two hours later when the lovers reached the outskirts of Le Touquet, where Michel stopped the car and kissed Josette.

"Here we are, chérie, the beginning of our new life together" he said.

"I do love you, petite" replied Josette.

"Bon, now let's find Henri's house, I hope he's home" said Michel without thinking. It then dawned on him that Henri and his wife were probably still with Monique at Grambois. His heart sank to his boots and he said to Josette "although it might be that we have to stay in an hotel tonight."

"Why, petite?"

"Because Henri is still in Grambois."

"You don't know that" she replied.

"True."

"Well let's go to his house and if he's not there, you could 'phone Grambois and see if he's left" she replied

"OK." Michel drove towards the centre ville and as they passed the elegant and spacious houses, set back from the road in amongst the pine forest, he said "Mon Dieu, there's some money around here, chérie."

"Oui, the houses are beautiful" she replied, and added "I hope Henri's is one of these."

"I shouldn't think so" replied Michel, then he wondered, Monique had said that Henri had been very successful. They proceeded, soon reaching the casino at the end of the Rue Saint Jean. Michel stopped the car and looked in the glove compartment for the slip of paper with Henri's address and that of his deceased Aunt .

"Henri lives at 23, Rue Saint Jean, now I wonder where that is?"

"Ask someone" said Josette.

"Non, we don't need to do that" replied Michel as he drove off.

"Can you see the street names anywhere?" he asked.

"Non, chérie, it's dark, look just ask someone" she persisted.

"Non, all these people will be tourists, they won't know" he replied.

"What, tourists in December?"

"Probably."

"Michel, this is stupid, stop the car and I'll ask that man" she said impatiently.

"Alright, but you'll make a fool of yourself" he replied as he pulled up by the kerb. Josette wound down her window and called out to an elderly, well dressed gentleman.

"Excuse me, monsieur, do you know where Rue Saint Jean is, si'l vous plait?"

"Oui, Mademoiselle" replied the elderly man, "you're in it" he added with a smile.

"Bon."

"It goes from the casino back there, right through to the promenade" he said.

"Merci, monsieur." She closed the window and said "there."

Michel did not reply, he felt it was diplomatically correct to remain silent. They drove off and Michel kept half whispering "number 23." They peered out in the darkness at the houses along either side of the road. Rue Saint Jean is quite a long thoroughfare and neither of them was able to spot a house number. Then it began to rain and Michel tut tutted as he switched the wipers on. This was all they needed, late at night in a strange place. Michel stopped the car and said "I'll have to get out and look."

"Oui, chérie." He slipped out into the pouring rain and rushed up to the front door of a house close to the road. He peered at the number and hurried back to the warmth of the car.

"That was number 43" he said.

"Ten more houses then" replied Josette.

"Oui." They pulled up outside number 23 and it was in total darkness.

"They must still be in Grambois" said Michel.

"Looks like it."

"Well, we'd better find an hotel" said Michel in a gloomy tone.

"Oui, but before that, could we just see the house that we're going to have?" asked Josette brightly.

"What now?"

"Oui."

"But it's dark, you won't see anything."

"Please, chérie, for me, please."

"Alright, it's number 19, Rue de Londres, I think it's just here somewhere" said Michel as he drove off slowly. They looked vainly for street names at every cross road as they moved towards the centre ville. Michel spotted a man with an umbrella hurrying along, and full of new found confidence he said "I'll ask him." He wound down his window and called out "monsieur, excuse me, do you know where Rue de Londres is?"

"Haven't got a clue, monsieur, I'm a stranger here" he replied and hurried on by. Josette burst out laughing and Michel said "I'm glad you think it's funny!"

"Well it is" she replied, still laughing. They continued until suddenly there was the sign 'Rue de Londres', dimly lit by a nearby street lamp. Michel turned into the road and they looked for number 19. The house was in darkness but they could make out that it appeared reasonably large and was detached from its neighbours. In the dim light it looked slightly faded and jaded.

"I expect it'll need some work doing to it" said Michel.

"I expect so."

"No one's lived there since Henri's Aunt died" remarked Michel.

"Did she die there?" asked Josette in a whisper.

"I don't know, but I expect so."

"I hope it's not haunted" whispered Josette.

"I doubt it, now have you seen enough?" he asked.

"Oui."

"Bon, now let's find somewhere to stay" Michel said firmly as he accelerated off down the road. They soon reached the promenade and turned right into the Boulevard de la Canche where the Park Plaza Hotel stood like a welcoming beacon in the rainy, wind swept, night.

"We'll stay there" said Michel firmly and he swung the Mercedes into the entrance.

“I expect it’ll be expensive” she said.

“I don’t care, I’ve had enough for today” he replied.

Half an hour later they were booked into a very comfortable room and Michel was on the telephone to Grambois.

“Hello” answered Monique.

“Hello, Monique, it’s me” said Michel.

“Michel, ma petite, where are you?” she asked in a delighted tone.

“In Le Touquet.”

“Oh” her voice dropped.

“We’ve just arrived.”

“We? Who’s ‘we’?” she demanded. Michel cursed himself and searched for a quick answer.

“A business associate” he lied.

“You mean a woman, probably Josette LeFranc………”

“Monique” interrupted Michel in a calming tone.

“Surely you remember her, Michel, you announced your engagement to her at Ricky’s, it was in all the papers” she replied sarcastically.

“Monique, you’re being too emotional” he replied.

“I am emotional, Michel, a woman gets like that when her husband walks out on her………”

“I’m here on business” he interrupted.

“Business? You must think I’m a complete fool, Michel.”

“Look, I haven’t got time for all this now, is Henri there?”

“Non, they left this morning and let me tell you, they are pretty disgusted at your behaviour.”

“Really?”

“Oui, and I shouldn’t expect too much from Henri in this so called ‘business venture’.”

“Oh?” Michel queried.

“I can tell you that Jackie’s dead against it” said Monique in a forceful tone.

“Go on.”

“Dead against it, Michel” she repeated.

“We’ll see.”

“Give it up, Michel and come home before it’s too late.”

“Goodbye, Monique” he replied and he put the ‘phone down and sat thinking for a moment. He hoped Henri wasn’t having second thoughts, after all, he did appear to be easily persuaded and he was henpecked by his ugly wife. Never a good sign and such a limiting factor when one was trying to build a business empire with a partner who is under his wife's thumb.

"They left this morning, ma petite" he said to Josette.

"Bon."

"They'll be here by tomorrow night."

"Bon, then we'll be able to move into our new house" she replied with a smile.

"Let's hope so" he said, knowing it was unlikely.

They slipped into bed, too tired for love and fell asleep in each others arms.

CHAPTER 3

Josette was already up and dressed when Michel awoke.

"Up you get, chérie, it's getting late, and we've a new house to move into today" she said. Michel groaned and rolled over in the warm bed. He was not ready for all this, just yet.

It was quite some time later before they emerged from their room and went in search of coffee and croissants. After breakfast Michel decided to book the room for another night, much to Josette's disappointment.

"Be sensible, chérie, Henri and Jackie are not going to be here until probably late tonight and Henri is not going to spend any time then opening his Aunt's home for us" said Michel as they made their way to the hotel car park.

"I am sensible, ma petite, why pay for a hotel room when we've got a perfectly nice house to live in?" she queried.

"Look, we don't know the state of it inside for a start" he replied.

"I'm sure it's alright" she countered. Michel was not convinced and he suggested that they should look at it as the very first thing on their agenda. She seemed happy at that and they set off in the Mercedes to view 19 Rue de Londres. The house did not look very appealing in the grey light of the overcast day and Michel was sure that booking the room at the hotel for another night was the most sensible thing he could have done.

"What do you think?" he asked after he had stopped the car outside Aunt's house.

"It will look better after it's had a good clean and a lick of paint" she replied. They left the warmth of the car and looked round the small, paved front garden and then tried to peer through the shuttered windows. What they could see appeared gloomy to say the least.

"We'd better have a look around the town and wait for Henri to arrive" said Michel in a hopeful tone.

"Oui, and we have to find a solicitor for your divorce" she reminded him   Michel did not feel like talking to a solicitor and after finding the offices of Monsieur Robardes, Notaire, in the Avenue Duquesne he promised to arrange an interview tomorrow, without fail. Josette seemed content for the moment. It was almost lunch time before they finished their tour with a slow walk along the Boulevard de la Plage, stopping occasionally to look out at the grey, choppy English Channel. The day was cold as well as overcast and they were glad to turn into the Rue Saint Louis out of the wind and find a petite restaurant for lunch. After a very good meal at a reasonable price Michel decided that he had had enough of walking about in the cold so they set off in the car to explore further afield. As they drove out through the pine forest they were again impressed by the grand villas set back amongst the trees. Each villa had an immaculate garden and several luxury cars parked on its spacious driveway.

"There's money here" he whispered encouraged by the wealth on display. They reached the nearby airfield and stopped out of curiosity. After parking the car they were surprised at the large number of light aircraft standing on the huge tarmac apron near the control tower.

"Henri said that all year round lots of English fly over just for le weekend" said Michel.

"Good for business then" replied Josette.

"Oui, they bring their girlfriends and spend easily" he laughed.

"All men are the same" she replied.

"What d'you mean?"

"They'll show off and spend money like water to get a woman's knickers off" she said with feeling.

"Good, that's just what we want" he replied and she laughed. They drove out into the surrounding countryside, using the back roads and were surprised at the greenery of it all. Michel began to feel more relaxed and was looking forward to seeing Henri again.

"I just hope that they don't get back too late" he said.

"We'll just wait outside their house until they arrive" replied Josette.

They returned to Le Touquet, found an agreeable restaurant and enjoyed an early dinner. Michel then drove to 23, Rue Saint Jean and parked outside Henri and Jackie's house to await their arrival. He and Josette sat in the darkness for some time, listening to the radio and chatting about the future and then the plans that Michel had in his mind for his office in Aunt's house.

"An office?" queried Josette.

"Oui."
"In the house where we're going to live?"
"Oui" he replied.
"Well, only if there's room" she said firmly.
"Ma petite, we're here to start a business…." Michel was interrupted by a tapping on his side window. He turned to see the pale, austere face of a Gendarme. He wound down the window.
"Monsieur?" he queried.
"I have been observing you and the lady for some time, monsieur" said the Gendarme.
"Oh" replied Michel.
"What are you doing, parked here?" asked the Gendarme.
"Waiting for someone, monsieur" replied Michel.
"And who would that be?"
"My cousin and his wife" said Michel.
"And when do you expect them to arrive?"
"Soon, very soon, I think they may of got held up on their journey, they've been staying with my wife and I over Christmas" replied Michel.
"I see that your taxi is registered in Marseille, monsieur" said the Gendarme gravely.
"Oui, that's correct."
"A long way from home then?"
"Oui."
"And is this lady your wife?"
"Non, I'm his fiancé, but we're to be married as soon as his divorce comes through" said Josette brightly.
"You appear to lead a complicated life, monsieur" said the Gendarme.
"It is a bit hectic at the moment" replied Michel with a silly laugh. The Gendarme was not amused.
"May I see your driving licence, monsieur?"
"Of course" and while Michel struggled to find his wallet the Gendarme shone his torch into the back of the Mercedes.
"You seem to have a lot of luggage in the back, monsieur, are you planning a long vacation?"
"Non, we're moving up here for good" replied Michel as he at last produced the document.
"We're starting a business" said Josette helpfully.

"Really" mused the Gendarme as he perused the licence.

"Oui" said Josette.

"Michel Ronay" said the Gendarme slowly.

"Oui, that's me" replied Michel.

"Well, Monsieur Ronay, is it a taxi business you're starting up?"

"Non, I'm going into the tourist business with my cousin Henri" replied Michel.

"Henri?......" mused the Gendarme.

"Oui, Henri and his wife, Jackie, they live here at number 23" said Michel hoping that the Gendarme's curiosity would at last be satisfied.

"Very well, monsieur, I have made a note of your licence plate and will of course check it out with the Marseille authorities, just routine, you understand" said the Gendarme as he handed Michel's licence back to him.

"Of course" said Michel.

"Bonsoir, Monsieur Ronay and Mademoiselle" said the Gendarme as he wandered off into the darkness.

Michel's thoughts raced away, if the Gendarme did contact the Marseille authorities then Gerrard would know where he was for certain. The thought of Gerrard tracing him to Le Touquet and being a blasted nuisance was almost too much to think about at the moment. Several cars drove by and then one pulled up behind the Mercedes and Michel was delighted to see Henri emerge from it followed by Jackie.

"They're here!" Michel exclaimed as he opened his door and left the car to greet his cousin and his wife.

"Henri."

"Michel, ça va?"

"Oui, bien sûr, and Jackie, ma petite" Michel said as he kissed her on both cheeks.

"Have you been here long?" asked Henri.

"Non, just a short while, now then let me introduce you to Josette" said Michel as his Fiancé stepped forward "Josette, this is cousin Henri and his lovely wife, Jackie."

"Enchante" said Henri as he took Josette's hand whilst Jackie just nodded and spoke her name in a decidedly cool tone.

"Now come on in" said Henri as he led the way to the front door of his imposing detached house. Sometime later, after they had all enjoyed several brandies and relaxed a little in the warmth of the elegant lounge, Jackie seemed a little more amenable and talked about Aunt's house and gave Josette a long list of jobs that needed to be carried out to make the place a comfortable home. Michel cringed inwardly at the thought of having to spend days fixing up the place before he could start the business. However, he was grateful that Jackie did not mention Monique. Actually, she saved that little arrow until the lovers were just about to leave for their hotel. As they kissed goodbye, Jackie said to Michel, in a firm voice "Monique sends her love as always and she said she hopes you know what you're doing this time."

"Thank you, Jackie" replied Michel politely as he could.

"See you tomorrow then" said Henri cheerfully and Michel shook his hand. Once in the Mercedes, Josette started.

"What did she mean 'this time'?"

"I don't know, chérie" he replied truthfully.

"Mon Dieu, how many other times have their been?" she asked.

"Chérie, I honestly don't know what she's talking about, I promise you, you're the only one for me" replied Michel with conviction, but that was before he met Madame Sophia Christiane. Whether it was the cold, grey day or Monique's message that upset Josette's normally warm disposition, Michel did not know, but the end result was that they fell asleep without making love. A new and disturbing trend.

The next day was brighter and Michel felt relaxed as they booked out of the hotel and drove round to Henri's house. The only little moment of concern came as he turned into Rue Saint Jean, when Josette reminded him to make an appointment with Monsieur Robardes to discuss his divorce. Michel promised he would, provided he could fit it in with Henri's plans for the day. She was not too happy about that, sensing a certain reluctance on Michel's part.

It had been decided that Henri would open Aunt's house for them and leave the lovers to move in and sort themselves out. After lunch, Henri would then take Michel to his shoe shop in the Rue Saint Jean and discuss business, whilst Jackie would give Josette a helping hand at the house. In the evening Henri had invited them to dinner, to celebrate their arrival, at his favourite restaurant, Flavio's, in the Avenue du Verger.

The inside of Aunt Claudette's house smelt damp and musty and Josette was apprehensive about the amount of work needed to make it comfortable.

"I know it needs a little tidying, but I'm sure you'll soon have it up to scratch and the way you want it" said Henri cheerfully.

"Oui" replied Josette with a note of uncertainty.

"I think we'll have to paint the place throughout" said Michel.

"Possibly" replied Henri.

"That's too big a job for us, we'll have to get somebody in" said Michel, happy to distance himself from the work.

"And some of this furniture will have to go" said Josette firmly as she surveyed the gloomy lounge.

"As you wish" said Henri as they set off on a guided tour of the house. They were impressed with the size of the rooms and although it had only two bedrooms they were very spacious. The furniture in every room was old, dark and very heavy and it added to the general sad atmosphere of the place.

"Did your Aunt die here?" asked Josette.

"Oui, in that very bed" replied Henri as they left the main bedroom. Josette shuddered inwardly and said "I think we'll want to buy a new one then."

"We will, chérie" said Michel, anxious to please his fiancé.

Henri arranged to collect Michel after two o'clock to show him his shop and discuss the plans for the future and then left them to move in.

After he had gone Josette said "this house is in a bloody awful state, it's going to take ages to make it anything like reasonable."

"We can do it, chérie, come on let's get the car unloaded" replied Michel.

They worked tirelessly until lunch time and then wandered off in search of something to eat.

As good as his word, Henri arrived just after two with Jackie and her mother, Josephine, to help Josette, whose face dropped with dismay as she was introduced to a rather plump, curious looking, older version of Jackie. After the introductions Josette gazed at Michel with a resigned look.

"I'm here to help, dear" said Josephine with a smile.

"I'm very grateful" replied Josette.

"Don't you worry about a thing, Jackie and I will sort every thing out" said Josephine forcefully.

"That's what I'm afraid of" murmured Josette under her breath.

"We'll see you ladies later then" said Michel, happy to be leaving the house to the women and after he and Henri had left, Josephine said to Josette, in a knowing way "Jackie's told me all about you, dear, and I want you to know that I only live a few streets away in the Rue D'Amiens so I'm nice and close if you want to talk to me about anything, any problems, just anything at all."

"You're very kind" replied Josette in a diplomatic tone.

"Not at all, I mean, that's what mothers are for."

"Oui, how true."

"Now then, let's get on and tidy up and you tell me all about Michel and why he left his wife" said Josephine whilst her daughter stood by with a smirk on her face.

"Oui, and why not" replied Josette lamely.

"Bon, now I've asked my brother, Pascal, to come and give a hand, he'll be along later today" said Josephine.

"Oh, bon" replied Josette, now feeling numb with exposure to Jackie's relations.

"But don't say too much in front of him, he's a terrible gossip" said Josephine.

"Non, I won't" replied Josette, grateful for the warning.

"Let's get on then."

Henri's shoe shop was more sophisticated in every way from that which Michel had expected. It was situated in a prominent position, quite close to the promenade, and boasted a small car park at the rear for customers. Henri parked the car in his designated space and Michel followed his cousin into the glamorous interior. Festooned with intimate wall lights and grand ornate mirrors it exuded poise and sophistication. Heavy drapes in royal blue, decorated with gold Fleur-de-Lys tied back with tasselled braids, revealed wall niches that were lit from beneath to exhibit very expensive shoes. Pretty sales assistants, all in elegant black uniforms wearing costume jewellery, wished their boss 'bonjour, monsieur Henri' as they flitted silently about on the deep pile golden carpet, attending to several well dressed women seated on plush chairs.

"Come upstairs to my office" said Henri and Michel followed, slightly open mouthed as he surveyed the scene before him. Henri's office was just so and as he slipped into the large, black leather, executive chair behind his huge glass top desk, Michel asked "why on earth do you want to start another business when you've got all this?"

"I want more, Michel, much more, and I'm bored with it all, I've told you before, Jackie wants me to go on like this until I have to retire and then buy some out of the way cottage in Normandy and wait to die!"

"Oui, I do remember" replied Michel as he relaxed into a plush chair opposite Henri.

"And she gets more like her mother every day" said Henri firmly.

"Oh, dear."

"Quite, and I pity poor Josette at home with those two all afternoon" said Henri.

"We'd better not leave her too long then" said Michel with concern as he thought another upset day for Josette would ensure that there would be no sexy loving tonight.

"The other thing is that my dear mother-in-law has 'phoned her brother, Pascal, to come and help today, she claims he's a 'do it yourself' wonder, well, I wouldn't let him oil my wheelbarrow if I had one" said Henri emphatically.

"That bad, eh?"

"Michel, what ever you do, don't let Pascal touch anything" said Henri. Just then there was a knock at the door and an elegant middle aged lady wearing the same costume as the assistants entered.

"Bonjour, monsieur Henri" she said with a smile.

"Ah, bonjour, Elaine, let me introduce you to my cousin, Michel Ronay."

"Monsieur" she smiled as she shook hands with Michel.

"Madame."

"Please call me Elaine, everybody does."

"Elaine."

"Michel has moved up to Le Touquet from Marseille and will

be here on business" said Henri.

"Oh, bon."

"Oui, it will be a new venture for me" said Michel.

"Welcome to our petite ville, Monsieur Michel" she said with a smile.

"Merci."

"Monsieur Henri, I'm sorry to disturb you but Madame Christiane has arrived and is complaining, will you please come down?"

"Oh, Mon Dieu, oui, tell her I'll be with her in a minute, give her a coffee or something" replied Henri.

"Oui, Monsieur" Elaine said as she left the office.

"Elaine is my manageress, I'd be lost without her" said Henri. Michel nodded and replied "well at least you've got somebody you can rely on."

"I need her to deal with the difficult customers"

"Not all of them by the sound of it"

"Non, that's true."

"Tell me about Madame Christiane then, it'll help you face her" said Michel with a smile.

"She's very attractive, very rich and married to a Paris Banker, she spends time here at Le Touquet because she's bored as her husband is always working, often travelling to London or Brussels. She spends money like water and behaves like an out of work chorus girl. In the summer she goes to Monte Carlo and we have a break from her" said Henri in a lame tone.

"Doesn't she have any friends in Le Touquet?"

"Only at the casino where she apparently looses a lot."

"She sounds fascinating, perhaps I should come downstairs with you and watch how you handle her" said Michel with a grin.

"Please do" replied Henri.

When Michel first saw Sophia Christiane he was totally mesmerised. Henri had said she was 'very attractive' and that had to be the understatement of the year. Sophia was stunning and Michel could not take his eyes of her as he followed Henri to the sales counter where she stood. Her blonde, shoulder length hair was beautifully fashioned and her makeup was light and enhancing. Michel guessed that she was about forty as she had that look of supreme confidence that a rich woman of that age exudes from her very being. Sophia stood with her mink coat open, one hand on her hip and clutching several expensive looking carrier bags in the other. As Henri approached she held up the carrier bags and said, in a wonderfully deep and commanding voice "Henri, my heel has broken."

"Oh, Madame Christiane, I'm so sorry, I'll put the matter right immediately I…….."

"You cannot, Henri, all the damage is done" she interrupted.

"Mon Dieu! Have you been hurt, Madame?" he enquired earnestly.

"Desperately" she replied loudly and everyone in the shop stopped talking and listened.

"Mon Dieu! What happened?" Henri asked as he tried to imagine the size of the impending legal action. When Sophia was sure that she had everyone's rapturous attention she continued.

"My heel broke last night as I was coming out of the casino in the pouring rain!" Henri was struck dumb with fear at that and Michel began to realise the significance of the situation.

"I then fell down the steps into a puddle and ruined my dress, one of the latest creations from Paris by Givenchy, I wish you to know." Henri groaned and held onto the counter to steady himself before giving Elaine an imploring look. Elaine looked pale but unflustered.

"Madame, what can I do to……….."

"Nothing, Henri" she interrupted "as I said, the damage is done, and on top of that, I was left struggling and hobbling about in the rain for all to see, like a drunken peasant woman in torn clothing, trying to get into my Mercedes." 'She knows how to hurt' thought Michel and he smiled gently at the lovely woman before him and he fancied there was a flicker of a smile directed back.

"Madame Christiane, I will do anything I can to put matters right" wailed Henri.

"Well, you can start by giving me another pair of shoes in exchange for these disasters" she replied firmly, holding out the carrier bag to Henri and shaking it.

"Of course, of course, Madame, Elaine, show Madame our new collection from Milan immediately" said Henri as he took the bag from her gloved hand.

"Oui, Monsieur" replied the loyal Elaine and she rushed away

up the stairs.
"If Madame would care to take a seat, I will attend to you personally" said Henri now pale and shaking slightly.
"Merci, and a coffee would be nice to steady my nerves after the shock of last night" Sophia said more calmly as she wandered off to a nearby plush chair.
"Of course, of course, er, Michel, get Madame a coffee, s'il vous plait."
"Certainly" replied Michel and not knowing where any coffee could be found he went upstairs to look for Elaine. He found her in a large stock room next to Henri's office, struggling to open several boxes containing the latest Milan collection.
"Henri has asked me to get her a coffee but........"
"Don't worry, Monsieur Michel, I'll get it as soon as I've taken these down to her."
"Merci, Elaine."
"I hope we've got enough shoes in her size" said Elaine as she checked several boxes.
"Does she complain a lot?" enquired Michel.
"Non, not really, but she is difficult sometimes, very fussy really, likes a lot of attention" said Elaine.
"Really" said Michel.
"Oui, I think she's a bit of an exhibitionist" she replied, and then clutching several boxes in her arms rushed off downstairs, leaving Michel wondering how he could see more of the beautiful, wealthy exhibitionist.
When Michel casually followed Elaine downstairs he saw Henri on his knees fitting an elegant red shoe to Sophia's extended foot. She glanced up at Michel as he approached and again he thought he saw a little smile on her lips. She returned her gaze to the shoe as Elaine arrived with the coffee to calm Madame's nerves and placed it on a glass topped table close by.
"These look quite nice, Henri" said Sophia as she toyed with the other shoe.
"Indeed, Madame, they are the very latest from Milan and the quality is......"
"Oui, I can see that for myself, Henri, I'm a very good judge of quality" she interrupted.
"Of course, Madame."

"I think that they fit rather well" she said as Henri slipped on the remaining shoe to her proffered foot.

"They look comfortable, Madame" replied Henri as Sophia stood up and looked into the floor mirror. She twirled one or two times and then looking hard at Michel asked "what do you think, monsieur?"

"Elegant shoes worn by a beautiful woman just enhance her beauty" he replied with a smile.

She smiled back for a moment and then said to Henri "who is this charming stranger?"

"Ah, my cousin, Madame, Michel Ronay from Marseille" stammered Henri.

"Are you sure he's not from Paris?"

"Quite sure, Madame."

"Pity."

"It's not a pity, Madame, because if I was in Paris I would not have the pleasure of seeing you" said Michel as he held out his hand and she smiled as she took it gently in her gloved hand.

"You're a touch smooth for a Marseille man" she replied coyly.

"There's only two of us in Marseille, the other one is presently in Monte Carlo" he replied. She burst out laughing at that and Michel saw Henri beaming and relaxed. A difficult, rich customer who is happy is a glorious sight to behold and Henri was very grateful to his cousin.

"I'll take these Henri, as Michel approves"

"Certainly, Madame, certainly, Elaine, wrap them for Madame" said a relieved Henri. Sophia returned to the chair and Elaine slipped the shoes from her feet as Henri stood by smiling and gently wringing his hands. Sophia sipped her coffee whilst the shoes were wrapped and after small talk and general enquiries from Henri regarding her health and that of her husband, Sophia Christiane glided out of the shop holding a carrier bag, containing her Italian shoes, and slipped behind the wheel of her white Mercedes sports coupe. In a moment she was gone from Henri's private car park. Only then did Elaine see Madame's petite leather handbag propped up under the chair.

"Monsieur Henri" she said as she pointed at the handbag. Henri went white and exclaimed "Mon Dieu!"

"Don't worry, I'll catch her" said Michel as he snatched the bag from the floor.

"Michel" said Henri in an anxious tone.

"Quick, give me your car keys" demanded Michel and without a moments hesitation Henri did as he was asked. Michel was into Henri's new Citroen and out of the car park in moments. He saw the white Mercedes some way ahead and he accelerated hard to catch up quickly. He was driving in unfamiliar streets and was anxious not to lose sight of Madame. The white coupe drove to the end of Rue Saint Jean, swung left then right into Avenue du Verger and continued into Place du Hermitage before turning into the Avenue du General de Gaulle where Michel caught up. He saw Madame Christiane glancing in her rear view mirror at him and it was obvious that she was a little unsure who it was driving closely behind her. Michel decided to drop back a little and follow her to her home. Madame Christiane's villa was set back from the road and surrounded by an elegant and well kept garden. The driveway up to the villa curved round in a long gentle arc up to the imposing front door and Michel followed the Mercedes, pulling up behind as she slipped from her driving seat. She smiled as Michel held up her handbag.

"You left this behind, Madame" he said.

"My word, you are attentive" she replied as she took the bag from him.

"All part of the service" he said.

"Merci, well you'd better come in for your reward" she said coyly.

"You're too kind" he replied.

The grand interior was like a film set and Michel was more than impressed with the luxury of the villa. Sophia threw off her mink coat and waved him towards the cream coloured settee that graced the centre of the lounge opposite the huge open fireplace.

"What will you have to drink, Michel?"

"A brandy, s'il vous plait" he replied as he lowered himself into the comfort of the settee whilst admiring her statuesque figure.

"So, as I've not seen you before I suppose you've only just arrived from Marseille" she said as she went to a large drinks cabinet and from a crystal decanter poured brandy into matching glasses.

"Oui."

"And are you on vacation or will you be working with Henri?"

"Working with Henri, but not in the salon."

"Oh?" she enquired as she handed him a brandy.

"We're going into the tourist business."

"Henri's not closing the salon is he?" she asked in an alarmed tone.

"Non, not at all" he replied.

"Bon; that would be a catastrophe" she said as she sat in a large armchair close to Michel.

"It would."

"Have you brought your wife with you?"

"Non" he replied truthfully and slightly taken aback by her directness.

"She's conveniently back at home then?"

"We're getting a divorce" said Michel.

"Is that wise?"

"I think so."

"Well, I'm not sure, you see, women get so serious over divorced men these days and want to rush them back into marriage as soon as they become available" she said.

"Really" he replied and he thought of Josette for a moment and remembered that he had promised to call at Monsieur Robardes office to make an appointment.

"Oui, I'm not sure that divorce is the answer to everything that goes wrong in a marriage" she said with certainty.

"Bon chance, Madame" he said as he raised his glass and sipped the golden liquid.

"Bon chance, Michel and call me Sophia please" she replied.

"Well, Sophia, tell me what I should do with my life" he said with a mocking smile.

"After you have started your business with Henri you should buy a nice villa, meet lots of new friends and entertain them at home, and remain married to your wife, who you can visit once in a while."

"That simple?"

"Oui, by staying married it'll keep hordes of silly women from trying to make a fool of you" she laughed.

"They succeed at that already, I can promise you" he replied.

"The secret of life is to enjoy it, live it and not get caught!" she laughed again.

"And you're sure you've found the secret?"

"Oh, I most certainly have" she replied, with her blue eyes flashing.

"And what does your husband have to say about your secret?" asked Michel.

"He doesn't know about my secret because he's never with me, he's always at work, and what he fails to understand is that he's missing out on so much" she replied.

"He certainly is" replied Michel with a grin.

"You think so too then?"

"Oui, Sophia, if I were married to you I'd make sure I worked from home so I didn't miss any of the fun" he laughed and she smiled.

"I've learned to take what I want when I want it, and believe me, it's the spice of life" she said with enthusiasm. Michel was really warming to this lovely woman and he was receiving all her messages loud and clear. He guessed that raw and uninhibited sex would soon follow, it only remained to decide where and when. The settee looked accommodating and the carpet in front of the fire was a possibility but he was sure Madame had already chosen the place and probably was leaving it up to him to set a time.

"Would you like to see round the villa?" she asked.

"Oui, with pleasure" replied Michel as he thought 'she has somewhere in mind to get her clothes off.'

"Let's finish our drinks then" she said with a smile. Michel smiled back and took his time to finish his brandy. He sensed her impatience and fancied that she had become a little flushed, a good sign for impending love making.

He followed the extraordinary woman around the ground floor, making the right appreciative noises at the diplomatically correct moments. Michel was genuinely impressed at the opulence and wealth on display in the spacious and grandiose rooms.

"Now come up stairs and see if I can impress you a little more" she said as she started up the curved staircase. Michel followed obediently, now sure that Sophia would make an unmistakable gesture in one of the bedrooms that would lead to unbridled, passionate sex. After viewing one of the guest bedrooms and the main bathroom with its bath for two, sunken in Italian marble, they moved into the master bedroom. Michel was taken aback by the size of the room as well as its furnishings. The predominant colour was peach, with deep, white fur rugs scattered over the soft carpet. The bed was enormous with a large padded headboard and matching side tables with low level lampshades in peach. Directly opposite the bed there were sliding glass doors that opened out onto a balcony where Michel could see a table and chairs set to one side. The view from the window was exquisite, the pine forest stretched away into the distance and with no other property in sight, absolute privacy was assured. Michel stood close to the doors admiring the view and said "this is superb."

"You like the view?" she asked from behind him.

"Oui."

"And what d'you think of the view over here?" she asked. Michel turned to see her standing by the bed with her legs apart, hands on her hips wearing only red bra and pants with stockings held up by matching red garters. She had her red Italian shoes on that Henri had just supplied in exchange for her broken shoe and she looked fabulous.

"The view is much better than the pine forest, it's a touch too green for me" he replied with a smile.

"Do you approve of Parisien lingerie?" she asked with a coy smile.

"Always" he replied and then added "but I like to look at it up close, I find that I always appreciate it so much more."

"You have such good taste for a Marseille man" she said as she walked towards him. He put out his arms to embrace her but she stepped away and said "you can sit in that chair and watch me if you want to." Michel eased himself down into a plush chair by the glass doors, knowing that he would enjoy Sophia dominating him whilst she made an exhibition of herself.

"I could tell the very first minute you saw me you wanted me" she said as she paraded backwards and forwards across the bedroom.

"You must have read my mind" he replied.

"Non, the look in your eyes told me everything I needed to know" she said.

"It was that obvious?"

"Oui, to me it was."

"You're very perceptive."

"I hope I'm very attractive" she replied as she turned again and Michel noticed how her breasts swung with the momentum.

"You are very beautiful" he said.

"I'm glad you think so, now tell me what really impresses you most? My legs? My hips? My breasts? Just tell me."

"All of you" he replied as he began to sweat a little.

"My breasts are so firm, I don't need a bra, look" and with that she unclipped the red, lace Paris creation and flung it to the floor. She was right, her breasts hardly dropped at all, but bounced seductively as she continued to pace up and down.

"Indeed you don't need a bra" he said.

"Would you like to feel how firm they are?"

"Oui, most certainly."

"Just a little feel then" she said as she came over to the chair and bent gently forward so he could touch. Her breasts were smooth and firm and he held them as gently as he could before rubbing his thumbs over her hard nipples.

"That's enough for the moment" she said as she moved away.

"Maybe for you, but not for me" he said.

"Just be patient Michel."

"I'm finding it hard, you are just so lovely."

"Now then, tell me, do these pants make my bum look big?"

"Enormous" he replied with a grin and she laughed.

"I'll have to do something about that then" she replied and turned her back on him before elegantly slipping her panties down stepping out of them and kicking them away.

"How's that now?" she asked.

"Perfect." She bent forward and touched her toes and Michel was impressed with the sight of her gentle curves.

"Does that look good?" she asked.

"Oui."

"Good enough to kiss?"

"Certainly."

"Come and kiss it then, my man." Michel rose from the chair slowly and placed his hands on her hips before he began kissing the cheeks of her naked bottom. He enjoyed every touch with his lips and he savoured the smell of her body as well as its softness.

"Mon Dieu, you're fabulous" he mumbled against her bottom.

"Now you can kiss the front" she said as she stood up and turned towards him. He buried his face in her pubic hair and kissed until he was breathless.

"Now lick it" she commanded and he did as he was told. He could hear her moaning with pleasure as he flicked his tongue all around and in and out of her.

"That's enough, Michel" she gasped and he realised she was close to an orgasm.

"I want you now" he said firmly and pushed her towards the bed.

"Oui, oh, oui, now" she replied as she fell back onto the soft covers.

Michel tore off his trousers and pants and lunged on top of Sophia with erection that took her breath away as he thrust it inside her. He was more brutal than usual as he felt she should be slightly punished for her teasing. But with every thrust he realised that she was enjoying it more than he expected.

"Oh, Michel, you're so big, but I like it" she gasped.

"It's all the fish we eat that does it" he replied and she giggled.

"I'll put it on the menu every night" she gasped.

"Oh, Sophia, I'm coming" he shouted as he felt the unstoppable surging sensation which meant the end was near.

"Keep going a little longer, chérie, please" she implored him, but it was to no avail and he slammed with all his might into Sophia's elegant body. Happily, it was so aggressive that it brought her a very sharp and pulsating orgasm to which she cried out repeatedly "Mon Dieu! Mon Dieu!"

As their passions subsided Michel kissed her gently on her perfect lips and then, as they parted, he said "you are the most beautiful woman I've ever seen."

"Merci, ma petite." She had just finished speaking when Michel heard a noise outside the bedroom door and felt himself go cold inside. There was a knock at the door a moment before it opened and a young woman entered.

"Pardon, Madame, but are you in for dinner tonight?" enquired the young woman apparently oblivious to her naked mistress fixed beneath a trouserless, perfect stranger.

"Er, non, Evette, I'll be dining out, merci."

"Very good, Madame, and bonjour monsieur" said the girl who

then promptly left the room closing the door gently behind her.

"Mon Dieu!" exclaimed Michel.

"Don't worry, chérie, its only Evette, my maid, she never takes any notice and she's very discreet" said Sophia.

"This must be a regular sight then?" asked Michel.

"I told you, I have fun when I want it" she replied with a smile. Just then the telephone on the bedside cabinet rang and Sophia picked it up.

"Hello, Madame Christiane speaking....oh, Henri, oui, kind of you to call....oui, Michel caught me, oui,.... Oui, he's given me my handbag, oui....non, nothing missing, oui, he's still here, would you like to speak to him?.....oui, here he is" and she handed the receiver to Michel as he remained on top of her.

"Hello, Henri."

"Hello, Michel, everything OK?"

"Oui, Henri."

"Are you alright, Michel?"

"Oui, why do you ask?"

"You sound a bit breathless, have you been running?"

"Non, I'll tell you later."

"Bon, are you coming back to the salon now?" asked Henri.

"Oui, I'll see you soon."

"Bon, and by the way, well done Michel, I can't thank you enough for keeping Madame happy."

"My pleasure" replied Michel as he replaced the receiver.

An hour later Michel returned to the salon, having promised an insistent Madame Christiane that he would meet her the next day for lunch at Le Café des Arts, in the Rue de Paris. He had grave concerns about the proposed lunch date but could not resist Sophia's beauty and sophistication, and as he had already made love to her, what further harm could there be in having lunch together?

After a coffee and thanks from Henri for saving the delicate situation, Michel and his cousin settled down to discuss future plans for the new business venture. The first priority was to set up an office in Aunt's house and Henri planned to leave that entirely to Michel. They discussed all the attractions that they could think of to entice the spendthrift tourist and eventually whittled the list down to a boat trip to Boulogne, a coach trip into Normandy, a gastronomic evening tour and bicycle hire service. Well pleased with the outcome of their deliberations they returned home in the late afternoon, leaving Elaine to close the salon as usual.

All was not well at 19 Rue de Londres, and although the house was a lot brighter and cleaner than when Michel had left it he felt an atmosphere which appeared as gloomy as before. He was introduced to Uncle Pascal by Josephine, who praised his 'do it yourself' abilities, whilst Henri rolled his eyes and Josette stood by, hands on hips, looking very sullen.

"I will do all I can to help you, Michel, anything at all, just ask me, I can do anything" said Pascal with confidence.

"Merci, Pascal, I'm sure that Josette and I will need your help getting everything in the house as we want it" replied Michel diplomatically.

"Of course, and I shall be there to see it gets done properly" said Pascal with gusto. Henri turned away, shaking his head slightly and said to Jackie "we'd better leave these good people to it then, chérie."

"Oui" she replied.

"We'll collect you about eight for dinner, Michel" said Henri as made his way to the front door followed by his wife, who stopped to kiss her mother and uncle 'goodbye'.

After they had gone Pascal, a short, rotund man with grey wavy hair and glasses, started stroking the wall and said "I think the place needs re-decorating throughout."

"I agree, Pascal, and it's too much for me to do, especially as Henri and I are starting up the business, I'll have to get someone in" replied Michel.

"Oh, non, non, I'll do it for you" replied Pascal.

"Pascal, that's very kind of you, but it's a big job."

"Nonsense, I can do it easily, I have a friend who has a little paint shop in Boulogne, near where I live, and I can get all the paint we need at trade price, for cash of course…"

"Of course" agreed Michel.

"And all you and Josette have to do, is choose the colours, I'll bring a colour card when I come tomorrow" Pascal said with a big smile and Josette slumped down in a nearby chair with a dejected look on her face.

"Bon" said Michel because he could not think of anything else to say.

"Pascal is so good at painting and decorating" said Josephine and her brother beamed in appreciation at his sister's comment.

"I'm sure" replied Michel uncertain of what he was letting himself in for.

"Well, I'd better be off now, see you tomorrow, mes enfants" said Pascal.

"Me too" said Josephine and after they had said their 'au revoirs' Michel closed the door and turned to be met by Josette's stony face.

"That lot have driven me almost out of my mind today" she said.

"Oh, ma chérie."

"And don't you ever leave me alone with them again, do you hear me?"

"Oui, chérie, but I've a business to start up and….."

"Michel, one more day alone with them and I'm going straight back to Marseille!" she interrupted.

"Chérie, I think you're over reacting….."

"Michel, I've told you what I'm going to do, so you decide!" and with that she flounced out of the room and went upstairs.

They spoke very little as they washed and dressed themselves for dinner with Henri and Jackie. Michel understood, from the little that Josette would say about the day's events, that all the woman did was question her about Monique. Then Pascal had arrived and gone round the house moving furniture, tapping walls and switching the lights on and off. At last they were ready for dinner and were sitting enjoying a drink when Josette said "I've had a dreadful day and I bet you didn't make an appointment with Monsieur Robardes to discuss your divorce." It was like a cold knife going in. He had forgotten all about it.

"I will see him first thing tomorrow, I promise" he replied.

"I won't hold my breath" she said.

Henri's favourite restaurant in Le Touquet was Flavio's in the Avenue du Verger where the cuisine was par excellence. As they drove up Michel was impressed by the elegant white exterior of the restaurant that was lit up by a warm glow of romantic lighting. The welcoming interior was tasteful and refined with high back chairs surrounding tables set out with gleaming cutlery and crystal glasses.

"Bonsoir, Monsieur Henri" said Guy, the owner, as they entered.

"Bonsoir, Guy" replied Henri as Guy bobbed a gentle bow and welcomed the others with "Madame's and Monsieur." They followed him to a table in the centre of the dining room and were seated by an attentive young waiter. Henri acknowledged several other diners as Michel began to peruse the extensive menu. He looked up occasionally and smiled at his fiancé who had seemed a little more relaxed than earlier and Jackie was improving the situation with some light and amusing conversation.

"It's all very good here" said Henri knowingly.

"I'm sure" replied Michel.

"The langoustines baked with spices is one of my favourites" said Jackie.

"I'll try the Brill in rhubarb wine" announced Josette with a smile which Michel was relieved to see.

"Bon, chérie, I'll join you" he said and he smiled back at his beloved. After starters of various soups, rich pates and the first bottle of wine, they were waiting eagerly for the main course to arrive when Sophia Christiane walked in escorted by a tall, grey haired man with a bored expression. She looked stunning in a black, figure hugging dress enhanced with gold jewellery. Michel noticed her first as Guy brought the couple to the very next table. As they were seated Sophia acknowledged Michel with a smile and he nodded back just as Henri saw her and half whispered "bonsoir, Madame."

"Bonsoir, Henri, and Michel" she replied just loud enough for them all to hear. Josette looked daggers at Michel.

"How does that woman know your name?" she hissed in a whisper.

"She's Henri's best customer, I met her at the salon and she's very rich" replied Michel.

"I can see that" Josette replied with a woman's eye for the very best couture.

"Michel saved me from a disaster today" Henri whispered.

"Really?" said Josette with a touch of disbelief.

"Oui, Madame came into the salon to complain about a pair of shoes, the heel had broken on one, and Michel calmed her down, then when she left her handbag behind, he went after her and gave it back, she was very grateful" said Henri in a half whisper.

"Oui, Michel is very good with people, especially women" said Josette with the emphasis on 'women'. They all noticed her comment and Jackie smirked a little whilst Henri looked uncomfortable.

"Is that her husband with her?" enquired Michel.

"Oui, I think so, I've only seen him waiting outside the salon in a car, apparently he doesn't like shopping" replied Henri and Michel was grateful for missing what may have been a close encounter with the husband at the villa. He hoped Evette was as discreet as her mistress claimed. The main courses arrived and Sophia looked at the cuisine that was being served and said "I am pleased to see you are having fish, I can highly recommend it." Michel just smiled and nodded gently whilst the others looked surprised at her comment. The wine waiter refilled their glasses and although Josette had mellowed slightly she still kept giving her fiancé inquisitive looks. They finished the meal in a leisurely fashion and relaxed with liqueurs and coffee. Sophia had been exchanging glances with Michel throughout and Josette had noticed, keeping a careful score. Michel suspected that he was in for some tough questioning at bed time.

After thanking Guy for his excellent cuisine and acknowledging Madame Christiane and her husband, they left the restaurant and drove to Rue de Londres, where the lovers hurried inside after making arrangements for the next day. Once Josette had Michel to herself she started.

"Who was that damned woman?"

"I told you, she's Henri's best customer" he replied.

"She seems a bit too friendly for a rich customer" she said forcefully.

"Well, to succeed in business you've got to take care of them" he replied.

"Oui, but I'm not too sure about her."

"I understand, ma chérie."

"I hope you do."

"Oh, I do."

"Bon, then to make me believe that you understand, just keep that appointment with Monsieur Robardes tomorrow."

"I will, ma petite, I will."

"Bon, now let's go to bed, I'm tired, really tired." Michel knew by her tone that there would be no sexual pleasures tonight and he followed his fiancé upstairs to the cold bedroom and the hard old bed that Aunt had died in. A mixed day with some compensations and he looked forward to having lunch with Sophia as he cuddled up for warmth to Josette.

CHAPTER 4

The next morning Michel left Josette in the tender hands of Josephine, who had arrived early, and made his way to the Avenue Duquesne to make an appointment with Monsieur Robardes. This declaration of his firm intentions to get a divorce brought a smile to Josette's face and he left her in a happier frame of mind. He hoped that the later arrival of Jackie and Pascal would not have too much effect on her happy state.

The reception of Monsieur Robardes office was clean, bright and welcoming. An attractive female in her thirties greeted Michel with a smile and wished him "bonjour, monsieur" as he entered.

"Bonjour, Mademoiselle, I'd like to see Monsieur Robardes, si'l vous plait."

"Certainly, monsieur, when would you like to make an appointment?"

"As soon as possible please, you see it's an emergency."

"An emergency, monsieur?" the receptionist asked in a concerned tone.

"Oui, it's my fiancé you understand."

"What's wrong with her?"

"She'll leave me if I don't get a quick divorce" he replied.

"I am sorry to hear that, monsieur" replied the receptionist and she immediately glanced down at the diary on her desk and tried to hide her smile.

"Monsieur Robardes is free this afternoon at four o'clock, would that be convenient?"

"Oui, merci, Mademoiselle."

"Bon, he will see you then, monsieur, may I have your name, s'il vous plait?"

"Michel Ronay."

She wrote his name in the diary and he left the office feeling a little better but apprehensive. He wondered if he was being a little hasty in trying to do the right thing. He pondered on what Sophia had said about divorced men and the females like Josette, lurking around, waiting to entrap them back into marriage. Suddenly he felt a touch of home sickness for Marseille, he missed the freedom, Ricky's bar, Jacques, Antone, as well as his string of delightful mistresses and Jean Gambetta in his dusty old garage. Le Touquet felt cold and a little hostile in comparison and he hoped the financial rewards from the business would make everything worth while. He was concerned about Josette's changed attitude towards him and he could only wait to see if she became, once again, the lovely and loving young woman that she had been in Marseille. Perhaps he should fix a time limit on their stay in Le Touquet and if things did not work out fairly quickly he should consider returning to Marseille.

Michel felt he needed a drink and drove back to the Rue de Londres, where he had seen a suitable place to relax and gather his thoughts. He parked the Mercedes close to the Bar Americaine and wandered in to its dimly lit interior. It was quaintly old fashioned but had a warm and friendly atmosphere and Michel guessed that with a name like Bar Americaine it would attract a lot of trans Atlantic visitors during the summer. He ordered a Pernod from the young bar tender, Pierré, and then found a corner to sit and think.

The bar was relatively quiet and there were only a few locals drinking and reading papers. He thought it would be a good idea to go back to number 19 and let Josette know that he would be seeing Monsieur Robardes at four o'clock before joining Madame Christiane for lunch at Le Café des Arts. Hopefully the news of the appointment with the solicitor would keep Josette sweet and he would also be able to see what mayhem Josephine, her daughter and Pascal had caused.

Several Pernod's later he left the bar and walked along to his new home. Inside he found Josette up a step ladder in the lounge attempting to dust the picture rail, Jackie and her mother in the kitchen washing crockery and Pascal dabbing cream emulsion paint in patches on the dark grey wallpaper in the hall. They all greeted him with smiles, except Josette, who raised her eyes to heaven when the 'helpers' were not looking. After telling his fiancé about the afternoon appointment he was pleased to see her smile and then went to find out what Pascal was attempting with a very tiny pot of emulsion paint in the hall.

"This is better than looking at colour cards, it gives a true impression of what it's like on the wall" said Pascal with authority.

"Supposing we don't like the colour" said Michel.

“That’s alright, we just have to paint over it with another colour” replied Pascal.

“Oh” said Michel.

“Oui, I’ve got a pale green to try out in a minute” said Pascal with enthusiasm.

“Was this your friend’s idea?” asked Michel.

“Oui, he says it’s the best way of choosing colours.”

“You can tell him that I’m not so sure” said Michel and went off to talk to his frustrated fiancé.

She slumped into a chair and whispered “I’m trying to be calm but they’re driving me crazy.”

“I can see that, come on, I’ll take you for a drink in a little bar I’ve just found along the street.”

“Please do” she replied and Michel told the ‘helpers’ that they were going out.

Over drinks in a quiet corner of the Bar Americaine, Michel shared his concerns regarding their long term future in Le Touquet and she brightened visibly at the suggestion that they should return to Marseille if things did not work out fairly soon. He told Josette that he did not want to see her unhappy, no matter what rewards the business might bring and when he had finished telling her, she shed a little tear.

“I do love you, Michel” she whispered.

“And I love you to, ma chérie” he replied.

It was almost lunch time when the lovers returned from the Bar Americaine suitably relaxed after a reasonable amount of alcohol. Michel told his fiancé that he was going to Henri’s salon before his appointment with Monsieur Robardes and later they would go out for a quiet, romantic dinner. When he left her she appeared to be her normal, loving self, once more and kissed him with some passion before he left.

Driving to the Rue de Paris he determined to tell Sophia that he could have nothing more to do with her and that after lunch he would never see her again. He spotted Sophia immediately he walked into the restaurant. She was seated at a table for two, in an alcove, looking stunning in a black dress with a huge white collar and a matching white picture hat with a black bow on the side. She smiled as he approached and sat down.

“Bonjour, ma petite” she half whispered in a sexy tone.

"Bonjour" he replied, trying to be a little distant. She picked up the nuance immediately and asked "are you a little sad today, ma chérie?"

"Non."

"Are you sure?"

"Oui."

"Perhaps seeing me last night with my husband has upset you?"

"Non, not at all."

"Bon, I would not like you to be unhappy" she said.

"I'm never unhappy."

"Bon" she said as the waiter arrived with the menus.

"This place is famous for its nouvelle cuisine" she whispered once they were alone.

"Bon."

"And I do so enjoy it."

"Bon."

"It always makes me relax and excite my animal instincts" she said deliberately. Michel did not know how to reply to that so he just gazed at the menu and tried to gather his thoughts. He realised it was going to be very difficult to tell this lovely woman that this was their last time together.

"And after lunch I've planned a little trip for us" she said.

"Oh, non, ma petite, I have a meeting with Henri at the salon" he said nervously.

"Nonsense, it's a lovely day and I know Henri won't mind if you're a little late" she purred.

"Oh, he will" replied Michel.

"Don't think so, chérie, especially if I tell him you're with me." Michel felt hopelessly trapped by this beautiful woman.

"Well we mustn't be too long on this trip" he replied.

"We won't be, I promise, now, what are you going to eat?" she asked as the waiter returned to take their order. Michel was guided by Sophia's choice from the menu and realising the situation he was in, relaxed completely. He decided to let her have total control over him as it would be their very last time together. She asked him about his business plans as they leisurely enjoyed the cuisine enhanced with expensive wine chosen by her. Michel was quite open and he was impressed by how well Sophia grasped his ideas and realised the potential of his plans. As they lingered over a delicious sweet she stunned him by saying "I'd like to be a partner in your business and invest a lot of money in it." Michel's jaw dropped and for a moment he was totally speechless.

"Well, I don't know, I'll have to discuss it with Henri….."

"He'll say 'yes' believe me" she interrupted.

"How do you know that?"

"Because he's weak, he's a salon keeper."

"I'm not sure……."

"I am."

"How can you say that?"

"Look how he behaved yesterday when I complained about my shoe, he almost fell to pieces in front of me."

"That's understandable, you're a very important customer of his, with a very powerful personality" replied Michel. She smiled at that and said "I am impressed with your loyalty to him."

"What I said is the truth, you are very important to him."

"Am I important to you, Michel?"

"Oui, of course" he replied.

"Bon, because I want to be involved with you and I won't take 'no' for an answer on this business deal."

"I can't agree to anything without talking to Henri."

"Believe me, just tell him you've done it, fâit accomplis is always the best way of getting the decision you want!" Michel did not know how to handle this woman so for the moment he decided to play along with her. He sat thinking for a while, allowing her to believe he was contemplating an agreement.

"Now then, just suppose I agreed for you to become a partner…."

"An equal partner, ma petite" she interrupted.

"An equal partner, how much would you be prepared to invest?"

"As much as you need to succeed in the business" she replied, her eyes gleaming with excitement.

"And when would you want your investment back?"

"Never."

"Never?" he gasped.

"Non."

"Why not?" he asked incredulously.

"Because what ever you need for the business would be such a small sum of money to me, I quite frankly, wouldn't miss it."

Henri had said she was rich, but Michel thought she must be 'rich rich'. This certainly put a fresh complexion on the matter and if she did not want her money back, well, it was equal to having a bank vault open and being told to help yourself.

"I'll have to give it some thought" said Michel.

"Non, you won't, just shake my hand now and say it's a deal".

"I can't."

"You'll never regret it" she said as she held out her beautifully manicured hand.

"Mon Dieu!" gasped Michel, the temptation was too great, dizzy and with his mind in a whirl, he took her hand and gently squeezed it.

"Bon, we're partners, and now all you have to do, is tell Henri."

"Mon Dieu." he whispered and thought 'what have I done?'

"So, finish your sweet, ma chérie, and let's go for a little trip."

After paying l'addition Michel followed Sophia to her white Mercedes coupe in a dazed state of mind. Was it the wine? Had he really just agreed to have this woman in the business? How would he explain it to Henri? And even more important than that; to Josette? He would have to get out of it, that was the only answer. He had a flash of inspiration, he would seek advice from Monsieur Robardes on how to legally cancel a verbal agreement. He felt a little better as he sat next to Sophia whilst she revved up the car before roaring off down the Rue de Paris and out of Le Touquet.

"Where are we going?" he asked.

"To a quiet little place I know" she replied as they headed south along the coast.

"I hope we're not going to be too long" he said.

"It depends on you, ma petite" she replied.

"Me?"

"Oui." Michel remained silent at that as his mind went into over drive wondering what this woman had planned next. She was certainly full of surprises and he was still recovering from the shock over the agreement made in Le Café des Arts. How could he ever explain it all to Henri?

After about twenty minutes the Mercedes slowed and then turned right onto a track just wide enough for the car. On either side were gently sloping dunes with tufts of long grass blowing in the sea breeze. Michel had a good idea what was going to happen next, but he remained quiet and thoughtful. Sophia stopped the car in a little parking area almost on the beach. There was nobody else in sight.

"Come on, chérie, let me show you a sight that you'll enjoy" she said with a smile. He got out of the car and waited as she opened the boot and removed a large blanket and a petite leather case.

"Follow me, mon brave" she said as she walked swiftly towards the beach. He did as he was told, certain that she would soon expose her body and demand immediate sex. They walked along for about a hundred metres before turning onto a narrow path that lay between two steep sided sand dunes. At the top was a small open space that was surrounded by a raised area of the dune. It provided a sandy grass wall about a metre high which gave shelter from the wind and was only open towards the sea. Sophia spread the blanket on the sand and asked "do you approve of my little spot under the open sky?"

"Oui, it's very cosy" he replied.

"It was made for lovers by the sea gods" she laughed as she sat down and opened the case. Michel sat beside her and watched her remove a bottle of brandy and pour the amber liquid into two elegant tumblers. She handed him a glass and said "here's to us and the business."

"To us and the business" he said trying to keep the fear of impending disaster out of his voice.

Sheltered from the gentle breeze by the dune wall and with the winter sun shining down, Michel soon became quite warm and removed his jacket.

"What a good idea, chérie" said Sophia as she stood up, looked around and then undid all the buttons down the front of her dress. She stood in front of him and opened it to reveal that she was completely naked underneath except for her stockings held up by silk garters.

"This is one of my easy fuck dresses for outdoors, what d'you think?" she asked with a smile as she placed her hands on her hips to reveal her complete body for his pleasure.

"Absolutely perfect" he replied already feeling a stirring in his loins.

"Bon" and she twirled round to face the sea and allowed the dress to drop onto the sand. Now naked except for her white hat, stockings and shoes, she looked glorious and held up her hands and opened her legs before saying "I love to feel the sun on my body and smell the sea, it's wonderful, it makes me feel at one with the very elements and at peace with my soul."

"Bon, chérie" he replied as he enjoyed the sight of her statuesque body in front of him.

"Are you at peace with your soul, Michel?"

"Oui, very" he replied.

"Bon, that means you'll enjoy my body even more than yesterday" she said with conviction.

"Bon."

"When two souls are at peace together the sexual fulfilment is so very complete" she said as she lowered her arms and placed her hands back on her hips. Michel saw her lift her head to the sun before turning to face him.

"Do you know, chérie, the sea breeze makes my nipples as hard as little diamonds" she smiled.

"I can see that, and they do stand out" he replied.

"I do enjoy your appreciation of me, it's so flattering."

"You are very beautiful and that's the truth" he replied with certainty as she sat down beside him.

"Now, take your clothes off and stand up to face the sea and tell me if you are at one with the elements before we get down to the serious business of lustful pleasure" she said with a coy smile.

"Oui, ma chérie" he replied obediently.

"And meanwhile, I'll pour us another brandy." Michel stood up and looked around and was pleased that there was nobody on the beach. He undressed and kept his back to Sophia all the time conscious of his erection. He opened his legs and held up his arms and did admit to himself that it felt rather good. The sea breeze was gentle and the sun quite warm on his body. When he thought enough time had elapsed, he lowered his arms and turned to face his new mistress.

"It's the first time I've seen you naked and I like it" she laughed and took off her white hat.

"Bon."

"Now, d'you feel at one with the elements?"

"I do."

"Bon, come and sit down and blend your soul into mine followed by your body." He sat beside her and she handed him his brandy.

"Here's to love, wherever we find it" she said.

"To love" he replied and immediately thought of Josette and was pricked by his conscience. He was enjoying the moment and it was certainly very delightful being on a secluded beach with a beautiful, naked woman and was infinitely better than driving his taxi around Marseille. But what would be the outcome, he wondered.

When they had finished their drinks Sophia put her arms around his neck and kissed him passionately for a long time before stroking his erection, as they carried on kissing. He, meanwhile, gently tweaked her diamond hard nipples until she was gasping between kisses. She broke away from their embrace and laid face down on the blanket.

"Have me now, chérie, slowly from behind, as I watch the sea" she whispered. Michel eased himself on top of her and she guided his rigid penis into her moist body. He kissed her neck as she whispered "do it slowly, in time with the waves breaking on the beach." She began to gasp with pleasure as he reached right up inside her soft, compliant body, each slow thrust in time with the waves.

"Oh, Mon Dieu, you must keep this up until I tell you to stop" she gasped.

"Oui, chérie, I'll try."

"Don't you dare come yet" she commanded between gasps. Michel did not reply and concentrated on the rhythm of the waves. He thought the English Channel looked pretty good from his viewpoint and having meaningful sex in the open with a breeze wafting around his bare bottom and the sun warming his back was an enjoyable experience. Then he happened to glance at his watch, it was almost three o'clock and he remembered the appointment with Monsieur Robardes at four. He would have to hurry things along a little.

"Chérie, you are just so beautiful and your body is so soft, I just can't go on much longer" he said slowly.

"Alright, chérie, stop now and let me turn over, I must feel the sun on my face when I come" she replied. They quickly took up the new position and she wrapped her long legs around his waist, her stockings rubbing sexily on his bare skin, as he once again reached up into her very being. He was surprised when she soon began to gasp and gently cry out with pleasure as he increased the tempo of his rhythm. He felt her body tighten as she began to race to a sharp and unbelievable climax. He thrust with all his might and exploded inside her as she screamed a final scream of intense pleasure.

"Oh, Mon Dieu! Mon Dieu! Mon Dieu! That was so good" she gasped.

"It was."

"You must never leave me, Michel, never, you understand?"

"Oui" he replied nervously as the fearful realisation of what she was demanding became clear in his mind.

"I've never been fucked like that before" she gasped.

"Really?" he asked, feeling quite proud but agitated.

"Never."

"Bon, now then, chérie, I'm afraid I must get back……."

"Oh, Henri can wait, just hold me close, Michel" she interrupted. He felt trapped by this woman and did not know what to do. All his previous encounters with women had been different, less demanding and less certain than this one. He held her close for what seemed a long while before glancing at his watch, it was now three thirty and it was getting colder.

"I'm sorry ma chérie, but I must make a move" he said gently. She agreed and after hurriedly dressing they retraced their steps to the car, passing an old man with a dog on the way. He grinned and wished them 'bonjour' and Michel was sure that the old man knew what they had been up to.

Sophia parked her car behind his Mercedes outside Le Café des Arts, she kissed him passionately and asked "where shall we go tomorrow, chérie?"

"Nowhere, chérie, I have to get on with starting the business."

"Well you won't be doing that all day, will you?"

"Possibly."

"OK, I'll have to be patient and wait until the evening before I can have you again" she said firmly.

"I don't think…."

"We'll go to the casino" she interrupted.

"But….."

"Pick me up at home, about eight, we can eat later."

"Sophia I can't……"

"You'd better go now, you don't want to keep Henri waiting, besides you've got a lot to tell him about your new partner" she smiled and lost for words Michel left her with a wave of his hand and slipped behind the wheel of his car.

It was just a few minutes past four when Michel was shown into the office of Monsieur Robardes. The solicitor was a tall, rather gaunt looking man with iron grey hair and large horn rimmed glasses wearing a dark, ill fitting, suit that had seen better days. Michel was waved to a hard upright chair opposite a rambling dark brown desk covered with files and sheaves of loose paper. It struck him that the office was rather drab and a little severe compared with the reception outside.

"So, Monsieur Ronay, what can I do for you?" he asked slowly.

"I wish to get a divorce from my wife, Monique."

"On what grounds, monsieur?"

"Well" Michel hesitated, he was unsure and had not thought about it that much.

"I'm listening, monsieur" coaxed the solicitor.

"We're not compatible."

"I see, and what makes you think that?"

"Well, er…."

"My receptionist tells me that you have a fiancé who is, shall we say, a little impatient."

"Oui, that is true" replied Michel, slightly annoyed that Josette should be mentioned so early in the discussions.

"Ah, could it be that the new lady in your life is the real reason for your divorce?"

"Well, possibly."

"Tell me, when did you leave your wife?"

"A few days ago" replied Michel.

"And when did you become engaged?" enquired Monsieur Robardes with a smile.

"Just before Christmas" replied Michel.

"Whilst you were still living with your wife?"

"Oui, well it was sort of accidental" replied Michel, remembering the debacle in Ricky's bar with the press.

"An accident you say?"

"Oui."

"How does one become engaged by 'accident', monsieur?" enquired the perplexed solicitor.

"Well, it's a long story, perhaps we could move on?" asked Michel, conscious of the large hole he was digging for himself.

"Monsieur" protested the solicitor "it may be a long story but all very relevant and how can I give you my best professional advice if I don't know all the facts?" Michel was stumped and he realised that getting a divorce from Monique was going to prove a lot more difficult than he had hoped.

"True" he replied.

"Bon, now then, let us start at the beginning, please take your time whilst I make some notes" said Monsieur Robardes, conscious of the probability of a large fee in this complex case.

"I have believed for some time that my wife and I are not compatible and……"

"Forgive me, monsieur, before you begin, some details s'il vous plait, firstly your address?"

"19, Rue de Londres, here in Le Touquet."

"Bon, and where does your wife live?"

"At our villa in Grambois."

"The address, monsieur, so I can write to her." Michel gave the details and the solicitor was surprised when he realised Grambois was near Marseille.

"And where is your fiancé living?" he enquired.

"Here, with me."

"In the circumstances, monsieur, as you have run away with another woman, it might be better if your wife sued you for divorce!"

"She'd never do that."

"Why not?"

"Because she loves me too much" replied Michel before realising what he had said.

"Monsieur, have you considered a reconciliation with your wife before it's too late?"

"Non, I must get a divorce, my wife and I argue all the time and I just can't live with that."

"I argue with my wife, monsieur, but its not serious grounds for divorce" replied the solicitor.

"I'm sorry to hear that, monsieur, but as you experience it yourself, I'm sure you must have some sympathy for me." said Michel firmly. The solicitor faintly nodded and did not reply but carried on scribbling over the pad in front of him.

"Tell me what you and your wife argue over."

"Everything" replied Michel.

"Surely not everything, monsieur."

"Everything."

"Please give me some examples, the major ones will do for the moment" said the solicitor with pen poised. Suddenly Michel's mind went blank and nothing sprang to mind.

"There's so many, I'll just have to think for a moment or two" replied Michel, suddenly wishing he had never kept this appointment and spent more time with Sophia on the beach.

"Well….." and Michel paused to gather his thoughts.

"Oui, monsieur" said the solicitor as he waited for the long list.

"Er, the major thing we argue over is the long hours I work."

"And what do you do for a living?"

"I'm a taxi driver in Marseille, or at least, I was…"

"Until you ran away" interrupted Monsieur Robardes looking over his glasses at his unhappy client.

"Oui."

"But surely that's a sign of a loving wife, she wanted you at home so you could be together."

"Possibly."

"Have you any children, monsieur?"

"Oui, my stepson, Frederik."

"So have you both been married before?"

"Oui."

"What else have you argued about?"

"Er," Michel hesitated.

"Oui?"

"Her mother and her aunts"

"Do they live with you, monsieur?"

"Non."

"Tell me how your wife's relations are the cause of your arguments."

"Well, when they all visit at the same time, they all argue."

"With whom do they argue?"

"With each other" replied Michel with conviction.

"Do they argue with you and your wife?"

"Well, non, not usually."

"In that case, surely the best thing to have done would be to invite them one by one at different times."

"Possibly."

"Anything else, monsieur?" Michel realised that he was not making much of a case for his divorce.

"Well…." he hesitated.

"Monsieur Ronay, I suggest that you go away and think very carefully about your divorce and make another appointment with my secretary when you have some firmer evidence of the incompatibility with your wife, to discuss."

"Oui, that's good advice" replied Michel with relief.

"That's what I'm here for" replied the solicitor.

"There was just one other matter that I would like your advice on" said Michel warily.

"Oui?" said Monsieur Robardes as he looked over his glasses.

"Er, quite by accident…." he began.

"Another accident, monsieur?" interrupted the solicitor.

"Oui, I've recently met a lady, here in Le Touquet, and I, by chance, agreed verbally to a business proposition with her, and……"

"Is your fiancé involved with this 'proposition'?"

"Non, she knows nothing about it" replied Michel.

"I see" said the solicitor as he fixed his client through narrowed eyes.

"Well, its only just happened and I haven't had time to tell anyone about it, in fact, you're the first to know" said Michel with a helpful smile.

"What, may I ask, is the nature of this proposition?"

"The lady in question wishes to invest as much money as I need to start a business here in Le Touquet" replied Michel with some pride.

"Really, monsieur" said Monsieur Robardes with interest.

"Oui, but although I agreed verbally to her offer, I really don't want her as a partner" said Michel.

"Totally understandable in your position, monsieur, with so many women involved in your life at present."

"Only two in Le Touquet" replied Michel in a hurt tone, which the solicitor ignored.

"The law is quite clear, monsieur, if you have made an agreement with this lady, it does not matter that it is only verbal, the law will recognise that agreement and only if you, by due and delicate conversation, can persuade the lady to withdraw, then I have to advise you that you're stuck with it!" Michel felt sick with fright at that terrifying thought. Seeing the fear in his client's eyes and mindful of the substantial fees charged in advising 'small business start ups' Monsieur Robardes then continued with a smile "of course, good legal advice can mitigate many of the problems surrounding finance and small business, so lifting the burden of un-necessary worry from the individual." Michel gave the solicitor a sickly grin and said "I think I had better leave you now and take some time to consider both my domestic and business position."

"A sound idea, monsieur, please call my secretary when you are ready to discuss matters further." Once out in the Avenue, Michel felt slightly faint and blamed it on the expensive wine at lunch and the brandy on the beach. He sat in the Mercedes for some time, trying to rationalise his thoughts before driving round to the shoe salon.

He made his way to Henri's office where he found his cousin seated behind his desk looking at several poster 'mock ups' of tourist attractions.

"Ah, Michel, just in time, what d'you think of these for your office?"

"Wonderful" replied Michel without looking at them.

"You haven't seen them yet."

"Henri, we've got a serious problem" said Michel as he slumped down in the plush chair opposite Henri.

"What ever is it?"

"It's Madame Christiane."

"What about her?" asked Henri in alarm.

"Well it's......."

"She's not going to sue is she?" interrupted Henri in a strangled whisper.

"Non, she wants to invest in our business" replied Michel nervously.

"Invest in our business?"

"Oui."

"Never, Michel, never, our lives would be a misery from the time we got out of bed until we got back in, non, we'd never be free of her."

"Henri......"

"I can tell you, Michel, we pray for the summer when she goes of to Monte Carlo, it's a blessed relief."

"She says she'll invest what ever we need and doesn't want the money back" said Michel enthusiastically.

"I don't care, Michel, the answer is 'non' and I mean 'non' for ever!"

"Why are you so against the woman?"

"Because, I know what she's like, you've no experience of her...."

"Oui, I have" interrupted Michel with a grin.

"What d'you mean?" asked Henri in a concerned tone.

"Guess."

"Mon Dieu! You haven't......"

"I have."

"When?"

"At her villa yesterday and on the beach today" replied Michel with a grin.

"Mon Dieu, you bloody fool, d'you realise what you've done?"

"I do."

"Michel, the implications......"

"Henri, I promise you there are no implications" interrupted Michel.

"Go on."

"As long as I take care of Sophia Christiane's personal needs, she'll do exactly as we want."

"Michel, you over indulgence in sex has affected your brain!"

"Don't be naive."

"The woman is a scheming, manipulative, spoilt, exhibitionist who takes pleasure in eating men like you for breakfast and then leaving them all fucked up and totally bewildered!" exclaimed Henri.

"You can't say that!"

"I just did!"

"Well, the bad news is, I've shaken hands on a verbal agreement that in return for all the money we need to start the business, she is going to be an equal partner."

"What?"

"I've shaken hands on it."

"Well you'd better unshake hands, because it's not going to happen."

"I can't" replied Michel.

"You've done this behind my back, you didn't even discuss it with me, I tell you, Michel, this stupid move of yours could wreck our business before it's even started."

"I know I can handle her."

"You think you can, like all the others before you."

"I'm not like all the others."

"Non, you appear to be more stupid!" Michel was quite taken aback by Henri's attitude and really did not want to argue with him any more over Sophia. The two men sat in silence, each with his own thoughts on the situation before them. Michel did feel guilty that he had fallen into Sophia's trap, but he could not resist the woman, and Henri just did not understand.

"Michel, let me tell you now, for years I've taken a lot of money out of this business and put on deposit so that one day I could close the salon, pandering to silly, rich women and do something I really enjoyed whilst making a small fortune. When we discussed starting the business, I was overjoyed, as I really believed that together, we could have some real fun whilst we made a lot of money." Michel felt very uncomfortable at that.

"I'm sure we can, Henri."

"I have more than enough money to start the business and cover all the overheads, including a good salary for you, for a year at least." Michel was impressed by that and said "really?"

"Oui, and if you'd spoken to me about money before you got involved with Madame, you probably would have told her to piss off!"

"Probably."

"Well now you know, so go and tell her she's had it" said Henri firmly. At that moment the ornate telephone on Henri's desk rang out.

"Oui, Elaine….oui, put her through……. bonjour Madame Christiane, bonjour…….. oui, oui, he's right here with me…. oui….. oui" Henri then held out the 'phone to Michel and said in a loud voice "it's Madame Christiane for you." Michel felt uncomfortable as he took the 'phone from his angry cousin.

"Bonjour, Madame" he said firmly.

"Have you told him about me yet?" she asked.

"Oui."

"Bon, so, what did he say?"

"It's too early to say at the moment."

"What d'you mean ?"

"I will be discussing some details soon" replied Michel trying to stall for time whilst he gathered his thoughts.

"Just tell him, Michel, that's all you've got to do, I know him, he'll shout and bluster for a bit, but he'll agree in the end."

"Possibly, Madame."

"Now, I can't see you tonight, chérie, but make sure you pick me up by eight tomorrow evening because I've booked a table at the casino for dinner."

"Bon" he replied nervously.

"And, Michel, ma petite, I'm sorry but I can't be with you tonight, I've got to go with my husband to a boring party with his Banker friends."

"Pity" he replied, much relieved.

"Oui, I'm dreading it, the wives are all bitches and their husbands just want to get my knickers off."

"I'm sure, and who can blame them?" he said and she laughed at that.

"I'll see you tomorrow then, ma petite, and don't be late."

"I promise."

"Au revoir" and she was gone. Michel replaced the 'phone on its ornate cradle and looked at Henri.

"She's happy" said Michel.

"Well I'm not" replied Henri.

"I'll see her tomorrow night and tell her the deal is off' said

Michel now content in the knowledge that Henri had plenty of money put aside for their venture.

"You think you can get rid of her that easily?" enquired Henri.

"Oui, I've taken legal advice on it."

"When did you do that?"

"This afternoon, I had an appointment with a solicitor, Monsieur Robardes………."

"You've been to see Charles?" interrupted Henri.

"You know him?"

"Oui, of course."

"Well Charles told me all I have to do is talk her out of it and that's the end of the agreement" said Michel.

"I hope you can" smiled Henri.

"I know I can."

"Did you really go to Charles just for that?"

"Non, my appointment was to arrange for my divorce." Henri fell silent at that and studied his clasped hands for a few moments before saying "do you think that's wise, Michel?"

"Oui, you know I want to marry Josette."

"What for?"

"Because I love her."

"How can you say that when you've been screwing Madame Christiane?"

"She trapped me into that, I didn't want to do it, but I couldn't resist her once she was naked, and believe me, she's some exhibitionist."

"I expect she is, but what about Monique?"

"What about her?"

"Michel, you've got a wonderful wife there, she puts up with all your bad behaviour, all your mistresses and she still loves you."

"You think so?" enquired Michel.

"I'm sure."

"Henri, Monique and I are not compatible."

"That's bollocks!" And at that precise moment the telephone rang again.

"Hello, Elaine, oui, oui, put her through…… hello chérie, oui, oui, Michel and I were just having a meeting…. oui……… oui……… what's his name again?………. Gerrard" at that Michel's heart sank into his boots as Henri continued "oui…….

straight away.... oui.... the number, chérie" and Henri wrote it down on the pad in front of him. "Bon, see you later, chérie" and he hung up.

Michel looked at Henri who smiled and said "your friend Gerrard 'phoned Monique after he was told that you'd left Marseille, she just called Jackie with a message."

"Go on."

"Gerrard wants to talk to you urgently."

"That's all I need today" said Michel.

"There's the number, you can 'phone him from here" said Henri.

"Merci."

"I'm going down to the salon, so you can talk in private."

"Merci."

Michel dialled the number and waited for what seemed an age before he heard Gerrard's voice.

"Hello."

"Hello, Cyril, it's Michel here, you wanted to talk to me."

"Call me Monsieur Gerrard, s'il vous plait, this is serious Police business."

"Pardon, Monsieur."

"Now then, I've been informed that you've left Marseille with the LeFranc woman, is that true?"

"Oui."

"Where are you now exactly?"

"In Le Touquet."

"What for?"

"I've moved here, I'm going to start a business with my cousin Henri."

"Why?"

"I've started a new life....."

"Don't talk nonsense, monsieur, you are needed back here on Police business" interrupted Gerrard.

"Monsieur Gerrard, I have done......"

"Never mind what you've done, monsieur, it's your duty to assist the Police, and I require your services right now, here in Marseille!" exclaimed the Gendarme.

"Let me tell you....."

"You can tell me nothing, monsieur, but I can tell you that

Conrad Montreau, the 'Black Snake', that known criminal from Lyon, is in Marseille taking over where the Salvator's left off, and you'd better get back here pretty quickly."

"I'm not coming" replied Michel firmly.

"Then I shall have you arrested and brought here."

"On what charge?"

"Don't be naive, Michel, you know full well that we can fit anybody up, including you!"

"Mon Dieu" said Michel resignedly.

"Precisely, so get back here where you belong, as soon as possible, au revoir" and with that Gerrard was gone. Michel replaced the receiver and held his head in his hands. It seemed that there was no escape for him from his life in Marseille. He thought for a while and decided that he would not go back but wait until the Police arrested him. It might be that Gerrard was bluffing, and whilst he held on to that thought he felt better.

In a while, Henri returned to his office and Michel told him what Gerrard had demanded but purposely withheld the arrest threat. They then continued discussing the business plans and Henri seemed quite relieved when Michel assured him that he would tell Sophia Christiane tomorrow night, over dinner, that she could in no way be part of their new business.

Michel arrived back at number 19 to find is fiancé almost in tears with the mess of kaleidoscope colours splashed all over the hallway of the house. Pascal, Jackie and Josephine had all gone home having promised that just one more day would ensure that all the cleaning was completed. However, Pascal had insisted that once they had chosen a colour from the samples he had painted with some fervour, he would buy the emulsion in bulk from his friend and paint the whole house.

"I can't cope with it all much longer" said a tearful Josette.

"You won't have to, ma chérie, come on cheer up, let's get ready to go out and eat."

"Oui, but tell me first, did you see Monsieur Robardes?"

"I did" replied Michel and she smiled at that.

"What did he say?"

"He just asked me to get one or two things sorted out and then go and see him again so he can start the proceedings."

"Bon."

"And he's writing to Monique to tell her that everything is going ahead."

"Oh, Michel, I'm so happy, it means we'll have a spring wedding" she smiled.

"Oui, why not" he replied, hiding his concern at Josette's impatience.

Michel relaxed in a hot bath and was pleased to be free of the sand that had remained on his body after the outdoor liaison with Sophia. He decided to take his fiancé to Flavio's for dinner and although a touch expensive, he was prepared to spend a little to make her happy. He now felt confident that with Henri's money behind him, he could spoil the pretty woman he intended to marry and make up to her for the difficult time she had recently endured.

Guy was delighted to welcome them again to his restaurant and quickly showed the lovers to a romantic candle lit table for two in a corner of his establishment.

"Michel, I'm so pleased we've come here for dinner, it is so lovely" she whispered as she looked over the top of the menu into his adoring eyes.

"Bon, ma chérie, I'm glad because I only want to make you happy."

"I know."

"Things are looking good for us and most important of all, we're together" he said with feeling.

"Oui, now and forever" she replied with a generous smile. Michel was not quite sure about the 'forever' part as he had made up his mind to keep all his options open for the time being.

They both chose Bisque for a starter followed by Chateaubriand with a very expensive Burgundy to drink. The lobster and prawns in the Bisque were soft, exquisite and deliciously tasty and the fillet steak just fell away as they cut into it. The Burgundy was a superb balance to the meal and they both felt very relaxed as they lingered over a Pear Belle Hélène for Michel and a Soufflé au Grand Marnier for Josette. Coffee and several brandies made the experience complete and it was late when Michel paid l'addition and they left with the good wishes of Guy ringing in their ears. Owners of French restaurants do like customers to show their appreciation by coming back night after night, it makes such a difference to the profits.

Once back inside number 19, Rue de Londres they both had a fit of the giggles as they stopped to admire Pascal's wall painting.

"He's a real artist, isn't he?" gasped Michel through fits of silly laughter.

"Oui, and are you going to let him paint the whole place?" enquired Josette.

"Why not, no matter what he does it can't be any worse than it is, besides, it's Henri's house and we might be going back to Marseille soon."

"Oh, Michel, I hope so, but I mean, only after we've made some money here."

"Of course."

"We could go back after we're married" she cooed.

"Why not."

They went to bed in a happy and relaxed state, with both of them feeling amorous. After kissing for a long while in the warmth of the old bed, Michel rolled on top of his fiancé and entered her with ease. She was as hungry for him as he was for her and it was not long before they reached that blissful moment when they climaxed together. They soon fell softly asleep entwined in each others arms.

CHAPTER 5

After very little consideration of Pascal's fiasco of colours that had been splashed all over the hall, Michel and Josette decided on cream for the interior of the house. Although bland and uninteresting they both felt that it was a case of make do for the time being as Michel could not be bothered and Josette believed privately in her heart of hearts that they would soon return to Marseille. Michel thought that if Gerrard carried out his threat, then it was likely he would be going back pretty quickly in a police car.

The helpers arrived with smiles and everyone seemed relieved that it was likely to be the last day of disruption except for the re-painting of the house of course.

"There, Pascal, that's the colour we've chosen" said Michel as he pointed to a large flash of cream emulsion.

"Bon, Michel, that's a very good choice, very practical, it goes with everything" replied Pascal with a beaming smile.

"So will you please buy enough from your friend to paint the whole place, and I'll give you the cash."

"Certainly, Michel, I'll go back to Boulogne now and get enough to do downstairs first, OK?"

"Bon" replied Michel and after kissing Josette farewell for the day he drove to the salon where Henri appeared to be in a buoyant mood.

"Ah, Michel, good news" said Henri as Michel slipped into the plush chair opposite his partner.

"Bon."

"My cousin, Roger, works for a coach tour company based in Boulogne and he said he will fix up a meeting with his boss to see if we can sub contract our tour operations."

"Bon, that'll save us a lot of hassle" said Michel with enthusiasm.

"And that's not all, Roger gave me a contact who's got a boat that he uses for sea trips, I thought we could see him and try and do a deal" said Henri with a smile.

"Excellent, Henri, it seems you've really got things moving."

"Oh oui, Michel, I'm really getting the feeling that the business is going to be a great success."

"So am I, Henri."

"The only problem is Madame Christiane, and you're going to see to her tonight, no doubt in more ways than one."

"Oui, possibly, but it will be for the last time."

"I hope so, now then, let's 'phone Monsieur DeVere, the man with the boat."

Half an hour later Michel and Henri were on their way to Boulogne to meet Monsieur Maurice DeVere, who had shown great interest in their business proposal. Any income is always welcome, particularly in the winter months when the choppy English Channel often looked very grey and un-inviting to tourists. Monsieur DeVere did not hold out much hope of substantial business just yet but he was impressed with Henri's enthusiasm and so was prepared to meet the newcomers to the tourist industry.

Within the hour they had arrived outside Monsieur DeVere's little office in the Boulevard Diderot, which overlooked the harbour basin that was full of boats of all sizes.

"Now leave this to me, Michel, I'll do all the talking."

"OK, but how d'you plan to set this deal up?"

"I'm not sure, let's see what he wants first and then we can set our prices over the top."

"Sounds good to me."

"I just hope his boat is impressive enough for us to make the profits we want."

"Let's hope so" replied Michel.

"Oui, some of the Americans have got lots to spend when they come over here."

"Bon, and let's get them to spend it with us."

"Precisely."

Monsieur DeVere was a short, stocky man with grey unkempt hair and a ruddy complexion, dressed casually in an oversize dark blue jumper and grey, stained, trousers. His office was a veritable jumble of boat bric-a-brac, untidy papers and fishing gear. To Michel it appeared to be like a marine version of Gambetta's garage but with the added odour of fish.

"So you're Roger's cousin" said DeVere, as he held out his

hand to Henri.

"Oui, and this is my cousin, Michel, we're business partners."

"Keeping it in the family, very wise" replied Maurice DeVere.

"Oui."

"Please have a seat" and Maurice waved towards two chairs that had seen better days.

"Now then, tell me your proposal" he said as he settled behind his untidy desk.

"We're new to the tourist business and we want to offer a range of exciting attractions, boat trips being one of them" said Henri.

"Very good decision, with the right boat you can do very well indeed" nodded Maurice with a smile.

"Bon, now then, what we'd like from you is a list of the trips that you could offer and what you will charge us per passenger."

"That's easy, I can do it two ways, either you can pay for the charter of the boat for the day and go where you want or pay per passenger, whichever fits into your plans" replied Maurice.

"I see" said Henri thoughtfully.

"It depends whether you want to take a select few out for fishing, or pack 'em in like sardines for sea sick special along the coast to Dunkerque" replied Maurice with a grin. Henri was slightly offended by the notion of sea sick tourists but Michel laughed out loud whilst thinking that Maurice was very much like Jean Gambetta.

"What do you charge per day then?" enquired Henri after he had gathered his composure.

"That depends on how often you want to charter the boat, I mean in the summer I'm very busy and to accommodate you I'd have to turn some of my regulars away" replied Maurice.

"Well, say once a week to start" said Henri. At that Maurice pursed his lips, leaned back in his chair and gazed at the ceiling. Like Gambetta he was making it up as he went along whilst wondering what Henri would be prepared to pay. Roger had already told him that Henri owned an up market shoe salon for ladies in fashionable Le Touquet and had a few Francs to spare.

"For the whole day I'd have to charge a minimum of a thousand Francs, just to cover my overheads, fuel etc., you understand, hardly any profit" he said as he lowered his gaze from the grubby ceiling.

“Hmm” mused Henri, now entering into the game of businessman’s bluff. Maurice waited as Henri took a small pad from his jacket pocket and wrote something down. This slightly un-nerved Maurice, who anxious not to scare off a very lucrative charter, said “of course, if we cut down the amount of time at sea, obviously the overheads reduce and I can bring the cost down.”

“Give me an example” said Henri. Maurice returned his gaze to the grubby ceiling where he once again searched for inspiration before fixing Henri with his sharp grey eyes.

“Er, if we reduced the time to say, four hours, then we’d be looking at…..” he paused for effect before continuing “ about five hundred Francs.”

“Hmm” murmured Henri as he wrote the figure down on his pad. Michel was enjoying this, it reminded him so much of his dealings with Jean, Sayid and all the others in Marseille.

“I take it that would be a select fishing trip rather than one of your specials to Dunkerque?” asked Henri.

“I can do either in four hours, which ever you prefer” replied Maurice in the hope that the new price was acceptable.

“I think that figure might just fit into our scale of charges” said Henri slowly.

“Bon, that’s settled then” replied Maurice with a smile.

“Not quite” said Henri and Michel was amused to see a look of concern on Maurice’s face.

“Oh?”

“For the fishing trip do you supply the rods and bait in the price or will they be charged on top of the five hundred Francs?”

“Non, everything is included” replied Maurice hastily.

“Bon, now all that remains is for us to see the boat” said Henri at which Maurice went a little pale.

“Certainly, but please understand, she’s not at her best at the moment, she’s undergoing her winter repaint and repairs” said Maurice.

“That’s alright, we understand” replied Henri with a grin.

They followed Maurice out of his office and across the busy Boulevard to a hard standing close to the slipway. There on blocks, among several other large motor cruisers, stood the ‘Sea Goddess’, a twenty metre, rather tatty looking boat patched up here and there with daubs of red oxide anti fouling paint on her white hull and superstructure.

"As I said, she's not looking her best" said Maurice as they approached the sorry state.

"Quite" replied Henri.

"You're welcome to come aboard" said Maurice as he grasped at the ladder that was leaning against the hull.

"Merci" replied Henri and at that moment the tousled head of a young man appeared above them over the stern.

"That's Jacques, my son" said Maurice

"Bonjour, Jacques" said Michel as Henri nodded at the young man and began to climb the ladder.

"Bonjour, messieurs" replied Jacques as he held the top of the ladder steady for the visitors.

Once safely on board they surveyed the spacious open rear deck, which was obviously designed for fishing at sea. A large cabin area forward was fitted out with several rows of seats facing the bow and large picture windows for passengers to enjoy the views. Forward of that was a suitably sized bridge with all the necessary controls, overlooking a forward deck for passengers who wished to see where they were going and were prepared to brave the elements. First impressions of the 'Sea Goddess' were not good and the whole boat looked very basic as well as not offering quite the luxury that both Henri and Michel imagined their tourists would require. They wandered to the rear deck alone whilst Maurice and his son peered into an open hatch above the engine bay. Henri remained thoughtful for a few moments and studied the harbour before them.

"What do you think?" asked Michel.

"It's a bit basic, but I suppose it'll do for a start" he replied.

"How much could we charge our customers for a fishing trip?" enquired Michel.

"I don't know off hand, perhaps three hundred Francs each, and if we had about ten that would give us three thousand, five hundred to Maurice, I suppose that's not bad" replied Henri.

"Quite good, especially as we don't have to do much" replied Michel. Just then they were joined by Maurice who asked with a beaming smile "well, messieurs, what do you think of her?"

"She needs tidying up a bit and a good clean before we could send our customers out in her" replied Henri.

"But of course, Henri, and I can assure you that when we've finished her winter overhaul, you won't know her" replied Maurice with a grin.

"Bon, and when will that be?"

"Give me a month or so."

"OK, Maurice, we'll be in touch then, of course we'll want to look over her again and have a short trip out with you before we offer boat trips to our customers" said Henri firmly.

"Bon, then that's settled."

"Oui, and we'll firm up on prices and trips nearer the time, I've made notes" said Henri.

"Of course, Henri, and here's to a profitable season ahead" smiled Maurice.

They climbed down the ladder safely and only when they were both about to shake hands with Maurice did they see the red oxide paint stuck on their fingers. Jacques handy paintwork had managed to contaminate the top of the ladder and three of them stood gazing at the mess on their hands.

"Jacques!" roared Maurice and the boy's head appeared.

"Oui, Pa?"

"Get something to clean this mess of our hands!" shouted Maurice in anger as he held up his hands to show his son the result of his carelessness. Jacques disappeared from view and Maurice apologised profusely to Henri and Michel.

"Don't worry, Maurice, these things happen" said Michel with a smile.

"Better us than some of our customers" said Henri with a stern look. Jacques appeared with a tin containing a cleaning solvent and with a grubby rag tried to remove the red oxide from their hands without making things worse than they were. He only partially succeeded and Michel took it well but Henri was not amused. After they had left Maurice and his son, not on the happiest note, they returned to the car.

"We'll go to my Aunt Maria's place and get cleaned up, we can't go back to Le Touquet smelling of paraffin and paint" said Henri angrily.

"Good idea, where does she live?"

"Here in Boulogne, not too far away."

"Bon." Henri then drove quickly to the Boulevard Voltaire and parked outside a block of flats.

"Now, Michel, before you meet Maria, I've got to tell you that she's, well, she's…."

"Disabled?" interrupted Michel.

"Non, she's, well…."

"Well what then?" asked Michel impatiently.

"She's a bit...... she needs company…… er, male company……. and anyone will do provided they can walk and talk."

"I see" said Michel.

"You must understand that she was widowed at an early age and has never re-married."

"Shame."

"Oui, and quite frankly, she has needs and……"

"They must be satisfied" interrupted Michel.

"Quite, I only thought it fair to warn you as you seem to have so much going on in your private life at the moment."

"Thank you for the warning" replied Michel.

Henri rang the sonnette and after greeting his Aunt the door clicked open and they went upstairs to Maria's flat. She opened the door and gave her nephew a big smile and kissed him before turning her attentions to Michel.

"And who's this?" she beamed. Henri made the introduction and then Maria invited them into her lounge. It was nicely furnished with conservative taste but felt very comfortable and welcoming. Maria bade them sit and asked "what will you have to drink, ma petites?"

"A petite Brandy, Aunt, merci" replied Henri.

"I'll join him, if I may" smiled Michel

"You certainly may" replied Maria with a twinkle in her dark brown eyes, which Henri noticed and murmured "Oh, Mon Dieu."

Michel watched Maria as she poured the drinks and was impressed with her looks. For a middle aged woman, Michel guessed she was in her mid fifties, she had a lovely round, open face and a good plump figure, well proportioned, with large breasts, accentuated by the black roll neck jumper she was wearing, and long legs, full and firm looking. Her white skirt finished above her knee and with its petite slit up one side made her look very alluring. Michel wondered how Henri could have such a desirable looking aunt.

"Now, what are you boys doing in Boulogne?" she asked as she handed them their Brandies and then sat close by in an arm chair.

"We've been looking at a boat" replied Henri

"A boat?"

"Oui, it's for our new business venture" said Michel.

"Are you closing the salon, Henri?"

"Oh, non, this business will be running alongside it, aunt."

"How exciting, are you buying this boat?"

"Non, we plan to charter it for our customers" replied Henri.

"Who are?"

"Tourists" ventured Michel.

"You're going into the tourist business, well, I'm sure you'll do very well, this place gets packed in the summer, mostly English, you understand, but they're very good, apparently they never complain and just spend money" she laughed.

"That's just what we want" said Michel with a smile.

"Before we get too comfortable, Aunt, may we wash our hands?" asked Henri.

"Of course, ma petites."

"I'm afraid that when we were looking around the boat we ended up covered in paint and we've tried to get it all off, but we still smell a bit" Henri said.

"Come with me" she said and quickly led the way to a small bathroom where she said to Henri "you wash here and Michel can wash in the kitchen."

"Merci, Aunt ." Michel then followed Maria to the kitchen where she turned on the taps and then spun round to face him.

"There, Michel, use the washing up liquid, I can't have guests with smelly hands" she laughed and then purposely brushed past him so closely that her breasts touched his arm. He felt a tingle of excitement run through him as he proceeded to wash, whilst she returned to the lounge and poured more Brandy into their glasses.

"Here's to your new business, may it be a great success" said Maria as she raised her glass to her nephew and his cousin when they returned.

"To the business" they chorused.

"And if your business is going to be here, I'll be seeing a lot more of you both" she said smiling at Michel.

"Oh, definitely" replied Michel and Henri raised his eyes to the ceiling at that.

"Bon, it's so nice when a family remains close, don't you think so, Michel?" she asked.

"Oui, I'm all for it" he replied.

"The office is going to be in Aunt Claudette's old house, where Michel and his fiancé, Josette are living now" said Henri firmly, hoping to discourage his predatory Aunt.

"What a good idea" said Maria with a smile and obviously not discouraged by the news that Michel was engaged.

"Oui, I must have somewhere comfortable to work" said Michel.

"But I'm sure you'll be coming here quite often" replied Maria.

"Oui" smiled Michel.

"Bon, you must keep an eye on your boat, make sure everything is alright" she said.

"Oh, I will, Aunt, you can be sure" said Henri firmly and hoping that Maria would understand that he would be managing the boat operation rather than Michel but she remained undaunted.

"Now, ma petites, have you had lunch?" she asked.

"Non."

"Bon, neither have I, so Henri, you can take us to Estaminet's then" she said firmly before downing her Brandy with gusto.

Estaminet du Chateau in the Rue du Chateau offers a French traditional menu and was one of Maria's favourite restaurants. She intended to make the most of this chance encounter with her nephew and his attractive cousin from Marseille, an extended lunch therefore would be ideal to develop the acquaintance further. They arrived at the restaurant and although Henri insisted that they were a little pressed for time as duties back at the salon required his attention, Maria launched into the menu with enthusiasm and was obviously not concerned.

"I'll start with potage aux champignons, followed by boeuf en daube" she said firmly.

"Bon, I'll join you" said Michel.

"Melon and carré d'agneau for me" murmured Henri.

"Do order a good wine, won't you Henri?" she pleaded.

"Oui, Aunt."

"After all this is a special occasion isn't it?" she smiled at Michel who smiled back as Henri perused the wine list. The attentive waiter took their order and then Maria began a wide ranging conversation, touching lightly on the new business before moving on to family matters and then friends that she had not seen for some while. Only the food and an excellent bottle of red wine punctuated her non stop chatter. Michel was amused and entertained by Maria's obvious enjoyment of life and her enthusiasm for everything and everybody. They all laughed a lot and the twinkle in her eyes grew ever brighter for Michel. After sweets from a dessert trolley and coffee, Henri excused himself and went off in search of the men's room. He had been gone for only a moment when Maria opened her handbag and produced a little card.

"Here, Michel, call me sometime soon, so we can have lunch together, don't tell Henri, he's such a dear, but so old fashioned" she said as she handed him her card.

"Oui, lunch would be very pleasant, perhaps in a day or so?"

"I look forward to it, now tell me all about yourself" she said. Michel had only just begun to get into the details of his complicated life when Henri appeared and called for l'addition. After dropping Maria back at her flat Henri drove quickly back towards Le Touquet.

"Michel, I'm a bit concerned about Aunt" said Henri seriously.

"Why? she seems fine to me."

"It's her and you I'm worried about."

"Don't worry."

"Well I do, because I know what she's like, she'll be after you quicker than you can imagine."

"Really?"

"Oh, oui, I saw how she looked at you over lunch."

"She's very amusing and….."

"Michel, you're in enough trouble with women at the moment and any more involvement will take your eye off the ball"

"It won't."

"Michel, we're starting a business and you need to be concentrating one hundred per cent on that, believe me" said Henri firmly.

"OK, ok" replied Michel as he gazed out of the side window at the countryside whilst not appreciating his cousin's interference in his love life.

"I mean it" said Henri. They hardly spoke again, each deep in thought about the situation they were in. Michel had to admit to himself that matters did appear to be a little complicated at present, but he was optimistic and was sure everything would sort itself out.

When they arrived the salon was busy and the assistants were attending to a number of women under the watchful eye of Elaine.

"Ah, Monsieur Henri, I'm glad you're here" said Elaine as they walked in.

"What's wrong, Elaine?" asked Henri in an anxious tone.

"It's Madame Christiane" she replied.

"Better go up to the office then" said Henri with concern. As they climbed the stairs Michel was conscious of the assistants gazing after them.

Henri sat behind his desk and looked into the worried face of his manageress.

"Well, Elaine?"

"Monsieur Henri, I'm afraid we're all a little upset today" she replied almost in a whisper.

"Go on" he said calmly.

"Madame Christiane came into the salon just before lunch and bought two pairs of shoes from the Milan collection……"

"Bon" interrupted Henri with a smile but Michel was now feeling distinctly uncomfortable.

"And while Nanette was serving her, she told her that she was going into a new business with you and Monsieur Michel, and you'd be so busy you wouldn't be able to cope, we're all so upset, because we don't want you to close the salon, we all love working here, Monsieur Henri, please don't do it" and with that she started crying.

"Oh, mon Dieu! That bloody woman!" exclaimed Henri angrily.

"Mon Dieu" whispered Michel.

"It's all your fault, Michel, and now you'd better do something about it!"

"Oui" replied Michel with feeling.

"Now then, Elaine, please stop crying, and let me tell you that I will not be closing the salon or selling it, or doing anything with it, do you understand?"

"Oui, Monsieur Henri."

"It is all a total misunderstanding and after we've closed this evening there will be a staff meeting here in my office, where Monsieur Michel will explain everything and I will re-assure everyone that I am not closing the salon and everybody's job is secure."

"Oh, bon, Monsieur Henri" she smiled.

"Now please let all the staff know what I have said."

"Oui, Monsieur Henri, merci, merci" she smiled and left the office. Michel sat down as Henri glared at him and said "Michel, I promise you that Christiane woman is big trouble and if you don't end it tonight, I'm not going ahead with the business, do you understand?"

"Oui, Henri, I do."

"Bon, now I suggest we have some coffee and while I do some paper work you plan what you're going to say to my girls after we close."

The rest of the afternoon passed quickly and Henri took several calls, one of which was from Roger who had made an appointment for them to discuss coach trips with his boss, Monsieur Jean Ricard, the day after tomorrow. Henri told Michel that he would not keep the appointment if the problem of Madame Christiane remained unresolved. Michel assured his cousin that it would be brought to a head tonight and asked Henri to cover for him should Josette question his meeting with a 'potential business partner.' Henri reluctantly agreed, shaking his head slowly and fixing his cousin with an icy stare.

After the salon closed, Elaine, followed by six pretty assistants, trouped into Henri's office. He welcomed them all with a smile and invited them to sit on the chairs that Michel had brought from the stockroom.

"Mademoiselles, let me begin by saying that I'm very sorry indeed that you have all been upset by a remark made by one of our customers, Madame Christiane. I'm afraid that it is a total misunderstanding and Monsieur Michel will explain everything in detail to you, but to begin, let me put your minds at rest, I will not be closing the salon under any circumstances, we have a very good business here with an excellent clientele and I have no plans to ever change a thing."

"Bravo, Monsieur Henri" said Elaine.

"All your futures are safe, I promise you" said Henri with a smile. The girls all smiled and half whispered 'bravo'.

"And now Monsieur Michel, will explain his position with Madame Christiane, so you may fully understand how the misunderstanding came about" said Henri with conviction. Michel stood with his hands clasped in front of him and began "Mademoiselle's, as you may already know, I came up from Marseille to start a new business venture with Monsieur Henri. During a conversation with Madame Christiane at her villa, after I returned her handbag that she left in the salon, she asked, out of interest, about our plans for the business. I explained that we intend to open an office catering for tourists who came to Le Touquet; unfortunately, she misunderstood what I was saying and thought I was inviting her to be an investor in the business. I assured her that Monsieur Henri and I had sufficient funds available and that we were not looking for further investment and how she got the idea that she was going to be a partner in the business, well, I really have no idea."

"She is so much trouble" said Elaine.

"Oui, and finally, I am seeing her this evening to tell her clearly, that she is not and never will be involved in our new business, I assure you." A chorus of 'bravo's' greeted him as he sat down.

"There we are, Mademoiselle's, tonight will be the end of it, so, please all go home safely and I'll see you all tomorrow" smiled Henri. The girls left the office chattering happily and when they had all gone Henri said "make sure you leave that woman in no doubt that she'll never be a part of our business."

"I will, I promise" replied Michel.

When Michel returned to number 19 he found Josette in a happy frame of mind busy arranging crockery in the kitchen cupboards. Pascal had made great progress and although he had left it a little messy, he had painted the hallway and the lounge in cream emulsion. The house looked so much brighter and had a warmth to its atmosphere where it had been so cold before.

"What d'you think, chérie?" she asked as she waved her hand at the fresh paintwork.

"It's so much better, and despite what Henri said about him, I think he's made a pretty good job of it" replied Michel.

"Oui, so do I, now I just want him to hurry up and get the rest done"

"I'm sure he will, he seems a good old boy."

"Bon, now, I hope you've been working hard with Henri today and that you're ready for a special dinner" she smiled.

"Well……."

"You can tell me about it later, because I've been out shopping with Jackie and she took me to a superb butcher and I've bought us fillet steak for our first meal together here" she beamed and Michel did not know how to tell her that he had an appointment with a 'potential business partner'.

"Ma petite" he began as he put his arms round her "I'm afraid you'll have to keep the steak until tomorrow night."

"Oh, non, you're not going out again?"

"I'm sorry, but……….."

"Michel, non."

"It's business and I have to go, Henri has insisted I deal with it" he said truthfully.

"Why can't he go?"

"Because he has another important meeting that he has to go to."

"Are we ever going to have some time together in this place?"

"Of course, ma chérie, as soon as things have settled down."

"Bon, and whilst we're talking about settling down, when are you going to see Monsieur Robardes again?"

"Soon, chérie."

"You always say that."

"Because it's true" he replied and kissed her gently.

It was almost eight when he kissed a sulky, suspicious Josette goodbye and set of to drive to Sophia's villa. He was wearing his only suit, it was dark grey with a fine pinstripe and with it a rather flamboyant gold tie that he had bought in Marseille. He felt that he was properly dressed for dinner at the casino and then perhaps a little flutter at the tables as he was certain that Sophia would try her luck.

Evette opened the door of the villa, welcomed him with a broad smile and conducted him into the lounge.

"Madame will be with you shortly, monsieur."

"Merci."

"May I get you a drink whilst you're waiting?"

"Oui, a petite Brandy, s'il vous plait."

He was sitting on the settee and just finishing his Brandy when Sophia walked in. She looked stunning in a red satin dress with a plunging neckline, gathered at the waist and then falling in large pleats to below her knee. Matching shoes and handbag completed the ensemble. Her makeup was flawless and with her blonde hair swept back into a French roll she was a vision of perfection. A diamond necklace with matching ear rings giving extra sparkle that was breath taking.

"Mon Dieu, you look fabulous" said Michel as he rose to meet her.

"Merci, chérie" she replied before kissing him. Her Chanel perfume then invaded his senses and he kissed her again passionately.

"I've looked forward to seeing you this evening" he whispered..

"Bon, and I have too as I expect it to be a night to remember, now, chérie, pour me a Brandy while I compose myself." Michel did as he was asked, thinking how right she was and he hoped that he would have the courage to tell her that she would not have a future in the business and tonight was their last night together. He then poured a large measure of Brandy for himself. They talked for a short while about the salon and then as the conversation began to touch on the new business Michel persuaded her it was time to go. She slipped into her mink coat before they drove off in her Mercedes to the casino.

They were greeted at the entrance by Paul, who looked sophisticated and elegant in his dinner jacket, before being shown to a table for two in a secluded part of the splendid restaurant.

"May I say how wonderful you look this evening, Madame?" smiled Paul.

"Merci, Paul."

"Will Madame grace the casino with her presence at the tables later?"

"Oui, certainly" she replied with a smile.

"Bon, I'll advise Monsieur DeVaux that you've arrived with a guest."

"Merci, Paul."

"Phillipe will attend to you now, may I wish you both 'bon appetite'?"

"Merci" said Michel as the elegant Paul gave a little bow and left them.

"He's always so attentive, I do approve, don't you?" asked Sophia.

"Oui" replied Michel slightly offhand as Phillipe arrived with two large menus and a wine list.

Michel ordered an expensive white wine to begin and then they took some time before choosing Moules Marinieres as their hors d'oeuvres followed by Boeuf bourguignon for Sophia and Tournedos Rossini for Michel. He selected a rich Burgundy to accompany the main courses and once Phillipe had taken their order they relaxed together in the luxurious ambiance of the restaurant.

"I feel lucky tonight" said Sophia as she sipped at her wine.

"Bon."

"Do you, ma chérie?"

"I'm always lucky" he replied with a smile.

"I love lucky men" she giggled.

"I've noticed" he replied and felt uneasy about having to tell this glamorous woman that it was their last night together.

"I've an idea, as we both feel lucky, I'll give you half my winnings tonight if you'll give me half of yours" she said with a sparkle in her blue eyes.

"Agreed" he replied instantly.

"Bon, shake on it" she said as she proffered her immaculate, slender hand to him.

"Why do I worry when I shake hands with you?" he asked and she laughed as he took her hand and squeezed it gently.

"We're partners, so you shouldn't worry because we can't lose" she said.

"True."

"And what did Henri say when you told him about our agreement?" she asked with a glint in her eye.

"Ah, well" replied Michel and he paused, desperately struggling to think how to answer her question diplomatically.

"Oui?" she quizzed.

"Well, first of all, we went through our business plan for the year to see how we could fit you in……."

"Fit me in?" she exploded.

"Of course, chérie, in business start ups, everything has to be carefully planned……"

"Listen, Michel" she interrupted "there's no 'fitting me in' I'm in from the start with as much money as you need!"

"I know, chérie" he replied holding up his hands in an attempt to diffuse her anger "I was only using a figure of speech……"

"And I've told you, I don't want the money back!"

"I know, chérie, that's very generous of you" replied Michel noticing that several diners close by overheard her angry outburst. Just then Phillipe arrived with the Moules Marinieres and provided Michel with a heaven sent distraction while he gathered his thoughts.

"They look good" he said as Phillipe placed the dishes before them.

"Bon appetite, Madame and Monsieur" said the little waiter before leaving.

"I hope you're not trying to back out of our agreement" she said as she picked up her fork to tackle the mussels before her.

"Non, of course not, chérie" replied Michel feeling very afraid of this difficult woman that he could not handle. Somehow, Josette and Monique seemed so wonderfully easy compared to Sophia. He took several sips of wine to steady himself before saying "it's got nothing to do with trying to 'back out' as you put it……."

"What is it then?" she interrupted.

"Business planning, ma chérie, making sure that the right amount of capital is available at the beginning and then increasing the investment as the business develops and requires more funding, too much money at the start up will only attract the tax man, and we don't want that do we?"

"Non" she replied through a mouthful of mussels.

"And Henri and I have more than sufficient capital to start, so, it's a question of when we can phase in your generous investment without attracting the tax man" said Michel with confidence, being quite sure his answer would satisfy her.

"Bon, that means I'm a partner without having to make any investment, sounds perfect, chérie, you've thought of everything, so what else did Henri say?" Michel was so shocked that he almost choked on his first mouthful of mussels.

"Can we talk about the business later?" he asked.

"Non, I'm curious, chérie, and I want to know" she replied firmly.

"Henri is very excited about your involvement in the business" he said truthfully.

"Oh, bon" she smiled.

"And because he knows that we are close and have an understanding, he wants me to make all the necessary arrangements with you."

"Bon."

"I promise you, he really doesn't want to be involved" said Michel.

"This is exciting, that means as he'll be busy running the salon, it'll just be us in charge of the new business" she said gleefully.

"Precisely, ma chérie" replied Michel.

"You know, this is the first time I've had my own business" she said with a smile.

"Really?" said Michel feeling a little apprehensive as he realised that her disappointment would be profound when he told her of Henri's refusal to agree to her involvement.

"Oui, Charles, my husband, has always taken care of our finances and I've never been allowed to do anything on my own."

"What a shame."

"Oui, but you know what they say, a successful man is one who earns more than his wife can spend!"

"Oui, but I'm sure you're doing your best to catch up" replied Michel with a grin.

"I do have expensive tastes and luckily Charles has the necessary money to match" she quipped and Michel gave a little chuckle.

They finished the mussels and sipped the wine whilst gazing into each others eyes with the flicker from the ornate table candles making her diamonds sparkle. Michel felt he was being totally mesmerised by this glamorous, ambitious woman and he wondered how he could ever say goodbye to her. Phillipe then arrived with the main courses and then proceeded to open the Burgundy with a flourish, pouring a sample for Michel to taste.

“Bon, Phillipe” he said.

“Merci, monsieur” he replied, pouring amounts into both glasses before leaving the lovers alone.

“I think I’m either going to win or lose a lot tonight” she said.

“Win, surely.”

“Non, chérie, I can’t be certain, I just somehow feel a little sadness within me, as if everything is going too well between us and I’m afraid that our pretty bubble may burst.” Michel felt quite moved by what she had just said and he sought to re-assure her.

“Non, chérie, we’ll be lucky tonight and we’ll carry on being lucky, always, believe me” he smiled.

“I hope you’re right” she replied before starting to eat her meal. They lingered over the delicious cuisine enjoying every mouthful as well as each other’s company. When they had finished and after a reasonable time had elapsed, Michel ordered Crepes Suzette for them both. It was while Phillipe was attempting to extinguish the flaming Brandy over the crepes that Monsieur DeVaux arrived at the table.

“Madame Christiane, how nice to see you this evening” he said with a broad smile.

“Merci, Monsieur” she smiled back.

“May I say how lovely you look tonight, Madame.”

“You may” she replied.

“I understand from Monsieur Paul that you and your guest will come to the tables later.”

“Oui, and I must warn you that I and Monsieur Michel, my escort and new business partner, feel very lucky tonight” she replied as Michel went cold inside.

“Non, Madame, it is we who are lucky to have you and Monsieur Michel” he replied and nodded to Michel. Phillipe then served the Crepes Suzette whilst Monsieur DeVaux gave a little bow and said “I look forward to seeing you both later, Madame and Monsieur.”

When they had finished the crepes they chatted for a while about the prospects for the new business and Michel just relaxed as he could not bring himself to deter her enthusiasm. He was being drawn deeper and deeper into a situation from which he could not escape. He was utterly powerless to say anything and he hoped that his courage might return before he was forced to tell her the news that would shatter their relationship. Coffee and delicious mints followed by liqueurs completed the evening meal and it was almost ten o'clock when Michel escorted the dazzling Sophia into the busy gaming room. Several people acknowledged her as they made their way to one of the Roulette tables. There was just one seat available on to which Sophia lowered her shapely form whilst Michel stood behind her attentively.

"Bonsoir, Madame Christiane" said the croupier.

"Bonsoir, Pierré" she replied.

"What would you like to start with, Madame?" he enquired.

"A thousand Francs, I think" she replied as Michel swallowed hard and Pierré deftly placed a pile of chips in front of Sophia as she gave him a thousand Franc note from her handbag.

"Mesdames and Messieurs, place your bets, s'il vous plait" commanded Pierré. Sophia placed chips on the numbers ten and twenty three. When everyone had finished Pierré spun the Roulette and they all waited for the clatter to stop.

"Rouge twenty three" stated Pierré.

"Bravo, we've won!" exclaimed Sophia and she turned to Michel as he put both hands on her shoulders.

"Bon, ma chérie, I told you we are lucky together" he replied. Pierré then cleared the table and placed a large pile of chips in front of Sophia.

"Place your bets, s'il vous plait" said Pierré and Michel was aware that several of the women watched Sophia place her bet before they followed suit. She placed chips on sixteen, twenty-one and thirty. Pierré spun after everyone had placed their chips and when the clatter stopped he called out "noir, thirty."

"Oh, Michel!" whispered Sophia as some other players called 'bravo'. Michel could hardly believe what he was seeing and felt sure that her run of luck would end with the next spin of the Roulette wheel. Pierré cleared the table and then placed her winnings in front of Sophia.

"Mesdames and Messieurs, place your bets, s'il vous plait." Sophia chose seven, twenty five and thirty two with everyone at the table waiting and watching. With all bets placed Pierré spun the wheel and announced when the clatter stopped " rouge, twenty five!"

"Oh, mon Dieu!" exclaimed Sophia as Michel felt suddenly

very hot.

"Three in a row" he muttered as Pierré cleared the table and placed an even larger pile of chips in front of Sophia. She then placed bets on twelve, twenty seven and thirty four. Pierré spun the wheel and number six came up. From then on Sophia did not win again and when she had lost all her chips she turned to Michel and said "you choose now, chérie, I seem to have used up all my luck."

"Oui" he replied and Sophia placed another thousand Franc note on the table. With the chips in front of her, Michel chose fourteen and twenty six and she placed the bet accordingly. Number twenty came up and from then on Michel lost every time until all the chips were gone.

"Shall we stop and have a drink at the bar?" he whispered.

"Oui, that's a good idea" she replied.

They left the table and wandered across to the bar where she sat on the only stool available and was immediately welcomed.

"Bonsoir, Madame" smiled the elegant barman.

"Bonsoir, Rafael" she replied.

"What can I get you, Madame?"

"Well, as I'm losing at the moment you'd better open a bottle of champagne" she complained.

"Oui, Madame."

"Champagne, ma petite?" queried Michel.

"Oui, it always brings me luck" she said as Rafael struggled to open a bottle of Môet Chandon.

The cork then popped and the glorious, sparkling liquid was poured into two elegant flutes.

"Here's to us and lady luck" said Sophia and she touched her glass with Michel's.

"Bon chance" he replied before they drank, each savouring the clean and invigorating taste.

"Do you really want to go back to the table or shall I take you home?" he enquired.

"Oh, non, we must try our luck again, chérie" she replied.

"If you wish."

"Oh, I do, and I must use my system to win" she smiled.

"You have a system?"

"Oui, it's very simple, I just bet double each time I lose until I win!"

"Mon Dieu" whispered Michel.

They drank half the bottle of champagne before returning to the table and Rafael promised to keep the remainder on ice for their return. True to her word, Sophia bet double the amount on her new lucky numbers, seven, twelve and twenty one. The wheel spun and they waited.

"Rouge twenty one" called Pierré to their delight.

"You see, chérie, the champagne and my system work well together" she smiled. From then on her luck changed again and when all the chips had been lost they returned to the bar.

"Don't worry, chérie, I just keep on going until I win" she said before she sipped at her champagne. Michel smiled and thought it would be wiser to return to the villa. After they had finished the bottle they returned a little unsteadily to the table where two vacant seats allowed the lovers to sit next to each other.

"Are you ready to play, Madame?" enquired Pierré.

"Oui, Pierré, give me ten thousand, s'il vous plait" she replied and Michel swallowed hard.

"Are you sure, ma petite" he whispered in her ear.

"Of course, chérie, I told you, I just go on 'til I win."

Sophia doubled her bets on the first three numbers and lost. Michel relaxed after realising that there was not the remotest possibility of him being able to influence this foolish, rich woman. She played twice more and lost both times and then put a large stake on two numbers only, seven and twenty three. The wheel spun and when the clatter stopped Pierré called out "rouge seven."

"Bravo, chérie" said Michel and he kissed her neck.

"You see, my system works" she replied calmly.

From then on her system let her down and when she had at last lost all her chips and admitted defeat they returned to the bar where she insisted they drank more champagne.

"Let me take you home, chérie" Michel pleaded.

"Non, we must make a night of it" she replied.

"But, chérie……."

"I think you're in the habit of giving up too easily" she interrupted scornfully.

"Not at all………"

"I don't want our bubble to burst" she interrupted as Rafael opened another Môet Chandon.

"It won't. I promise you" he replied as Rafael poured the champagne. They touched glasses and looked hard at each other.

"Here's to us and our future together" she said with a slight slur. Michel felt very nervous at that and wondered what her reaction would be when he told her the truth about the business and their relationship. They slowly drank most of the champagne before Michel at last persuaded her that it really was time to go home. After she signed her husband's account for the dinner and champagne and then bidding fond farewells to all the staff at the casino, Michel drove Sophia's Mercedes back to the villa quite slowly. He was tired and emotional after a very heavy night with his mistress, who then demanded that he stay the rest of the night to comfort her in her hour of need following her losses. Michel followed her in to the lounge where she flopped down on the settee.

"Pour me a Brandy, then carry me upstairs to bed and fuck me gently" she said.

"I think you've had a little too much champagne" he replied.

"OK, cut out the middle man and take me to bed then" she replied. Michel did not want to stay the night and was becoming anxious.

"Do you have any idea of how much you've lost tonight?" he asked hoping the question might sober her up.

"Non, and I don't care, Charles can afford it" she replied.

"You know, Sophia, you must……"

"Stop asking questions, chérie, and take me to bed!" she interrupted. Michel realised that any further conversation was useless and he bent down and kissed her gently.

"Come on then, ma chérie" he said as he helped her from the settee and then slowly guided her upstairs to her bedroom. She undressed quickly and lay naked on the bed for him.

"Ma chérie, I need comforting" she whispered and within moments he had joined her. They kissed for a while before she guided him into her moist, soft body and he then began a slow rhythmic movement that made her gasp each time he thrust all he had into her very depths.

"Mon Dieu, this is good" she whispered.

"Oui."

"You'll never stop loving me, will you, Michel?"

"Non, never" he replied then instantly regretting it.

"Bon, because now we have found each other we must stay together."

"Of course."

"Now hurry up and finish off, chérie, as I'm too tired to go on" she demanded. Michel increased the speed of his rhythm until he reached the point of no return and relaxed into her, enjoying every pulsating moment.

"That was good" he gasped and she kissed him passionately.

"Bonne nuit" she murmured as she closed her eyes.

"Bonne nuit" he replied and rolled off her warm body. Sleep came easily to them both and was some time later before Michel's instinct forced him to wake up and look at his watch. It was just quarter to four in the morning and he knew he had to leave right away if he was to stand any chance of pacifying Josette. He dressed quickly and silently before bestowing a light kiss on Sophia's lips and leaving her to sleep. The morning air was crisp and cold as he manoeuvred his car out the drive and headed back home. Josette was awake as he quietly slipped into their bedroom.

"Was it a good meeting?" she enquired suddenly out of the dark.

"Oui, ma petite, it was, you startled me, I thought you were asleep" he replied as he struggled out of his clothes.

"You mean, you hoped I was" she said.

"Oh, non, ma petite" he said as he snuggled into bed with her.

"Oh, oui, Michel, because if I was asleep I wouldn't be able to smell your business client's perfume." His heart sank and he thought 'what a night!'.

"Ma chérie………" he began.

"Michel, you must think I'm a complete fool, and if you don't stop right now, I'm going back to Marseille and you'll never see me again, do you understand?"

"Ma petite……"

"Do you understand?" she demanded.

"Oui."

"Bon, so go to sleep" and with that she turned her back on him and began to cry quietly.

CHAPTER 6

It was late morning before Michel was out of bed and sitting at the table in their cream kitchen eating croissants and drinking black coffee. He looked at his red eyed fiancé across the table and said "sometimes I think we don't understand each other."

"You're wrong, I understand you too well" she replied.

"Really?"

"Oui, you're a man who just can't resist getting involved with people, especially women" she said without emotion.

"Ma petite.........."

"And I've got to either accept that and live with it or leave you" she interrupted.

"I never, ever want to lose you, ma chérie" he whispered.

"Then do something about the way you behave" she replied angrily.

"I promise, I will, I really will."

"We'll wait and see" she replied as the front door bell rang.

"That'll be Pascal" she mumbled and went off to open the door. Michel realised that he had to lavish some sincere attention on Josette otherwise she would certainly leave him. Suddenly Pascal's beaming face appeared and after greeting Michel, he asked "what d'you think of the colour now it's up?"

"Very nice, clean looking, you've transformed the place" replied Michel.

"Bon, I'm glad you're pleased, I'm going to start upstairs today" said Pascal as he sat at the table.

"Bon" said Michel.

"A coffee before you begin?" asked Josette.

"S'il vous plait" he smiled.

"When will you be finished?" asked Michel.

"Soon" replied Pascal as he looked at Josette pouring his coffee.

"Your eyes look a little red, Josette, I hope it's not the smell of the paint."

"Non, it's the smell of another woman" she replied as she offered him his cup and then left the kitchen.

"Oh, dear, I'm sorry I spoke" whispered Pascal.

"Don't worry, it's just a little misunderstanding" said Michel.

"There's no such thing where a woman is concerned" replied Pascal before he sipped his coffee.
"True."
"Now then, how's the new business going?" enquired the old man with a smile.
"Very well, we've organised boat trips from Boulogne and tomorrow we're having a meeting with Roger's boss to discuss coach tours and Henri has already organised posters, printing and so much more."
"Bon, it already sounds like a great success."
"Oui, I'm sure it will be and I can't thank you enough for all this work you're doing here."
"You're welcome."
"I really wouldn't have had the time to do it myself, I'm just so involved with the business" said Michel.
"I understand." At that moment Josette returned and said to Michel "it's late, hadn't you better get going?"
"Oui, ma petite."
"After all, you wouldn't want to miss any 'potential client' meetings" she said in a sarcastic tone.
"Non" he replied and Pascal gave him a knowing look.
"I expect I'll see you sometime later then" said Josette.
"Oui, I'll be back in time to take you out to dinner at a very nice restaurant in Boulogne" he replied and he watched her face brighten into a faint smile.
"Bon" she replied before he kissed her gently.
The salon was busy when Michel arrived and after greeting Elaine he went straight up to Henri's office.
"Well, did you tell her?" asked Henri as Michel slumped into his chair.
"Sort of."
"What d'you mean 'sort of'?"
"I tried to explain the position clearly but she'd had too much to drink" replied Michel.
"Look, unless you get this mess sorted out, I'm not going ahead and I've told you that over and over again."
"Just give me a little more time, she's a very difficult woman to deal with" pleaded Michel.
"Mon Dieu! I've been telling you that from the moment you set

eyes on her!"

"I'll make arrangements to meet her and get it finally sorted."

"When?"

"Er" Michel hesitated "tomorrow."

"Do it now" said Henri forcefully and he picked up the 'phone..

"Elaine, call Madame Christiane for me, s'il vous plait." They fixed each other with an icy stare while they waited for Sophia to answer her 'phone. Michel heard her voice and Henri then passed it to him.

"Madame Christiane, it's me, Michel, how are you this morning?"

"Better now I've heard from you, why did you leave me last night?" she asked in a disappointed tone.

"Oui, I'm sorry about that but I'm in a meeting with Henri at the moment" he replied in an attempt to change the subject.

"I don't care where you are, chérie, why did you leave?"

"I'll explain later."

"When?"

"Tomorrow, let's meet for lunch at Le Café des Arts" he suggested.

"I want to see you today, chérie."

"Not possible I'm afraid, business meetings you understand."

"What about tonight then?" she asked.

"Too busy still, so let's make it tomorrow, say one o'clock?"

"Alright, but make sure you keep the rest of the day free" she replied firmly.

"Certainly."

"Bon, I'll see you tomorrow then, au revoir."

"Au revoir" he replied and handed the 'phone back to Henri.

"Satisfied?" asked Michel.

"I'll only be satisfied when I know for certain that she is not going to be involved in the business" replied Henri in a firm tone.

"I understand."

"I hope you do."

It was just before lunch when Henri telephoned Roger's employer to make an appointment to discuss the possibility of organising coach tours around Normandy. Monsieur Jean Ricard said he would be pleased to see them at his office in Boulogne at ten o'clock in the morning. Michel felt relieved that Henri appeared to accept his guarantee that Sophia would definitely be told over lunch tomorrow that her investment would not be accepted. Henri had only just finished his call to Monsieur Ricard when Elaine buzzed him to tell him that Aunt Maria was on the line.

"Bonjour, Aunt ."

"Bonjour, Henri, are you well?"

"Oui, merci, and you?"

"Oui, and how's Michel?"

"He's OK."

"Just OK?"

"He's fine Aunt, I promise you."

"Bon, now then, when are you next coming to Boulogne?"

"As it happens, we're coming tomorrow, on business, Aunt."

"Bon, could you call in and collect some things for your Mama?"

"Of course."

"Bon, what time?"

"Oh, say about eleven thirty."

"I'll see you both then, au revoir, Henri."

"Au revoir."

As soon as he had replaced the receiver he fixed Michel with a firm stare and said "Aunt Maria has got you lined up, I can tell, and I'm warning you to stay well clear of her."

"Henri as if.........."

"You've got enough on your plate with Madame Christiane" he interrupted.

"OK" replied Michel whilst wondering whether he should telephone Maria in the circumstances. He was very tempted because she appeared to be such a lovely, un-demanding, mature woman. He decided to just relax and see what transpired in the next day or so.

They went to the Bar Americaine for a lunch of baguettes and coffee before returning to the office to discuss financial matters. Henri had prepared a substantial and well detailed business plan with all the expenditure and expected income clearly identified. Michel's proposed salary was no more than just adequate and in any other situation he would have raised an objection but in his current position he decided to remain quiet. Their business discussions continued for the rest of the afternoon, punctuated occasionally by Elaine requiring Henri's attendance for a customer who requested his personal attention.

When Michel arrived home he was pleased to be greeted by his smiling fiancé.

"So, where are you taking me tonight?" she asked as she poured him a coffee.

"To a very nice, romantic little restaurant that I know you'll just love" he replied.

"Have you been there before?" she asked.

"Oui."

"Who with?" she demanded.

"Henri and his Aunt Maria" he replied and she smiled and said "oh."

"Now then let's make a night of it."

"Bon" she smiled.

"Oui, and after dinner I have a little surprise for you" he said.

"Oh, what is it?"

"You'll have to wait until after dinner."

"Give me a clue."

"Non" he replied and kissed her.

They took their time getting ready and it was almost eight o'clock before they set off in the direction of Boulogne.

"You look lovely tonight, chérie" said Michel as he swung the Mercedes out on to the coast road.

"Merci, ma petite" she replied glancing down at her elegant little black dress.

"The colour suits you."

"Oui."

"But you always look lovely to me" he whispered, hoping she was warming a little more towards him.

"I hope so" she replied gently.

"I know things have been a bit difficult since we first arrived here, but I'm sure everything will settle down."

"Oui."

"And then we can get married."

"Oh, Michel, I do love you so."

"And I love you, chérie, I really do and I can't wait for you to be Madame Ronay."

"Oh, Michel, neither can I."

"I just know we'll always be happy together" he said quietly and she just sighed.

When he parked outside Estaminet du Chateau he was surprised to see the restaurant appeared very busy, which is always a good sign unless you intend to eat quite soon. Michel escorted Josette into the warm, comfortable interior and was greeted by a harassed looking waiter.

"Monsieur, I'm sorry we are very busy at the moment, can you come back in, say, half an hour?"

"We'd prefer to wait, if we may" replied Michel not wanting to sit in the car or wander around the streets of Boulogne on a cold, dark night.

"Certainly, monsieur, if you like to go to the bar, I'll call you as soon as I have a table free."

"Merci" replied Michel.

There was just one bar stool vacant and Josette slipped onto it with elegant ease as Michel caught the bar man's attention.

"What will you have chérie?"

"Pernod, ma petite" she replied.

Michel ordered two Pernod and then turned his attention to the busy, noisy restaurant before him.

"The cuisine must be good" said Josette.

"It is" he replied as the barman placed their drinks in front of them.

"Here's to us and our future" said Michel.

"To us" she replied with her eyes sparkling with happiness.

The half an hour wait turned into three quarters of an hour with all the noisy customers apparently in no hurry to go. Michel chatted happily with his fiancé as they waited patiently and continued drinking. An hour passed and they were both feeling a little woozy and quite hungry when the harassed waiter appeared.

"Won't be long now, Monsieur, I'm sorry you've had to wait."

"It's alright" replied Michel and the waiter nodded before he disappeared into the back of the restaurant. It was another fifteen minutes before some customers got up from a table in the window and the waiter hurried to clear the debris of their meal before attracting Michel's attention. He and Josette made their way unsteadily to the table where they almost fell down onto the chairs.

The waiter produced the menus and wine list then rushed away to a table close by where the customers appeared particularly boisterous. Michel glanced towards them and said "I think that noisy lot are English." Josette turned to look at them for a moment before smiling at Michel and replying "oui, tourists, our future."

"I hope that they're not all like that" he said as one, rather plump, red faced Englishman spoke loudly in schoolboy French to the waiter whilst his three male companions laughed.

"Never mind them, chérie, what shall we have to eat?" asked Josette. Michel then turned his attention to the menu and perused it for a few moments.

"I'll have the Bouillabaisse to start, followed by Chateaubriand, ma petite, and you?"

"The same as you, chérie" she whispered as she gazed into his eyes.

"Bon, and I'll choose a light wine for us, otherwise I'll never be able to drive home to our all cream house." She laughed and Michel smiled back at his lovely fiancé. She was so easy to be with and so un-demanding compared with Sophia and he regretted ever becoming involved with her. Henri was right, Sophia ate men for breakfast and then discarded them by lunchtime, always searching for something that was never there. Michel was sure that she would never be content and would eventually end up alone and unloved leading an evermore frantic existence.

"Are you ready to order, Monsieur?" enquired the waiter.

"Oui" he nodded and gave the order in a louder than usual voice to overcome the noise from the English.

"I'm sorry about them, Monsieur, but they're English" said the waiter apologetically.

"That's alright" replied Michel with a smile.

Michel had chosen a light Rosé to drink and they had consumed half the bottle before the waiter returned and served them the Bouillabaisse.

"Bon appetite" said Michel with a slight slur and Josette smiled and whispered her reply. The soup was delicious and quickly eaten, they then waited patiently for the Chateaubriand. Michel ordered another bottle of the Rosé in the meantime which they continued to sip whilst whispering sweet nothings to one another. The loud conversation from the English table continued and the air of romance surrounding the betrothed was being overshadowed and then punctuated by outbursts of laughter. By the time that the harassed waiter served their main course the second bottle of Rosé was empty and Michel ordered a half bottle to finish the meal. They had now become very hungry and they hardly spoke as they devoured the Chateaubriand. Just as they were finishing the English party rose unsteadily from their table and staggered gently out of the restaurant.

"Thank heavens they've gone" said Michel as he poured another glass of Rosé for Josette.

"Oui, peace and quiet at last" she replied.

"Now then, what dessert tempts you, chérie?" enquired Michel.

"Nothing, ma petite, I've had enough and so have you."

"Nonsense, I need something to soak up the wine."

"We've had too much to drink" she said and then began to giggle.

"I know, but my little surprise will sober us up" he replied.

"Oh, Michel, what is it, I want to know!"

"I'll show you later" he replied.

"I can't wait 'til later, tell me now!" she giggled. At that moment the waiter arrived and Michel ordered a Pear Belle Hélène for himself and coffee for both of them. Josette continued to press him about the 'surprise' in between giggling fits but Michel remained steadfast and only after he had finished his sweet and was lingering over coffee did he give a hint of the 'surprise'.

"It's to do with the business" he said.

"Will I like it?"

"I'm sure you will" he replied.

"Well, what is it then?"

"Be patient, chérie, just be patient."

"Michel, sometimes you're such a pain!"

"I know, but you still love me, don't you?"

"Oui, unfortunately." He laughed at that and signalled the waiter for l'addition.

It was quite cold outside and they waited in the Mercedes for a few moments for the heater to warm up before driving off. Michel was feeling the effects of all the alcohol he had consumed during the evening and as a precaution he drove slowly down to the Boulevard Diderot where he parked outside the office of Monsieur

DeVere.

“Here we are” he said.

“Where?”

“This is from where we’re going to operate our sea trips for tourists.”

“Is this the surprise?” asked Josette.

“Oui, part of it, chérie.”

“And the other part?” she asked.

“Over there” he replied nodding towards the cruisers on the hard standing.

“It’s not very romantic.”

“Come with me and you’ll see” he replied.

“Michel it’s cold out there, can’t we go home?”

“In a moment, chérie, I just want you to see our ocean cruiser.” She raised her eyebrows and got out of the car before wrapping her coat around her. They wandered unsteadily, arm in arm across the deserted Boulevard to the hard standing where Michel guided them to the place where the ‘Sea Goddess’ stood on her hull supports looking like a huge beached whale.

“This, ma chérie, is the ‘Sea Goddess’, what do you think of her?”

“Very nice, ma petite.”

“Bon.”

“Can we go home now?”

“Non, not yet, you haven’t seen round her.”

“Oh, Michel…….”

“Non, non, come with me, chérie” he interrupted before leading Josette round the boat for her closer inspection. Josette made all the right appreciative comments as to the size of the ‘Sea Goddess’ and her condition and was hoping that that would be enough to satisfy Michel. They then reached the paint covered ladder that had previously caused problems and Michel said “let’s go on board for a quick look around.”

“Non, Michel, it’s late and besides I’m sure the owner wouldn’t like it.”

“Nonsense, ma chérie, Maurice wouldn’t mind at all, come on” and with that he climbed the ladder and slipped over the side onto the deck. He then peered back down at his fiancé and said “come on, chérie.”

"Michel……."

"Come on, you'll love it up here, the view is great." She reluctantly climbed the rickety ladder to the top and was grateful when Michel put his arms around her and pulled her up and onto the deck. At that point she accidentally kicked the ladder away and it fell with a loud crack onto the hard standing below and slithered some distance away from the hull.

"Oh, mon Dieu!" exclaimed Michel.

"What have I done?"

"You've only knocked the ladder down you stupid creature!"

"Mon Dieu!"

"Now we can't get off the bloody boat!" At that, she started to giggle and as it turned into laughter it became infectious and Michel started to laugh as well.

"What are we going to do?" she asked.

"As we're here we might as well have a tour of the boat and then I'll try and think of how we can get down."

"Aye, aye, mon capitaine, lead the way!" He laughed again and kissed his lovely fiancé passionately.

"It's good being on a boat" she said.

"Really?"

"Oui, I know where you are and I can keep my eye on you" she laughed and Michel kissed her again. They stood for some while on the rear deck looking over the harbour at the myriad of small boats bobbing gently at anchor. It was quiet and serene with only the occasional car driving along the Boulevard disturbing the peace of the late night. With his arm around her shoulder he led Josette into the passenger cabin with its rows of seats, and then onto the bridge. She was fascinated by all the controls and Michel pretended he knew what most of them did. They wandered around the deck in front of the bridge and stood there kissing for some while.

"Come on, chérie, take me home" she whispered.

"Oui, of course" and they returned to the rear deck where Michel looked down and wondered how they were going to descend to the hard standing. It was far to high for them to jump down and it was obvious they needed help, but from where at this time of night?

"It's no good, ma petite, I'm just going to have to shout for help otherwise we'll be here all night."

"OK, you'd better do it then." Michel took a deep breathe and put his hands to either side of his face and shouted as loud as he could. He did it three more times and waited but no one came.

"Try again, chérie, but louder this time." He did his best once again and after the third shout he thought he saw the figure of a man walking along the Boulevard.

"Look, there's someone there" he said pointing at the distant figure.

"Call again, quickly, before he disappears" she said. He shouted once more as loudly and for as long as he could. To their delight the man stopped walking and looked around. Michel shouted again and they both waved their arms as the solitary figure looked in their direction.

"I think he's seen us" gasped Michel excitedly.

"Bon, shout some more and keep waving" she said. He continued to call as the figure made his way unsteadily in the direction of the 'Sea Goddess'.

"I think he's drunk" said Michel.

"Doesn't matter, chérie, he's seen us."

"True."

"And we only want him to put the ladder back." As the man came closer Michel noticed he was more than a little unsteady on his feet. He called again and heard the man mumble something.

"Merci, Monsieur" called Michel to which the man looked up and replied in English "its OK, mate I'll save you and your girl."

"Mon Dieu! He's English" said Michel.

"Well I'm sure he's still able to pick up the ladder" replied Josette.

"We're good at saving you Froggies" said the man with conviction.

"What did he say?" asked Josette.

"I've no idea" replied Michel and then he recognised him.

"Mon Dieu! It's the red faced man from the restaurant!"

"Oh, non" she whispered.

"Monsieur, pick up the ladder, s'il vous plait" shouted Michel.

"What?" came the reply.

"He doesn't understand" whispered Michel.

"Is that because he's drunk or English?"

"Both, probably, Monsieur, the ladder, the ladder" shouted Michel pointing down in the direction of the rickety object.
"How did you get up there, mate?" queried the man.
"The ladder, la, la" shouted Michel in exasperation.
"And what's more to the point, how did you get the girl up there?" asked the Englishman.
"Monsieur, the ladder……."
"Up to a bit of hanky panky are we?" enquired the man with a grin.
"Monsieur…."
"Don't blame you, mate, she's very attractive" he interrupted.
"Mon Dieu! He's stupid!" exclaimed Michel.
"Now how are we going to get you down" said the man as he put his hands on his hips and then looked around him.
"Ah, there's a ladder over there, it looks as if it might just reach."
"What did he say?" asked Josette in a whisper.
"I've no idea" replied Michel as the man made his way unsteadily towards the ladder.
"Oh, mon Dieu, he's seen the bloody ladder at last" gasped Michel and watched fascinated as the drunk Englishman attempted to pick up the ladder before falling forward on top of it.
"Oh, non" whispered Michel and Josette looked on in horror as the man attempted to pick himself up. As he struggled on the ground he resembled a lunatic fighting a giant stick insect and seemed unable to detach himself from its clutches. Josette started to laugh and Michel joined her as their only hope of rescue carried on with the one sided fight for supremacy. At last he managed to roll off his protagonist and slowly stood up before reaching down, with legs splayed apart, and lifted the ladder from the hard standing.
"Bravo, Monsieur" called Michel as the man stood the ladder against the hull. Michel grabbed the top to steady it for Josette to climb down but to his horror the Englishman was already climbing up towards them.
"Non, non, Monsieur, please go down, we can manage" shouted Michel.
"Don't worry, mate, I'll save you" said the drunk.
"He's coming up, Michel" said Josette in an anxious tone.

“I can see that! Monsieur, please go down!”

“Don’t panic, mate, I’m here, you’ll be alright.” Suddenly he was face to face with them at the top of the ladder and was attempting to climb over the side of the boat. The man faltered slightly and Michel was concerned that he might fall backwards so he held onto the Englishman’s arm and at that moment, as he clambered over the side, he accidentally kicked the ladder away. Michel heard it clatter on the hard standing before it slithered away.

“Oh, bollocks!” exclaimed the Englishman

“Are you alright, Monsieur?” enquired Josette as Michel turned away and looked up at the starlit sky and exclaimed “I don’t believe it!”

“Now what do we do?” asked Josette.

“I’ve no idea” replied Michel as the man composed himself and then began tapping his chest.

“I’m Terry, Terry Watson, from England.”

“Oh, mon Dieu!” whispered Michel.

“Bonsoir, Monsieur Terry Watson” replied Josette.

“D’you speak English at all?” enquired Terry.

“Non” replied Josette.

“Pity” said Terry as he shook his head.

“Ask him where his friends are” said Michel.

“I don’t know how to say that” replied Josette. Michel then held up four fingers and said to Terry “where are your friends?” Terry looked confused until Josette grabbed one of Michel’s fingers and said “Terry Watson.”

“Ah, I realise who you are now, you were in the restaurant tonight” replied Terry.

“What did he say?” asked Michel.

“I’ve no idea” replied Josette as she waggled Michel’s finger once again and said “Terry Watson.” The Englishman looked even more confused as Josette then counted “one, two, three” and tapped Michel’s upright fingers.

“Oh, you mean my mates” smiled Terry.

“Oui” replied Josette as she realised that the drunk understood.

“I’ve no idea where they are now, after the restaurant we went to a bar somewhere near here and I left them drinking, I needed a bit of fresh air, so I was going back to our boat, it’s moored somewhere over there" replied Terry as he waved his arm towards the fleet anchored in the harbour.

"What did he say?" enquired Michel.

"I don't know, chérie."

"This is a fine mess" said Michel.

"How we going to get off this boat?" asked Terry and as neither Michel or Josette could understand what he said they just shrugged their shoulders.

"Typical, not got a brain cell between them" mumbled Terry.

"I think I'll just have to shout for help again" said Michel.

"Oui, ma petite." Michel cupped his hands once again and called for help three more times.

"That's the answer, make a noise, wake 'em all up" said Terry and he wandered off towards the bridge. Michel and Josette watched in fascination.

"What's he going to do?" asked Michel and Josette just shook her head. It did not take the Englishman long to find what he was looking for amongst the controls on the bridge and he stabbed his finger with pleasure onto the large red button that he guessed was either the starter for the engine or the siren. The siren screamed out in one long burst that seemed to last for ages before Terry released the button for a moment and he then followed it up with three more short ones with the sound echoing around the harbour and beyond.

"Mon Dieu, he must have woken up everybody in Boulogne!" exclaimed Michel.

"At least someone will have heard that" said Josette with confidence. Terry then re-appeared on the deck with them and asked "what did you think of my toot tooting then?"

"Bon, Monsieur" replied Michel guessing at what Terry had said.

"Look, there's some people over the other side of the Boulevard" said Josette pointing in the direction of their parked Mercedes.

"I'll call them" said Michel and he cupped his hands and shouted at the three distant figures. In the pale light of the street lamps they saw the figures stop and look in the direction of the 'Sea Goddess'.

"Call again, Michel" said Josette as she waved her arms at the men. Michel shouted as loud as he could and watched with relief as the figures started to cross the Boulevard slowly towards them.

"That's Frank, and Dave...... and Mitch" said Terry as his friends made their way unsteadily towards the boat.

"Mon Dieu!" exclaimed Michel.

"Hey, Frank, it's me!....... Dave!........ Mitch!........ I'm up here!" shouted Terry. The three figures then hurried a little and one called out as they became closer "Terry, what are you doing up there for God's sake?"

"I've been trapped by this bloke and his girlfriend" replied Terry.

"How?" asked the man.

"Don't ask, Frank, just pick up that ladder down there and get us off this bloody old boat!" exclaimed Terry.

"We'd thought we'd lost you" said another man as Frank went for the ladder.

"And I thought I'd never see you lot again, Dave" replied Terry as Frank and Mitch placed the ladder back against the hull much to the relief of Michel and Josette.

"Come on sweetheart, you first" called Frank.

"They don't speak any English" said Terry as he gestured towards the top of the ladder for Josette to descend first.

"Merci, Terry" she smiled as Michel helped her over the side of the boat. With Frank and Mitch supporting the ladder she anxiously began the slow climb down very aware that her little black dress would reveal everything to the men below.

"Come on, Mademoiselle, don't be scared" said Frank.

"We'll catch you if you fall" said Mitch.

"Coo, she's got lovely legs" said Frank.

"I'd like to catch her anytime" said Mitch as he reached up to steady Josette.

"Merci, Messieurs" she said as she stepped down the last rungs onto the hard standing.

"You're very welcome" replied Frank.

"Now you, Monsieur" said Terry and Michel swung his leg over the side and began his descent. He arrived safely at the bottom and after thanking the men holding the ladder, he put his arm affectionately around his fiancé. It was at this moment that the Gendarmes arrived in two cars with flashing blue lights. Terry had begun his descent and he saw the Gendarmes first as the assembled crowd below were busy watching him.

"Oh, bollocks!" he exclaimed.

"What is it, Terry?" asked Frank.

"It's the police!" he replied. They all turned to see six or more Gendarmes racing towards them in the moonlight.

"Mon Dieu!" exclaimed Michel. Terry was almost at the bottom of the ladder when the Gendarmes arrived and grabbed Michel and Dave first before manhandling the others. The Englishmen started shouting their objections whilst they were carrying out a rescue mission as Terry descended the last few rungs into the arms of a large Gendarme. At this point Frank became a little overwrought at his arrest and lashed out at the Gendarme holding him. His fist connected with the Gendarmes nose and then a nearby colleague produced a truncheon and whacked Frank on the head. This was the signal for all hell to break loose and despite the cries for restraint from Josette and Michel, a true Anglo French meleé commenced. However, it was only a matter of time before the Gendarmes had overcome the drunk Englishmen and were leading them away in handcuffs towards the Police cars.

"Monsieur, monsieur, these people were only trying to rescue us from the boat" said Michel to the senior Gendarme as he was hurried towards the Boulevard.

"And what were you doing on the boat at this time of night, Monsieur?" enquired the Gendarme.

"I was showing it to my fiancé…."

"Really" interrupted the Gendarme.

"Oui, Monsieur."

"And are you the owner of the boat in question?" demanded the Gendarme.

"Non, not exactly, you see………"

"Well you can explain everything down at the station" interrupted the officer.

"Monsieur, I'm a business man from Le Touquet, you shouldn't be arresting me!" exclaimed Michel.

"As I said, Monsieur, you can explain everything later."

"Look, I don't want to leave my car parked over there" said Michel nodding towards his Mercedes.

"Is that taxi yours?" asked the Gendarme.

"Oui."

"Give me the keys, Monsieur and we'll bring it along" replied the Gendarme and he held out his hand.

"Josette, get my keys out of my pocket, chérie." She then fumbled nervously before retrieving the keys and handing them over.

"Merci, Mademoiselle." By then a large police van pulled up and the Gendarmes opened the rear doors and started to load the struggling and complaining Englishmen into the back. A small crowd had gathered to watch in comparative silence and Michel heard several snatches of their conversations where the words 'English thieves', 'drug smugglers' and 'illegal immigrants' were spoken in murmured half whispers.

"This is all a dreadful mistake" complained Michel to the Gendarme as he was half lifted up into the blue, corrugated Renault police van.

"I don't think so, Monsieur" replied the senior Gendarme.

"Well I know it is!" exclaimed Michel.

"Mademoiselle, you'll please come in my car to the station" said the Gendarme as he ignored Michel.

"Oui, Monsieur" she replied quietly. With all the miscreants now loaded safely the Gendarmes returned to their cars and with cries of 'bravo' from the gathering crowd, the convoy set off back to the Gendarmerie with all blue lights flashing.

Captain Orteu looked sternly at the prisoners assembled before him and then glanced at the paperwork on his desk.

"Michel Ronay, according to this information on the charge sheet, you are French and you live in Le Touquet" said the Captain.

"Oui, Monsieur, I am a business man involved in the tourist industry" replied Michel.

"And you are Josette LeFranc, also a French national, living with Michel Ronay in Le Touquet" said the Captain as he fixed Josette with inquisitive eyes.

"Oui, Monsieur, we're engaged to be married as soon as his divorce comes through" she replied. The Captain ignored her and returned his gaze to the charge sheet for a moment before addressing the others in English.

"Terence Watson, Frank Richards, David Mason and Mitchell Cooper, you have been arrested and charged with trespass, property damage, disturbing the peace, drunkenness, common affray, resisting arrest and assaulting police officers, you will remain in custody overnight and will be brought before the court for further investigation by the judge tomorrow………"

"Oh, no! This is all a mistake, we were only trying to help this bloke and his girlfriend get off the boat" interrupted Terry as the others chorused their protests.

"Silence!" shouted the Captain. The room fell silent and Michel, feeling guilty that the situation was entirely his fault, said "Monsieur Captain, these good people came to our rescue, without them Mademoiselle LeFranc and I would have been trapped on the boat all night."

"Possibly, Monsieur" replied the Captain.

"We might have died from exposure, we had no food or anything to drink…….."

"Monsieur, the law is the law and you, along with Mademoiselle LeFranc and these four Englishmen, were caught in the act of trespass and damaging property by my officers" interrupted the Captain.

"What property?" demanded Michel. The Captain studied the charge sheet for a moment and then replied "a ladder, Monsieur."

"We didn't damage the ladder, it kept falling over, that's why we were trapped!" exclaimed Michel.

"And then, when you were arrested by my officers, you started fighting" replied the Captain sternly.

"They were heavy handed and wouldn't listen" said Michel.

"You can explain that to the judge" replied the Captain.

"You're not keeping us here, are you?"

"Oui, Monsieur, you are under arrest and will be held in custody until tomorrow" said the Captain.

"But we've got to get back to Le Touquet, I've got an important business meeting in the morning" said Michel in a worried tone.

"Your meeting has been cancelled, Monsieur."

"Oh, non" said Michel.

"Oh, oui, Monsieur Ronay" replied the officer.

"Now then, Captain, would you please tell Terry and his friends that Josette and I are very grateful to them for saving us tonight and I'm sorry that they've ended up in so much trouble through no fault of their own."

"Oui, Monsieur" replied the Captain and he then translated everything that Michel had said.

Terry and the others smiled broadly then shook Michel by the hand and Josette bestowed little kisses on all four Englishmen, all of whom blushed slightly.

"Take them away" ordered the Captain and the prisoners were then escorted to their solitary cells for the rest of the night. Michel had a fleeting moment to kiss Josette before she was led away in tears by a statuesque police woman.

CHAPTER 7

Henri was just about to leave his house to collect Michel when the telephone rang.

"Oui?"

"Henri, it's Michel."

"Why are you calling me, I'm just about to come round for you?"

"Don't bother."

"Why not?"

"Because I'm not at home."

"Michel, we have a meeting at ten with Jean Ricard in Boulogne."

"I know, and I'm already there."

"What with Monsieur Ricard?"

"Non, in Boulogne."

"I'll pick you up there then" replied a surprised Henri.

"Don't think so, Henri."

"Why not?"

"I'm in prison."

"Mon Dieu! What have you done now?"

"Nothing serious I promise you."

"Tell me, will you?" demanded Henri angrily.

"I was trapped on Maurice DeVere's boat with Josette…….."

"What!" exclaimed Henri.

"Look, I can't stop now, the Gendarmes are taking us into court."

"Mon Dieu!"

"You'll have to keep the appointment with Monsieur Ricard and I'll call you at the salon when we get out of here."

"Alright, Michel, but remember you've a lunch date with the Christiane women."

"Don't remind me."

"You'd better not miss that."

"Thanks, Henri, the day just gets better and better."

"It's all your own fault, Michel."

"Au revoir, Henri."

"Au revoir."

The presiding judge was a thin grey haired man with thick glasses who viewed the six accused before him with a long, hard stare. The charges were read out in both languages to the judge's irritation and at last when the prosecuting officer had finished the catalogue of misdemeanours there was complete silence whilst his honour made some notes.

"I will question Michel Ronay first of all, followed by Josette LeFranc, the English will have to wait" he said slowly and with all the legal gravity expected of a prosecuting judge. Michel braced himself and glanced anxiously at Josette as the judge began.

"Firstly, Monsieur Ronay, explain to me all the events last night that led to your arrest and your appearance in my court this morning." Michel then gave the judge a full and detailed statement of everything that had happened in the early hours of the morning on board the 'Sea Goddess.' He ensured that the judge was made aware of every moment of the incident and ended by complaining about the refusal of the Gendarmes to listen at the scene and their un-necessary heavy handling of the brave English who had come to their aid in their moment of need. The judge listened impassively and when Michel had finished he made some notes. The questioning then began.

"What were you and Josette LeFranc doing on the boat in the early hours of the morning, Monsieur?" enquired the judge.

"I was showing her around."

"Surely that would be more appropriate in the daylight, Monsieur."

"Well, we'd had a romantic dinner in the Estaminet restaurant, where we first met our English friends, and as a surprise I wanted to show my fiancé the 'Sea Goddess' as I have recently concluded a deal with the owner, Monsieur Maurice DeVille, to offer boat trips to my clients, you see I'm a business man in the tourist industry." The judge seemed un-impressed and made some notes.

"Would Captain Orteu please find this Maurice DeVille and ascertain if he knows Monsieur Ronay?"

"Oui, Monsieur le judge" replied the Captain before he hurriedly left the court with a Gendarme. The judge continued with his investigations and went over and over in minute detail all of Michel's statement of events. At last, when he had finished with Michel he turned his attention to a nervous Josette. Once again the events were thoroughly rehearsed and he finished with one last question.

"And when are you getting married, Mademoiselle LeFranc?"

"As soon as Michel's divorce comes through" she replied brightly.

"Ah, the old 'as soon as my divorce comes through' ploy" he said with a grin.

The Englishmen were then fully examined by the judge through an interpreter and one by one they corroborated Michel's explanation of events. They all waited for a while before Captain Orteu and his assistant returned to the court accompanied by a concerned looking Maurice DeVille who informed the judge that he knew Michel and confirmed that no harm had been done to the 'Sea Goddess' except for her ladder which showed signs of accidental damage. Having satisfied himself that no serious incident had taken place, the judge commended the Gendarmes for their swift action when called to duty by an irate citizen of Boulogne, whose new born baby had just gone to sleep for the first night in weeks before being woken by the siren. The judge then solemnly discharged all those before him and the elated prisoners made their way out of the court.

Once outside, Michel thanked Terry and the others before apologising to Maurice who took the matter lightly and smiled throughout. Having said goodbye to Terry and his companions and wishing them a safe journey back to England, Michel and Josette went to the police pound and recovered the Mercedes. It was now nearly lunchtime and they hurried back to Le Touquet as quickly as they could. They found Pascal waiting outside their house surrounded by several tins of cream emulsion paint.

"Bonjour, mes amis, I was just about to go home" he beamed as they arrived.

"Sorry, Pascal, but we were unavoidably detained" replied Michel as he unlocked the front door.

"Everything alright?" enquired the old man as he gathered up his tins of paint.

"Oui, it is now" said Michel.

Once inside Michel rushed upstairs to wash and shave, leaving Josette to prepare a light lunch for them all. When at last he appeared in the kitchen, fresh and with a clean shirt he said "I'll just have a coffee, ma petite."

"But I've made some soup and baguettes for us all" Josette protested.

"I know, chérie, but I've an appointment in about ten minutes with Henri and a customer of his, and I can't stop."

"Oh, Michel……."

"I know, I know, just pour me a coffee, chérie" he interrupted and Josette did as she was asked. He drank the hot coffee, whilst Pascal looked on bemused, and then kissed Josette.

"I won't be late tonight" he said.

"Bon, because I'm going to cook the steak for dinner."

"Ah, oui, I look forward to it" he replied and then wishing Pascal a productive afternoon painting, he left the house and drove quickly to Le Café des Arts.

Sophia sat in her usual place in the alcove and looked radiant in a dark blue, fitted dress with a cheeky little white pill box hat tipped at an angle. She smiled broadly as Michel entered the restaurant and gave him a little wave as he approached.

"Here at last" he said as he sat opposite his lovely mistress.

"I was beginning to wonder if you were coming" she replied with a smile.

"Would I let you down for a moment?" he asked as the waiter handed them the menus.

"Possibly, but not yet" she smiled.

"Why are you so suspicious?" he enquired.

"I've told you before, it's all to good to be true and I'm afraid our bubble will burst."

"Not if we don't let it."

"Ah, but you may not care if it does."

"What are you going to have?" asked Michel as he changed the subject and glanced down at the menu.

"I'm not sure, I feel restless today, so I'll have to think."

They sat in silence before Michel decided on potage julienne followed by canard a l'orange and Sophia, being undecided, was prompted to have the same. Michel perused the wine list before ordering a light Rosé to accompany the meal.

"So why were you nearly late?" she asked after the waiter had left with their order.

"Tricky business in Boulgone" he replied.

"Really" she said with a sparkle in her eyes.

"Oui, I can't go into too much detail but…….."

"Oh, please do, Michel, I'm anxious to hear anything about our business" she interrupted eagerly. He was beginning to feel trapped again and a touch of cold fear closed over him. He knew for certain that, come what may, she had to be told that it was all over. He could not possibly return to the salon and face the wrath of Henri once again. So true to form, Michel romanced the story, all the time gaining strength of purpose and iron resolve to face the anger that Sophia would unleash upon him when she was told the unpalatable truth.

"It started last night after the client and I had had dinner at a restaurant in Boulogne….."

"Which restaurant?" she interrupted.

"Estaminet's"

"I don't know it."

"Never mind………."

"Was the food good?" she interrupted.

"Oui."

"Bon, you can take me there then."

"I will, now after…….."

"Who was the client?" she asked and Michel was stumped for a moment.

"You wouldn't know them" he replied.

"Of course not, chérie, that's why I'm asking."

"It was Monsieur DeVere, an important ship owner, with offices in Boulogne" Michel replied as the picture of Maurice sitting at his desk in his poky, clutter filled office sprang into his mind.
At that moment the waiter arrived with the wine and after opening it, poured the sparkling liquid into their glasses, giving Michel time to gather his thoughts.

"To us, chérie" he said.

"To us, for ever" she replied and hearing that, fear returned to him like a damp coat over his shoulders.

"Now, where was I?" enquired Michel as he placed his glass down on the table.

"With Monsieur DeVere" she replied.

"Oui, so after dinner, and by then it was quite late, Maurice invited me to inspect one of his ships" said Michel and then he paused.

"Go on, chérie."

"Well, I hesitate to tell you what happened next" he said.

"Why?"

"It's a little embarrassing."

"It doesn't matter, please go on" she pleaded.

"We left the restaurant and drove to his office before walking across to the harbour where his ship, the 'Sea Goddess' was on blocks for its annual maintenance."

"The 'Sea Goddess', what a romantic name, it reminds me of me, facing the sea, naked and in harmony with it" she whispered.

"Oui, quite so" he replied and at that point the waiter arrived with their soups and wished them 'bon appetite'. Conversation then halted until they had finished the potage and resumed after they had consumed more wine and spent a few moments gazing into each others eyes.

"Then what happened, chérie?" she enquired.

"Maurice and I climbed aboard the ship up a ladder which had seen better days….."

"You didn't fall off did you?" she asked anxiously.

"Non, I fell on" he replied.

"Fell on?"

"Oui, I fell onto the deck and accidentally kicked the ladder, which slid to the ground." At that, she started to laugh and Michel was slightly taken aback.

"We were in a serious position, chérie" he said and her laughter subsided.

"Do go on" she giggled.

"So, as Maurice and I were now trapped on the 'Sea Goddess', with no means of escape, we had no option but to shout for help." She giggled again at that.

"Luckily, a man who we'd seen in the restaurant earlier, heard us and came to our rescue."

"Bon, a lucky moment."

"The trouble was, he was English…."

"Mon Dieu."

"Precisely, and he didn't understand us….."

"A catastrophe."

"It was, because he picked up the ladder, put it back against the ship and climbed up."

"Non!"

"Oui, and when he got to the top he fell on board, as I did before, and kicked the ladder away!"

"Mon Dieu! So you were all trapped on the ship!"

"Oui" and she started to laugh loudly, pausing only to say "next you'll be telling me that everybody in Boulogne ended up on the ship!" Her laughter became uncontrollable and she was by now attracting the attention of other diners.

"Shhh, ma petite, you're embarrassing me" he whispered.

"But Michel, it's so funny!"

"It's not, and it gets worse" he said firmly to which she laughed all the more.

"It can't" she replied her eyes now moist with tears.

"Then, the Englishman, Terry, who was drunk by the way, went up to the bridge and sounded the ships siren………."

"Mon Dieu! Did anybody hear it?"

"Oui, everyone in Boulogne." At hearing that, Sophia went once again into fits of laughter and only the arrival of the waiter with two portions of canard a l'orange forced her to subdue her outburst.

"Don't tell me any more 'til we've finished this" she said with a grin.

"OK" replied Michel, pleased to have another break to gather his composure for what could turn out to be a very difficult afternoon. The nouvelle cuisine at Le Café des Arts was as delicious as it was simple and beautifully presented. Michel ordered another bottle of Rosé and other than knowing glances and furtive smiles the lovers took their time over the main course with little conversation. Diners nearby were grateful for the silence and other than a few raised eyebrows, the customers settled down to enjoy the cuisine.

When they had finished, Sophia smiled at Michel and said as she sipped at her wine "so, tell me the rest then."

"Where was I?"

"Terry had just woken everybody in Boulogne with the siren" she giggled.

"Ah, oui, then by chance, three friends of his, who he'd left in a bar somewhere, arrived in a drunken state, and heard him shout."

"He started shouting?"

"Oui."

"I'm surprised that anyone didn't call the police" she said.

"I'm coming to that" replied Michel as she started to laugh.

"Oh, Michel"

"So the three friends came over to the ship, found the ladder and were starting to rescue us…."

"Bon" she interrupted.

"And that's when the police arrived."

"Mon Dieu."

"And as they started arresting everybody, me included I might add, the English started fighting….."

"Each other?"

"Non, the Gendarmes."

"Typical."

"Then we were all carted off to the Gendarmerie for the night and then had the pleasure of facing a sour faced old judge in court this morning."

"My poor petite business man" she cooed.

"I thought I was going to end up with a prison sentence" said Michel quietly.

"But you didn't, chérie, and now you're here, safe with me" she smiled as the waiter arrived.

Michel ordered salad des fruits for both of them followed by coffee.

"So, what have you planned for us this afternoon?" he asked as the waiter hurried away.

"It's a nice day again, so I think we'll just drive along to our spot in the dunes" she replied with a smile.

"What a very good idea" said Michel, believing that would be the ideal place to tell her the bad news. The meal and wine had given him confidence and now he just wanted to get it over with. They chatted aimlessly and lingered over the sweet and coffee before calling for l'addition and leaving the other diners in peace.

Sophia drove her Mercedes leisurely to the turning off the south bound coastal road and swung the car onto the track between the dunes. She parked and after retrieving the blanket and petite case from the boot, they made their way along the deserted beach to their lovers nest hewn out in the sand dune by the sea gods especially for them.

"I think I'll wait a while and enjoy the brandy before I go 'au natural' in the breeze" she said as she laid on the blanket and opened the case.

"Why not, ma petite, we're in no hurry."

"Bon" she replied as she poured two large brandy's into the crystal glasses.

"I could do with a little rest after this morning's excitement" said Michel with a sigh.

"Bon, because I want you to gather your strength for a long session today" she said as she handed him his brandy.

"Really?"

"Oui, I have a deep and longing need that won't be satisfied if I'm rushed."

"I see" replied Michel as they touched glasses.

"To us" she said.

"Bon chance" he replied.

They sat for some while, each quietly deep in thought, watching the waves breaking gently on the shore and enjoying the warm winter sun. Michel finished his brandy and putting the glass carefully down said, "Sophia, we must talk about the business……"

"Oh, not now, chérie, I'm relaxing and getting myself ready for you" she interrupted.

"Sophia" Michel persisted "I'm afraid I've got some bad news."

"Don't tell me, it was a woman you were trapped with on the ship not Monsieur DeVere" she said with a touch of anger.

"Look, this is serious" he said gently.

"Well, what is it for heavens sake?" she asked in an irritated tone.

"I don't know how to tell you this but…….."

"Oh, Michel, spit it out before I get really angry" she interrupted.

"You can't be a partner in the business" he blurted out and then felt better.

"What!" she exclaimed as her eyes narrowed.

"It just wouldn't work, chérie" he said as gently as he could.

"Who says it wouldn't work?" she demanded.

"It doesn't matter……"

“I can guess, I think dear Henri fits the bill!” Her anger alarmed Michel and he tried to calm her down with smooth diplomacy.

“Listen, chérie……”

“Non, you listen, Michel, we’re partners, equal partners, and whether Henri likes it or not, I’m in the business!”

“Ma chérie……”

“I mean it, Michel, and you can go and tell that pompous twit to get on and manage his salon and leave us to run our business!”

“It’s not going to happen” replied Michel.

“Oh, oui, it is.”

“Non.”

“I promise you that the best Parisian lawyers that money can buy will make it happen” she replied and Michel began to buckle under the threat.

“Ma chérie……..”

“Go tell Henri his future if he tries to stop me” she said with determination.

“Mon Dieu, how did I get into this?”

“Never mind how, you’re in it up to your eyeballs now” she replied.

“And don’t I know it!”

“Take me home” she demanded angrily.

“Ma chérie………”

“Now Michel!”

“But let me……”

“You’ve ruined my lovely afternoon and you can blame yourself as well as Henri for that!”

“I’m to blame?”

“Oui, you should have the guts to tell him to piss off!” With that she gulped down her Brandy, snatched his glass and packed the case before standing up and grabbing the edge of the blanket.

“Home” she said as she glared down at him still slumped on the blanket with a confused look.

They did not speak again until she parked behind Michel’s car outside Le Café des Arts.

“Michel, go and inform Henri that I, your partner, do not wish to hear anymore of his narrow minded, restrictive comments about our business.”

“But, chérie…….”

"Remember the Paris lawyers, Michel."

"Ma petite......"

"And when you've told him, you can 'phone me at home and we can make our arrangements for tonight, OK?"

"Sophia......."

"Off you go, ma petite."

Michel left her and walked slowly to his Mercedes and sank down in the driver's seat. He watched her in his rear view mirror for a moment before she roared off at great speed and his heart sank into a grey sea of despair. He dreaded telling Henri and prayed for a miracle.

The salon was busy and he nodded to Elaine on his way up to Henri's office, where he tapped gently on the half open door before entering.

"Ah, Michel, glad to see that you've escaped justice and are free once again" beamed Henri.

"Oui, for the moment" he replied as he sat in his chair.

"Before you tell me about prison, please tell me that you've seen the Christiane woman and she's now out of our way" said Henri in an anxious tone.

"I've seen her and I've told her that she can't be involved in the business...."

"Bon" interrupted Henri with a relieved look.

"But she wouldn't listen......"

"What?"

"And she's threatening us with Parisian lawyers if we don't........"

"Oh. Mon Dieu! Mon Dieu!" gasped Henri.

"I know how you feel" said Michel glumly as he looked at his cousin who then clasped his head in his hands.

"We cannot go ahead, it's all over, our dreams, our plans, everything, it's all come to nothing because of that dreadful bloody woman" complained Henri, shaking his head.

"There must be something we can do, surely?" asked Michel.

"What do you suggest?" Henri asked.

"I can't think for the moment...."

"That's the trouble with you, Michel, you just don't think" interrupted Henri.

"Look, can I help it if she's........."

"I warned you Michel, from the very beginning, this was all totally avoidable."

"The woman is a nightmare……"

"I know, and I told you!"

"OK, OK, I'm sorry, what more can I say?"

"I just have to wonder how many women you need in your life?"

"Only one."

"Really?"

"Oui."

"You amaze me, there's Josette, Monique, Yvonne and only God knows how many others."

"True, but I only really love Josette."

"Mon Dieu!" At that moment Elaine knocked and entered the office.

"Monsieur Henri, I'm sorry to interrupt but Madame Tetroux would like to see you, she has a complaint" said Elaine.

"Another one to contend with!"

"I don't think it's very serious" said Elaine attempting to lessen the stress.

"Not very serious? Why, that's the best news I've heard today" said Henri as he stood up from his desk.

"I'll leave you in peace for a while and come back later" said Michel.

"OK" nodded Henri.

"I'll have a good think about our little problem."

Elaine looked concerned at that and then followed Henri out of the office and downstairs to attend to Madame Tetroux.

Michel went straight to the Bar Americaine and slumped down in a corner seat by the window. He hoped that inspiration might flow into his troubled mind as he watched the myriad of passers by making their way along the Rue de Londres. He ordered a double Brandy and stared at it for a while before picking up the glass from the polished wood top table and gulping half of it down. He wondered how he was ever going to extract himself from Sophia's clutches. He felt he needed another person's perspective on the problem. Someone who did not know Sophia but could perhaps understand her motives, another woman, a mature woman was the answer. He immediately thought of Maria in Boulogne, she would be bound to help, after all, Henri had said that she had a soft spot for him, and Michel was absolutely sure that when he confided in Maria, she would have all the answers. He felt relieved after having decided to contact her and then he finished his Brandy before using the payphone at the back of the bar.

"Maria, it's Michel here, ça va?"

"Oh, Michel, what a lovely surprise."

"Oui, I was just thinking of you" he said.

"And I've been thinking of you."

"Really?"

"Oui, I hoped you'd call."

"Well, here I am."

"Bon, are you coming to see me?"

"But of course" he replied.

"When?" she giggled a little.

"Tomorrow."

"Bon."

"I'll take you to lunch at Estaminet's."

"Oh, Michel, I look forward to that, I'm in need of a long, leisurely meal."

"So am I."

"We have so much to talk about."

"We certainly do" he replied.

"You are coming alone aren't you?" she asked in a concerned tone.

"Of course, I want you all to myself."

"Bon, what time will you pick me up?"

"About twelve, is that OK?"

"Oh, oui, I'll be ready."

"Bon, 'til tomorrow then."

"Oui, au revoir, ma petite."

"Au, revoir."

He returned to his corner seat feeling uplifted and ordered another double Brandy to celebrate the certain downfall of Sophia Christiane. It was sometime later that he left the Bar Americaine and wandered back to number 19 to see Josette and discover how Pascal was getting on with the painting.

"Hello, ma petite, I'm home" he called as he entered the

hallway. He could hear voices in the lounge and made his way into the room where Josette and Jackie were sitting facing one another. They stopped talking and both fixed him with an icy stare.

"Hello, chérie, and Jackie" he said anxiously.

"I'm glad you're back" said Josette.

"So am I, chérie."

"I want to talk to you" said Josette firmly.

"Of course, chérie" smile Michel sensing danger.

"I'd better be going" said Jackie.

"Oh, don't go" pleaded Michel.

"I think I better had" Jackie replied and stood up.

"Au revoir, Jackie and thanks" said Josette.

"Au revoir, I'll see myself out" she said and was gone in an instant.

"Now then you'd better sit down" said Josette.

"Oui, ma petite" and Michel did as he was told.

"Jackie has told me that Elaine, the manager at Henri's salon 'phoned her yesterday about something or other, and said, quite innocently, that everyone at the salon was pleased that you'd been able to sort out the problems with Madame Christiane and Henri wouldn't have to close the salon now" said Josette in a measured tone.

"Oh, bon."

"So tell me, Michel, what the hell's been going on?" she exploded.

"Ma chérie, I promise you it's all been sorted out……"

"I don't believe you" she interrupted.

"Listen to me will you?"

"You'd better tell me everything, Michel, and I mean everything otherwise I'm going back to Marseille for certain."

"Right, just listen to me, the Christiane woman is a very good customer of Henri's, she spends a lot of money with him……"

"So how come you're involved with her?"

"I'm not really, she heard about our tourist business from some one, probably one of Henri's assistants and decided to invest money into it….."

"Go on."

"Well, she wanted to be an equal partner and both Henri and I said 'no' as we have ample funds to start up and we didn't want a partner, especially her, she's very difficult to handle."

"I expect you could manage it."

"The man hasn't been born yet..........."

"So, are you doing all the business negotiations with her?"

"I have been."

"And mixing a little pleasure with business, no doubt."

"Ma chérie, how could you think that?"

"I know you too well, Michel."

"Just trust me, will you?"

"I have no alternative at the moment, but I warn you, that much as I love you, I'll be on the train back to Marseille if I catch you out one more time."

"Ma chérie, you have my word."

Michel returned to the salon after promising Josette that he would not be late for dinner, and as he sat down in the office he hoped that between Maria, Henri and himself they could come up with a plan to stop Sophia and her lawyers.

"Any ideas?" asked Henri.

"Non, I'm still recovering from a difficult one sided conversation with Josette over the Christiane woman."

"Oh, dear me."

"Apparently Elaine told Jackie in conversation all about it and Jackie was at home when I arrived."

"Mon Dieu, I guess your overnight stay in prison in Boulogne was easy compared with the rest of today" grinned Henri.

"It was."

"Now then, I've had a thought, we can fight fire with fire and I've made an appointment for us to see my friend Charles Robardes tomorrow morning to discuss what we can do legally to protect ourselves" said Henri and Michel felt a great weight lift from his shoulders.

"That is good news."

"Oui, Charles is very astute and I'm sure he can find a way through this mess."

Michel felt much relieved as he left the salon and made his way to the Bar Americaine where he ordered a double Brandy and sat, in the corner that he had previously occupied, to contemplate. He tried to organise his thoughts and wondered what he could to say to Sophia when he telephoned her. He was looking for a very good reason for not seeing her tonight as well as skirting round the problem of what he had told Henri. When he had finished his Brandy he made his way to the payphone and dialled Sophia's number.

"Sophia, ma chérie."

"Michel" she replied coldly.

"Are you alright?"

"I'm fine." Michel knew that when a woman says she's 'fine' she is definitely not.

"Bon, now about tonight, chérie……."

"Have you told Henri his future?" she interrupted.

"I'm coming to that, chérie……."

"Get to it now, Michel!"

"Chérie…….."

"Now, Michel."

"Henri and I have had a long discussion about you…….."

"And?"

"Well, it's a bit complicated……"

"It better not be" she interrupted.

"The end result is that you can't be in the business" he said firmly.

"Is that final?"

"I'm afraid it is." There was a long pause before Sophia replied "right, that's your decision, it's the wrong one of course and I will have to think carefully about it all."

"Bon" replied Michel, somewhat relieved.

"Now then, pick me up at eight and we'll go to the casino" she said firmly.

"Sophia, ma chérie, not tonight."

"Why?"

"I've some urgent business to attend to and I won't be finished 'til late."

"Meet me in there then" she replied.

"OK, I will, but it will be late" he said.

"That's alright, chérie, I'll try not to lose too much before you arrive."

"Bon."

"Au revoir."

“Au revoir.”

Michel wandered back home with the worry of Sophia and her demands pressing down heavily on his shoulders once again. Josette looked pleased to see him and Pascal was anxious to show his efforts in refurbishment.

“What do you think?” asked the old man with a smile as Michel surveyed the ‘all cream’ bedroom.

“Very good, Pascal, you’ve done a wonderful job.”

“I’m glad you like it.”

They returned downstairs to sit and drink coffee at the kitchen table. It was after six that Pascal left for Boulogne, promising to return tomorrow and finish the other bedroom.

“What a day” said Michel.”

“Oui, it certainly has been” Josette replied.

“I’m glad I’m home with you, chérie” said Michel and he gave her a little kiss.

Later Josette prepared a delicious meal. The fillet steak was most tender and they managed to drink two bottles of rich burgundy before she presented the dessert of fresh fruit salad with cream. They were both full, almost to the point of discomfort and as they settled on the settee together, Michel made up his mind to remain at home with his fiancé and make gentle love to her later. Madame Sophia Christiane would have to play the tables and lose alone in the casino tonight.

CHAPTER 8

The morning was bright and sunny and after coffee and croissants with a very happy and contented Josette, Michel set off to meet Henri at the salon. Just as he was about to drive away, Pascal arrived with a young assistant, Pierré, eldest son of the paint supplier in Boulogne.

"He's come to help me today so I expect to get upstairs totally finished" said Pascal.

"Bon" replied Michel.

"Then when that's all done I can start on a few other little jobs that need doing" said Pascal.

"Such as?"

"Well, some of the wiring in the kitchen needs looking at" replied the old man.

"Really?"

"Oui."

"I'll leave you to it then, au revoir" replied Michel trying to hide his concern. Splashing cream emulsion all over the place was relatively easy but fiddling with old wiring was a very different matter. Michel hoped he would not return to an unlit home with a tearful fiancé nursing a candle.

Henri was in buoyant mood and seemed pleased to see his cousin, as Elaine brought coffee for them at the start of the day's business in the office.

"Charles is going to see us at ten this morning and hopefully he'll have some ideas to put forward" said Henri.

"Bon, I'm relieved to hear it" replied Michel.

"And I'm sure he'll advise you to stay well clear of Madame Christiane."

"Don't worry about that, I've had enough of her to last me a lifetime" replied Michel.

"Bon, now then, I saw Monsieur Ricard yesterday, whilst you were still in prison……."

"Thanks for reminding me" interrupted Michel.

"And we've got an outline agreement for coach tours round Normandy" said Henri.

“Good news.”

“Oui, the figures he’s quoted per passenger, are surprisingly low and I reckon we can make at least a hundred percent on every tourist.”

“Now that’s encouraging” replied Michel.

“Oui, now I’ve arranged for you to go on a half day tour that he’s running next Thursday for some Dutch tour guides, just to see how the operation works and if you think it’s suitable.”

“OK, it sounds good.”

“Oui, his coaches look clean and tidy and all his drivers wear a uniform, it seems to be a bit more professionally run than DeVere’s boat trips” said Henri.

“I look forward to it.”

“Now, how’s the office coming on at home?”

“Haven’t sorted that out yet as Pascal has only just finished painting downstairs.”

“Well as soon as the paint has dried I suggest you use the dining room, it’s big enough to start with.”

“OK.”

“I’ve ordered the posters that I showed you and most of the printing has arrived” said Henri.

“You have been busy” replied Michel.

“Oui, I had to get on with it whilst you were otherwise engaged.”

“Point taken, but from now on I’m fully focused on the business” said Michel with conviction.

“Glad to hear it.” They chatted on for a while and as they finished their coffee Henri glance at his watch.

“Time to see Charles.”

They arrived at Monsieur Robardes office just before ten and were shown promptly into the notaire’s inner office.

“Bonjour, Messieurs” he purred as he waved them to the seats in front of his paper strewn desk.

“Now then” he began ponderously “I’ve given the matter some thought and I believe that I may have found a way round your problem.”

“Glad to hear it, Charles” said Henri as Michel smiled with relief.

"Firstly, you must tell me exactly when you both agreed to start the business" said Monsieur Robardes as he peered over the top of his glasses at them.

"It was just before Christmas when Jackie and I were staying with Michel and his wife, Monique."

"Ah, oui, I know of the lady."

"We were on our way to pick up my two Aunts' that had been involved in a road accident" explained Michel.

"Oh, dear, were they alright?" enquired Monsieur Robardes.

"Oh, oui, it was the cyclist that suffered and the other driver, not to mention the van involved" replied Michel brightly.

"As I've said before, Monsieur, you seem to lead a somewhat eventful life" said Monsieur Robardes.

"He certainly does" said Henri.

"So, exactly on what date did this conversation take place?"

"Er, I think it was on the Saturday, that would have been the 20th……." said Henri.

"Non, Henri, it was on the Sunday" interrupted Michel.

"You sure?" asked Henri.

"Oui, because I didn't come home on Saturday night" replied Michel and Monsieur Robardes raised his eyebrows. Michel noticed that and looking straight at the notaire said firmly "I was working all night." Monsieur Robardes ignored him.

"Oui, you're right it was the Sunday, so that would have been the 21st of December" agreed Henri.

"Did you put anything in writing?" asked Monsieur Robardes.

"Non" replied Henri.

"No matter, now then, this is what I plan to do, I will draw up an agreement for you both to sign, which will confirm your verbal arrangements for the new business that you made in December and it will state that you are equal partners with, may I suggest, that Henri has the casting vote, and explicit in the contract will be a clause that prohibits any other person joining the business except as a member of staff."

"Brilliant, Charles" smiled Henri.

"Bravo, Monsieur" grinned Michel.

"And I think that will do the trick and keep you out of the clutches of Madame Christiane and her Parisian lawyers" beamed Monsieur Robardes with total satisfaction.

"And can she do anything at all?" enquired Michel as it all sounded a bit too easy to him.

"Oh, oui, she can sue you, Monsieur, but she can't join the business" replied the notaire.

"Sue me?"

"Oui, you had no right to offer her a partnership under the terms of your business agreement with Henri."

"Mon Dieu!" exclaimed Michel.

"I'm afraid you've broken your contract, and in fact Henri could sue you too."

"It gets worse" said Michel.

"Anyway, once you sign the contract your new business will be safe" said Monsieur Robardes.

"Merci, Charles" said Henri.

"I'll have it all drawn up by tomorrow, so if you could just pop in about midday and sign, the deed is done, the business will be secure, but regrettably, you Monsieur Ronay, will not be" said Monsieur Robardes with a smile.

"Well what can I do?" wailed Michel.

"I suggest you brace yourself for the impending law suit" replied the notaire.

"Oh, Mon Dieu!"

"But I assure you that once the Parisian lawyers have issued their writs, I will be at your service and I will ensure that my fees will be most reasonable" said Monsieur Robardes with due solemnity.

"Thank you so much for all your help, Charles" said a relieved Henri.

"What about me?" demanded Michel.

"Charles has just told you he'll look after you if the worst happens" said Henri.

"I think I need a drink" mumbled Michel.

"Until tomorrow then, Messieurs" said Monsieur Robardes as he stood up.

"We look forward to it" replied Henri as he stood and dragged the hapless Michel from his chair.

Once outside in the cold air Michel insisted they go for a drink in the Bar Americaine and Henri readily agreed.

"Oui, why not, I think a little celebration is in order" smiled

Henri.

"It may be a celebration for you but it sounds like the beginning of another nightmare for me" replied Michel.

"Don't worry, if it happens, I know Charles will take care of you" said Henri as they got into his car.

"Oui, but how much is it all going to cost?"

"Michel, if you get stuck for money, I'll help you."

"Merci, Henri."

The Bar was quite busy and the cousins found themselves an empty table at the back of the establishment amongst some of the locals wheezing through their own cigarette smoke.

"Well I think Charles has saved the day" said Henri as he sipped at his glass of Pernod.

"I hope so" replied Michel as he gazed forlornly at his drink.

"Have faith in the future, it's not all bad you know" said Henri brightly.

"Sometimes life seems so unfair" replied Michel.

"Oui, but sometimes it's unfair to your advantage" said Henri. At hearing that Michel brightened visibly, life was good, Charles had saved the business, Henri was relieved, Josette was happy, Pascal would finish painting today and soon he was off to see Maria for lunch. The day was improving steadily and Michel began to relish the prospects before him.

It was nearly lunch time when Henri returned to the salon and Michel drove off to Boulogne for his secret rendezvous with Maria. He was late and so he hurried the Mercedes as fast as he could and eventually parked outside her flat in the Boulevard Voltaire just after midday.

"Maria, it's Michel" he said to the sonnette when he heard her voice.

"Ah, Michel, come on in, ma petite" she cooed.

He was upstairs and in her flat within moments and he kissed her on both cheeks immediately he saw her. He followed her into her lounge and she waved him towards the settee and said "what would you like to drink, ma petite?"

"A Pernod, s'il vous plait" he replied as he sat down and looked at Henri's delightful Aunt .

For a woman in her mid fifties she looked superb, her dark hair was swept up into a French roll, her makeup, although discreet, was a little heavy on her plump, smiling face and her figure was almost statuesque with her prominent breasts pushing against the red v-neck jumper she was wearing. Her tight black skirt with a small side split accentuated her firm, long legs and her red high heeled shoes tipped her forward in a most provocative way. Michel was strongly attracted to her and decided that before he returned to Le Touquet he would do his utmost to tempt Maria into a deeply satisfying sexual experience. Remembering what Henri had said about her, he felt that might not be too difficult.

"There, ma petite" she said as she handed him his drink.

"Merci" he replied as she sat down beside him on the settee.

"Here's to us" she smiled as they touched glasses.

"To us."

"Now then, we've lots to talk about" she said.

"Oui."

"Tell me first of all about the new business with Henri."

Michel began to explain, in broad terms, what they planned to do but was frequently interrupted by Maria asking questions about the details of the operation and then giving her advice on how they should proceed. All the while he was explaining things she kept moving slightly closer to him and repeatedly whispered, at the appropriate moment, "you're so clever to do all this." To which he smiled his appreciation and continued whilst she fixed her big brown eyes on him. He began to feel slightly uncomfortable as Maria seemed to be controlling the pace of events and he felt that he was being seduced by this attractive woman. At an appropriate moment he glanced at his watch and said "I think we'd better go, we don't want to miss lunch."

"Of course, ma petite, it's just so interesting listening to you that I really have no idea of the time" she replied.

"Oui, it is exciting" said Michel.

"You don't have to rush off after lunch, do you?" she asked as she stood up.

"Non."

"Bon, then we can relax."

Estaminet du Chateau was very busy but the waiter, recognising Maria as one of the regular customers, found them a discreet table for two at the back of the restaurant.

"There, this is nice" she said as they perused the menus.

"The cuisine is good here" replied Michel.

"Oui, now, let me recommend the soupe a l'oignon gratinee to start, it's delicious" she enthused.

"OK."

"And then what do you fancy?" she asked with a twinkle in her eyes.

"Anything you suggest" he replied with a smile as he gazed back at her.

"Bon, I'll remember that."

"I think you're a little naughty" he replied.

"Non, ma petite, I'm a lot naughty, now then what are you going to eat?" she asked and Michel was then certain that Maria would take full advantage of him when they returned to her flat. He smiled and consulted the menu once more.

"I'll have the carré d'agneau" he replied "and you?"

"Boeuf bourguignon I think, I feel as if I need something substantial" she smiled as the waiter arrived. Michel chose a full, rich Burgundy to accompany the meal and the waiter hurried away with their order. Maria then placed her hand over Michel's and gazing into his eyes said "I hope you're going to spend a lot of time in Boulogne on business."

"Oh, oui, you can be sure of that" he replied.

"Bon, I'm so looking forward to getting to know you better" she smiled.

"And it's the same for me."

"I'm so glad to hear it."

"We've got so much to talk about" he said, thinking of the Sophia Christiane problem.

"We have" she agreed.

"Maria, you're a lovely, mature woman who obviously knows how to handle people and influence them….."

"Merci, ma petite, you're so sweet" she interrupted.

"I mean it, and I know that I can rely completely on your advice."

"You can, I promise you" she smiled.

"Well, I have a complicated problem, and I'd like to tell you all about it….."

"Oh, please do" she interrupted with a sparkle in her eyes.

"Before I start, I'd just like to know how to handle a difficult woman."

"Michel, I'm not difficult, I'm dead easy" she replied in a concerned tone.

"Non, ma petite, I don't mean you" he laughed.

"Bon, it's your fiancé then?"

"Non, I'd better start from the beginning" he said as the waiter arrived with their onion soups.

"After we've finished this" she said as they began the meal.

Michel could not remember when he had enjoyed such a delicious soup before and he commented on it to Maria who just kept smiling at everything he said. The waiter poured the Burgundy for them and they soon settled into a mellow and enjoyable state of mind. Michel decided to leave the story of Sophia and the problems surrounding her until they returned to Maria's flat. They chatted aimlessly with Michel sharing little details of his life in Marseille whilst Maria touched on her past life and the pleasures to be enjoyed now. Michel realised that this comely French woman lived life to the full and would let nothing stand in the way of her pleasures. She only stopped talking to eat and stopped eating to talk and Michel found it so easy to relax and be entertained by her.

Maria told him all about her late husband, Marcel, tragically lost in the China Sea when he fell overboard from his cargo ship during a typhoon, leaving her a widow at thirty. She explained that luckily Marcel, being ten years her senior, had been able to educate her sexually in all the ways of a well experienced merchant seaman, for which she was incredibly grateful. She told Michel that she had never re-married as she preferred to experiment with men, which was now her only pleasure.

The main course arrived and the friends took their time over the meal with Michel having to order another bottle of Burgundy half way through. They sat for some while before ordering a dessert and when it arrived they lingered until much of the ice cream had softened over the chocolate coated pears. Coffee was eventually served and it was quite cool when Maria stopped talking long enough for them to drink it. It was almost three o'clock when they left the restaurant and returned to Maria's flat.

Michel sat on the settee as he watched Maria pour two large brandies into cut glass goblets and wondered when she would make the first move.

"There, ma chérie" she whispered as she handed him his glass and sat beside him.

"Merci, to us."

"Oui, to us."

"Lunch was perfect" he said between sips.

"Oui, and unhurried" she replied.

"So, what have you got planned for the rest of the afternoon?" he enquired.

"Absolutely nothing, ma petite" she lied.

"Bon, I need a rest."

"You can sleep on my bed for a while before you go home" she said.

"You're very kind."

"Oui, I am, and very gentle" she said and with that she kissed him gently on his lips.

"So you are" he whispered and then taking her in his arms he kissed her warm generous mouth with passion forcing his tongue into her.

"That's better, ma petite" she whispered as they broke for air. He kissed her again and held her compliant body close for some time before releasing her, breathless and flushed.

"Ma petite, I'm ready for you now" she said quietly.

"Bon."

"My bed is very warm and comfortable" she whispered as she stood.

"It sounds very restful" he replied and followed her into her bedroom where the covers were already pulled back revealing the apricot coloured sheets. Michel sat on the bed and looked at Maria and said "let me watch you undress."

"Anything you wish, ma petite" she whispered and began by pulling her red jumper off over her head, revealing her white lace brassiere that was struggling to retain her impressive breasts.

Next she unzipped her skirt and allowed it to drop to the floor before stepping out of it. She wore matching white lace panties and garters holding up her stockings. Michel was now very aroused by her plump, statuesque body and he watched in delight as she undid the clip on her brassiere and slipped it off allowing her breasts to sway in the most alluring way. She then pulled down her panties to reveal a mound of thick, black pubic hair and after stepping out of them walked over to Michel.

"There, what do you think?" she smiled.

"Absolutely beautiful" he replied and putting his hands on her hips he kissed her soft stomach before transferring his mouth to her protruding nipples in turn. He heard her gasp as he sucked and gently nibbled at each one and then sliding one hand between her legs felt the moistness of her body.

"Oh, Michel, don't torment me, I'm ready now" she whispered as he carried on sucking, nibbling and touching.

"I can't stop" he replied before returning to her nipples now becoming more prominent by the moment.

"You'll drive me mad" she whispered as she attempted to unzip his trousers. At that point Michel relented and whilst she kicked off her shoes and slipped onto the bed, he undressed and once naked, made a show of his rigid penis.

"Mon Dieu, that looks good" she said as he climbed on top of her and then with consummate ease slid into her soft body.

"Do it slowly, ma petite" she whispered before kissing him so passionately that he had difficulty in controlling himself.

"You're so soft, ma petite" he said.

"I am for you, Michel."

"I think I'm going to have you several times this afternoon" he said.

"I look forward to it" she replied before kissing him passionately once again. Michel then began to push slowly into her and took pleasure at hearing the little gasp she made each time he reached as far as he could into her. It was only a matter of time before the wonderful sensations that heralded the beginning of his climax started and he had no control as he was forced to increase the speed of his thrust to which Maria gasped louder at every stroke until she cried out "Mon Dieu! Mon Dieu! Mon Dieu!" at which, Michel released his passion into her moist body. They lay, sweating and gasping for some while before their heartbeats subsided and Michel was able to slide out and roll off Maria's delicious body.

"That was so good" she whispered as she cuddled him.

"Oui, it was, you're very lovely and I enjoyed that so much" replied Michel with feeling.

"Rest now, ma petite, before we do it again" she said.

"I will." Whether it was the excellent meal, the brandy or the release of the tension of the day, Michel never knew, but he fell into a deep sleep and did not wake up until nearly five o'clock. He was conscious of being kissed and opened his eyes to see Maria's face close to his smiling down at him.

"There ma petite, are you ready for some more loving?" she asked gently.

"What time is it?" he asked.

"That's not very romantic" she replied.

"I'm sorry, ma petite, but I've a meeting with Henri at six" he lied.

"He'll have to wait a little for you" she said as she took his penis in her soft hand and started to excite him. It did not take long and he thought 'Maria's right, everybody will have to wait' and he kissed her passionately as she rolled on top and guided him into her body. She took him deep and moved up and down with ease, gasping at every penetration with her huge breasts swaying gently at every change of direction.

"This is so good" he said.

"It is" she gasped.

"I think we should do this at least once a week" he gasped.

"That arrangement would fit very nicely into my routine" she replied.

"Bon."

"It would help relieve the stress that builds up these days" she said, her words punctuated by gasps as she sank down hard on him.

"We obviously understand one another."

"We do, we do, and oh, Mon Dieu! I'm coming!" she screamed and with that she thumped her plump body down harder and harder on him. Michel pushed up and climaxed as he felt her tighten on him and then they reached a point of mutual ecstasy. When they had stopped moving and their passion had subsided once again she said "Michel, what ever happens, you've just got to see to me once a week."

"OK."

"Promise me, Michel."

"I promise" he replied and his heart sank once again as he realised that he had just committed himself to yet another tricky relationship. He seemed unable to resist the women who came into his life.

"Bon, now can you come over for dinner the day after tomorrow?" Maria enquired with a hopeful smile.

"Er, oui, I think so" replied Michel, slightly unsure.

"Bon, because I want you to meet a friend of mine."

"Oh, oui" replied Michel with a smile as his mind raced at the thought of a threesome with a similar, attractive middle aged lady.

"I know you'll get on so well together and Louis needs a man's reassurance."

"Louis?" queried Michel.

"Oui, he's an old friend and I'd like you to meet him" she smiled.

"OK, but won't that stop us from……"

"Non, he'll only stay for dinner then he'll go and we'll be alone" she interrupted.

"Oh, bon, I look forward to meeting Louis."

"That's wonderful, ma petite, so if you can be here at about seven, I'll get something delicious for dinner and you bring a couple of bottles of good wine" she smiled.

"It's a date" he replied and kissed both her nipples before gently smacking her soft, round bottom. She smiled at him all the time he was getting dressed and then after more kisses and many 'au revoir's' interspersed with confirmations that he would definitely be there for dinner at seven as arranged, Michel left the flat and drove to Henri's salon.

Although it was almost six thirty when he arrived, the salon was still quite busy with elegant women, mostly dressed in furs, trying on examples of the new Milan collection. Elaine and several of the assistants nodded in recognition as he climbed the stairs to Henri's office.

"How's your office coming on?" asked Henri as Michel sat opposite his cousin.

"Er, OK, I need to make a few alterations and Pascal is checking the wiring" replied Michel.

"I wouldn't let him do that" said Henri in a concerned tone.

"He's only checking it."

"I know Pascal, he'll start making 'adjustments' and the whole place will be in total darkness before you know it" said Henri grimly.

"He can't be that bad, I mean he's done pretty well with the painting" replied Michel and at that moment Elaine knocked on the half open door.

"Monsieur Henri, I'm sorry to disturb you, but Madame Christiane is downstairs and wishes to talk to Monsieur Michel privately" she said, her face clouded by concern.

"Oh, Mon Dieu" said Henri under his breath as he glanced at Michel's pale complexion "tell her Monsieur Michel will be down in a minute."

"Oui, Monsieur Henri" replied Elaine.

"Now what?" wondered Michel.

"I don't know, but you'd better see her."

"OK."

"And if it looks like she's going to make a scene bring her up here or take her outside into the car park" said Henri firmly.

"Alright, but please save me if she turns nasty" replied Michel.

"I will."

Michel left the office and walked purposefully down the stairs to meet a smiling Sophia.

"Michel, ma petite."

"Madame Christiane" he replied.

"Why so formal?" she asked.

"Because we are in the salon, Madame" replied Michel in a half whisper.

"Let's go somewhere more private then."

"Oui, in my car outside" suggested Michel.

"Non, mine, it'll be warmer than yours" she smiled and Michel was concerned because she appeared to be so pleasant. After they sat in her Mercedes, Michel waited for her to begin.

"Now, chérie, tell me first of all why did you not come to the casino last night?"

"I'm sorry, ma petite, but it was so late by the time our business meeting had finished ......"

"Michel, you let me down" she interrupted.

"I know, but….."

"I lost a lot of money at the tables."

"You can't blame me for……"

"Oh, oui, I can, without you, I have no luck."

"That's very touching and it's is nice to be your lucky mascot, but sometimes business comes first" he said gently, hoping that she would remain calm.

"Money is also business, ma chérie, and heavy losses can not be tolerated by anyone, me included" she snapped.

"What can I say?"

"My husband will have a fit when he finds out what I've lost."

"Don't tell him then."

"I couldn't deceive Charles like that!" she exclaimed.

"Deceive Charles! What about your affairs?" demanded Michel, shocked at her double standards.

"That's just fun and sex, absolutely nothing compared to money!"

"Really?"

"Oui, you don't take money seriously enough, that's why you haven't got any" she blazed.

"You don't know that" retorted Michel.

"Oh, I do, my chérie, just look at the way you dress for a start!"

"Mon Dieu!"

"And you drive around in an old Marseille taxi, I mean, what sort of impression does that give?"

"You're unbelievable, d'you know that?"

"Oui, all my friends tell me so" she smiled.

"Well what now?"

"I've given you a little tongue lashing for standing me up, don't ever do it again, so now it's time to make up after our first row, chérie" she smiled.

"You must be joking!"

"I'm not, so just kiss me, and make it good!"

Michel could not resist and thought if it kept her happy, so be it. He took her in his arms and kissed her passionately just as Henri tapped on the side window. The lovers jumped apart at the sudden interruption and when Sophia had gathered her composure she wound down her window with a touch of a button and said "oh Henri, do fuck off!"

"Madame!" he exclaimed.

"Oui, it's a shock I know, but please do as I ask."

"Madame….."

"Henri, I am the customer" she interrupted.

"You are indeed, Madame Christiane, but that does not excuse your behaviour!"

"You sound more like a school teacher than a salon owner" she retorted.

"Madame….."

"Michel, tell your cousin to piss off!"

"Ma petite……" began a horrified Michel.

"You call this bitch 'ma petite'?" demanded Henri angrily, throwing caution to the wind.

"He does, all the time" she retorted sharply.

"Mon Dieu!" exclaimed Henri.

"You'd better go back inside" said Michel fearing that the situation could easily get out of hand.

"I came to tell you, Michel, that Monsieur Gerrard, you remember him I'm sure, has just called and he wants you to 'phone him back right away" said a distressed Henri.

"Mon Dieu! That's all I need" replied Michel.

"So, bonsoir, Madame Christiane" said Henri in a sarcastic tone.

"Bonsoir, Henri, and Henri…."

"Oui, Madame?"

"Phone me when you've got the new Paris collection in, won't you?"

"Of course, Madame" he replied.

"Wouldn't want to miss any of that" she said. Henri returned to the salon and leaving Michel shocked and totally confused by the workings of Sophia's mind. She then looked at her lover and said "you can never have too many shoes, you know."

"Never."

"Now, what are we going to do tonight?" she said.

"I'm afraid that……"

"I think if you come about eight, we'll eat in, I'll tell Evette to rustle up something quick and easy, then we can have a chat about the business before we go for a romantic drive along the coast to a little bar I know."

"Ma petite….." protested Michel.

“About eight then, and don’t be late” she interrupted.

“Look, I can’t……”

“You’d better go in and ‘phone your friend Gerrard, it sounded terribly important to me” she said with a smile. Michel was totally overcome by this woman and mumbled “about eight” as he opened the door of the Mercedes and climbed out.

“Au revoir” she called brightly.

“Au revoir” he replied and slammed the door shut. He did not look at her again as she drove out of the private parking area but he felt as if he just wanted to cry.

Henri sat behind his desk with a glum expression and briefly looked up when Michel entered.

“Now what?” asked Henri.

“I suppose I’d better ‘phone Gerrard” replied Michel as he sat down.

“He sounded irate” said Henri.

“Oh, good, another one that’s going to cause me problems” replied Michel as he picked up the telephone and started dialling the Gendarme’s number.

“Bonsoir, Monsieur Gerrard” said Michel when he heard the Gendarmes voice.

“Ah, Monsieur Ronay, thank you for calling back.”

“My pleasure.”

“Just a quick word……”

“Oui.”

“When are you coming back to Marseille?” enquired Gerrard forcefully.

“I’m uncertain at the moment” replied Michel.

“Well you’d better firm up and give me a date, otherwise I’ll have you picked up and brought back in custody.”

“Merci, you’re too kind” replied Michel sarcastically.

“I mean it, Ronay.”

“Look, just give me a day or two will you?”

“Ronay, don’t stall me, I’m not in the mood.”

“I’ve got some problems to sort out and then I’ll ‘phone you the day after tomorrow, promise.”

“OK, I’ll write that in my diary now and if I haven’t heard from you, expect a knock at the door in the middle of the night” said Gerrard firmly.

"Merci, I look forward to it, au revoir" replied Michel before replacing the receiver.

"Mon Dieu, you must be in so much trouble" said Henri.

"I am" Michel agreed.

When he returned home Michel found Josette in the lounge sitting with a glass of brandy in her hand and an unhappy expression on her face.

"What's the matter, chérie?"

"Pascal has done something to the wiring and we've no lights in the kitchen" she replied.

"Mon Dieu!"

"Exactly, lucky the cooker is gas" she replied.

"Oui."

"He says he can fix it tomorrow, but I think we should get a proper electrician to look at it" she said.

"Oui, ma petite."

"So, I'm going to cook dinner by candle light" she smiled.

"How romantic" replied Michel.

"Oui, but don't get excited, it's just soup and scampi Provençale tonight."

"Bon, now can we eat soon as I've got a business meeting at eight" said Michel.

"Oh, chérie, not another meeting."

"I'm sorry, ma petite, but if you're going to marry a successful business man, then you just have to put up with these things" he smiled and poured a brandy for himself.

"OK, as long as you're not seeing that Christiane woman" she said at which Michel shook a little as he raised his glass to his fiancé.

"To us, ma petite" he said.

Josette prepared the food in record time and they enjoyed the candle lit meal at the kitchen table. Michel knew he would have to eat again at Sophia's, two dinners in one evening, which he fully recognised as the plight of a man with a fiancé and mistress. He also knew from past experience that over eating and then the worry of his situation would balance out his calories and help keep his weight down. After kissing his fiancé gently and promising he would not be late, he left the house and drove to Sophia's villa.

Evette opened the door and greeted him like a close friend and ushered him into the lounge.

"Madame will be with you soon" she said.

"Merci, Evette."

"May I get you a drink whilst you're waiting, Monsieur?"

"Merci, a brandy, s'il vous plait." Evette obliged with a smile and Michel slumped down onto the settee and waited for his drink.

"Dinner will be ready soon, Monsieur" said Evette as she handed him a cut glass goblet nearly quarter full of the golden liquid.

"Merci, Evette." Left alone, he sipped the brandy and surveyed his surroundings. The opulence of the room was very impressive and the high quality of the furniture was simply a reflection of the wealth of Monsieur Christiane and his wife. The oil paintings of the Normandy countryside together with magnificent sea-scapes that graced the walls were all originals and gave an elegance to an already spectacular room. Michel was deep in thought when Sophia came in to greet him.

"Ma chérie" she smiled and held out her arms to embrace him.

"Chérie, you look wonderful" he whispered as he stood and kissed her. Her low cut, black satin dress was figure hugging and short. Her blonde hair was loose and curled under at her shoulder and her makeup was perfect as usual. Diamond pendant earrings and a diamond studded black satin choker completed the ensemble with Chanel perfume exuding from her soft, desirable body. Michel was truly intoxicated by Sophia and he felt as if he would never escape from her influence. One moment he loved her and the next he hated her, he did not know what to do about the situation, and he thought that perhaps running away might be the only answer.

"Pour me a brandy, chérie" said Sophia as she lowered her elegant body onto the settee "and come and sit with me."

"Oui, chérie."

"I've had a very difficult day and the row with Henri has upset me" she said in a plaintive tone.

"Don't worry about Henri, chérie" replied Michel as he poured her brandy.

"Non, if you say so but I do need comforting" she said.

"I'll comfort you" he replied as he handed her a large brandy.

"Bon, here's to us" she said and they touched glasses.
"Now tell me, where are we going after dinner?" he asked.
"Ah, a petite secret" she smiled.
"Somewhere secret, I like the sound of that" he said.
"Oui, I know you'll love it."
"Mustn't be too late back, I've a busy day with Henri tomorrow" said Michel.
"I understand, chérie, I don't want to be late especially after last night" she replied.
"Stayed late at the casino then?"
"Oui, losing money whilst waiting for my good lucky mascot to arrive and save me."
"I'm sorry."
"Oh, forget it, chérie, I'm sure you'll never do it again." At that moment the door opened and Evette announced that dinner was served. Michel followed Sophia into the dining room that was situated across the hallway. The silverware on the highly polished oval table, set for two, glinted in the candlelight and Michel sat opposite his lover as Evette served Sophia with crevettes in a salad before placing a similar hors d'oeuvres before him.
"Bon appetite, chérie" said Sophia as they commenced their meal. Evette then produced a bottle of light, dry white wine that complemented the crevettes with its superb quality and bouquet. The lovers hardly spoke until they had finished the course and drunk more than half the bottle of wine. Sophia kept glancing at Michel and smiling, which un-nerved him a little as he wondered what this attractive and dangerous woman was up to.
"You look apprehensive, ma chérie" said Sophia as Evette cleared the table.
"I've got a lot on my mind" Michel replied.
"Monsieur Gerrard, for instance?"
"He's one of many problems."
"Who is he then?" she asked in a curious tone.
"Someone I know from Marseille."
"Is he a close friend?"
"Not really, he's a Gendarme" Michel replied and Sophia was a little startled at that.
"Mon Dieu! Are you involved with the police?" she asked and then Michel, seizing the opportunity to impress, paused for effect

and gazed into her blue eyes.

"Oui, I've been an undercover agent for some while now" he replied watching the expression on her face change to open mouthed incredulity.

"Oh, Michel, my brave, wonderful........."

"It's nothing really, I promise you" he interrupted.

"Chérie......"

"I can't tell you much, but I head up the undercover infiltration of organised crime syndicates" he said with pride.

"Mon Dieu! You're a national hero" she half whispered.

"So I'm told."

"Are you on a mission in Le Touquet?"

"I can neither confirm or deny that" he replied with a detached air of mystery.

"Oh, Michel, now I understand everything" she whispered.

"Do you?"

"Oui, the shabby clothes, the old Marseille taxi and you don't want me in the business because you want to protect me" she said with eyes wide open.

"As well as being beautiful, you're also a very clever woman" he replied gently whilst thanking Gerrard for his timely call. It was a gift and it seemed that with one bound he was free from her and a great weight lifted from his shoulders.

They looked at each other in stunned silence for a few moments before Evette arrived with the main course of Chateaubriand. She then poured a rich Burgundy into their glasses whilst wishing them 'bon appetite'. When she had left the lovers, Sophia said "I don't know if I can eat anything after what you've just told me."

"You must, chérie, the steak looks delicious" he replied.

"Michel, I think I'm in love with you."

"Sophia, that's so wonderful to hear, but I think you might be a little overcome by my revelation, which you must keep secret, for your own safety" he smiled.

"Ma chérie, you're wonderful" she whispered.

"I'm not a real hero.........."

"But you are" she interrupted.

"Enjoy the meal, Sophia, we can talk later when we're out."

They hardly spoke until they had finished their dinner, with Michel struggling with a very full stomach, he only just managed to drink a little coffee after cheese and biscuits.

Leaving the villa they drove off down the Avenue du General de Gaulle in Michel's car as Sophia had decided that she could not possibly drive tonight. He swung the car out onto the coast road and headed, at her direction, south towards Abbeville.

"You'll love this little bar" she said.

"I'm sure I will."

"I found it by accident, last summer."

"It has happy memories for you then?"

"Oui" she replied and remained silent and Michel guessed that it would have been a place that she had taken a lover to after an afternoon on the beach.

"Michel, what's going to happen to us?"

"Whatever we want to happen, ma chérie."

"You have a fiancé and a wife."

"True."

"And I have a husband."

"Oui."

"But I don't want him, Michel, I want you" and at that his blood froze.

"Chérie" he began.

"We've got to be together……"

"Chérie" he interrupted.

"I mean it, we'll both have to get a divorce."

"Let's leave this discussion for another time" he said gently.

"You won't leave me, will you?" she asked.

"Non, of course not" he replied.

"Bon." They drove on in silence and Michel was beginning to feel a little sorry for this lonely woman who appeared to have everything except someone who really loved her.

They drove on until they came to a junction where Sophia directed him to turn right to Berck-Plage. Soon they had reached the village and stopped outside a little bar that was lit up with coloured lights captured in fishermen's nets which were draped across the front of the building. Michel followed her into the smoky, noisy bar which was busy with the locals enjoying their evening. He bought red wine for her and a brandy for himself before they sat at a small table near the open fire, crackling with the noise of wood logs burning brightly.

"This is cosy" he said.

"A petite jewel" she smiled. They sat in silence for a while, soaking up the atmosphere of the bar both pleased to be in each other's company. Michel bought another round of drinks and was relaxing all the while, now that the revelation of his undercover mission had released him from Sophia's demands.

"You know, chérie, I think we both need a holiday together" she said with a smile.

"Well, at the moment I'm........."

"I usually go to Chamonix to ski in January" she interrupted.

"Very nice......."

"If we just have a week together, that'll be long enough to set us up for the spring" she said.

"What about your husband?" asked Michel.

"He doesn't ski."

"Possibly not, but won't he wonder where you are?"

"I'll tell him that I'm going to Chamonix as usual, he won't care."

"Mon Dieu" whispered Michel under his breath and wondered if there was any escape, however, he decided to play along.

"So when would you like to go?" he asked.

"In a couple of weeks time" she replied.

"OK."

"Oh, chérie, that's wonderful, I'll 'phone and book the hotel tomorrow!" she exclaimed.

"Bon" replied Michel with a heavy heart.

"Now take me home and make a fuss of me" she whispered.

As they drove back to Le Touquet, Sophia told him all about the attractions of Chamonix and went into the smallest detail to ensure that he would be able to relax and enjoy the holiday. He did not have the heart to tell her that, like her husband, he could not ski either. They arrived back at the villa and were soon inside cuddled up on the settee enjoying brandy whilst planning their holiday when suddenly Evette rushed in and said "Madame, Monsieur Charles has just arrived!"

"Mon Dieu!" exclaimed Sophia as she jumped up from the settee before her husband strode into the lounge.

"Ma petite, I didn't expect you back from Paris until tomorrow" she said.

"A meeting was cancelled" he replied as he looked hard at Michel and then asked "who's this?"

"Michel Ronay, a business partner of Henri………"

"What's he doing here at this time of night?" demanded Charles.

"I've been discussing a business investment with your wife, Monsieur" replied Michel as he got shakily to his feet.

"I take care of all the financial investments in this house, Monsieur" replied Charles.

"Indeed, Monsieur, well, I think I'd better be going" said Michel.

"Oui, Monsieur" replied Charles as he fixed Michel with a steady and hostile gaze.

"Thank you for an interesting discussion, Madame Christiane, I hope to see you in the salon when our Paris spring collection arrives" said Michel diplomatically.

"Thank you, Monsieur Ronay, Evette, please show Monsieur out."

"Oui, Madame."

Michel drove home sweating slightly and was glad when he closed the door of number 19 and went upstairs to his cream bedroom and his lovely fiancé who was sitting up in bed reading.

"Meeting go alright?" she asked brightly with a smile.

"Oui, better than I hoped."

"Bon, now come to bed and cuddle me."

"Oui, I need a cuddle to" he replied as he started to undress wearily.

They made love gently and slowly for some time before he relaxed gently into her as she kissed him passionately. He thought what a fool he was to be ensnared by other women when he had the woman he loved most of all with him.

CHAPTER 9

In the morning Pascal arrived at Michele's house just as a van, with two men inside, pulled up.

"Bonjour, Michel" beamed the old man.

"Bonjour, Pascal" replied Michel.

"Looks like you've got a delivery" said Pascal nodding in the direction of the van.

"They wouldn't happen to be electricians by any chance?" enquired Michel.

"Non" he replied and blushed a little.

"Pity, that means that you've got to try and fix the wiring in the kitchen on your own."

"Oui, I've brought all my tools and I'll have it done in a moment."

"Bon, I look forward to that moment" replied Michel.

"I'm sorry about last night……" began Pascal but he was interrupted by one of the men.

"Monsieur Ronay?" he called.

"Oui."

"I've got a desk for you" he said as his companion opened the back doors of the white van.

"Bon" said Michel. The man nodded and went to assist his colleague as Pascal stepped into the house and made his way to the kitchen. Michel went out to the front gate as the men struggled with a large, old fashioned, dark brown desk, which they dropped to the ground rather heavily before taking a rest. They looked at Michel and the older man who had first spoken to him, said "I hope this is going downstairs, Monsieur."

"Oui, it is."

"Bon, it's too heavy for us to move anywhere else" he said between gasps.

"I can imagine."

"This old stuff is OK if you like it."

"Oui."

"They don't make them like this anymore, thank God" said the man.

"Oui" replied Michel as he examined the desk. It looked in good condition and he guessed that Henri had paid a reasonable amount of money for it.

"Better show me where you want it, Monsieur" said the man.

"Oui" and Michel led the way into the house and pointed to the dining room.

"We can manage that, Monsieur, but you'd better tell us where you want it in there because you'll never move it on your own."

"Oui" replied Michel.

The men disappeared out the front door as Josette arrived from the kitchen. She waited and then watched the men struggling up the garden path before asking "where's that going, ma petite?"

"In there" replied Michel nodding towards the dining room.

"Oh, non, it's got to go upstairs into the small bedroom" she announced.

"Ma petite, I can't possibly have an office upstairs" he replied.

"Why not? Henri does."

"He's in a different business, and I've got to be seen by our clients, besides, it's so heavy they would never get it up the stairs."

"There's you and Pascal here to help them."

"Non, ma petite" replied Michel firmly.

"I don't want it in there, that's our dining room" she said placing her hands on her hips.

"Josette, please don't cause me any problems at the moment" pleaded Michel.

"Fine" she said and flounced off back to the kitchen and Michel knew he had not heard the last of it. The men struggled through the doorway, twisting the desk one way and then the other as they attempted to get it into the hallway before turning left into the dining room. The turn was too abrupt and after much discussion and some argument they advanced further down the hall towards the kitchen. At that moment Pascal left his coffee and came to assist, resting one hand on the edge of the desk as a display of help before giving advice to the two sweating delivery men.

"Messieurs, come towards me a little more and then tip it up on one end, then we can go backwards into the dining room" he suggested whilst moving his hand further along the edge.

"Non, it won't go that way, it'll be too high to go through the doorway" replied the older man.

“Non, once you get it closer to the door, you can lower one end” replied Pascal helpfully.

“Non, if we do that we won’t be able to turn it” said the other man.

“Why don’t you take it upstairs?” asked Josette from the kitchen. At that there was a stunned silence before Michel said “I have to go to a meeting now and I’ll have to leave you I’m afraid, so just do your best.”

“If we get it into the room, where do you want it, Monsieur?”

“In the middle, I think” replied Michel.

“Bon” said the weary delivery man. Michel then kissed Josette goodbye and promised he would not be late home. As he left them to the tricky manoeuvres with the old desk he heard Pascal warning them about the fresh paint on the walls followed by slightly raised voices from the men.

The salon was busy and Michel smiled at Elaine behind her counter before making his way up to Henri’s office that was the signal for her to follow on with two coffees.

“Remember we’re seeing Charles at midday to sign the contract” said Henri with a smile after they had finished their drink and relaxed.

“Oui, and I’m sure we’ll have no more problems with Madame Christiane from now on” replied Michel.

“Why are you so confident all of a sudden?” enquired Henri.

“Because I saw her last night and she has dropped the idea completely” replied Michel.

“You mean to tell me that we’ve run up a hefty bill with Charles for no good reason?” asked Henri in an angry tone.

“Just a minute, Henri, I didn’t know she was backing off until I spoke to her.”

“Bugger me, Michel, I really worry about you” said Henri.

“Well don’t” he replied as the telephone rang and Henri answered it.

“Hello, Monsieur Henri it’s Maurice here.”

“Bonjour, Monsieur Maurice, bonjour” replied Henri.

“Bonjour, Henri.”

“How’s the ‘Sea Goddess’ looking today?” enquired Henri.

“She’s looking good and you can tell Michel that I’ve bought a new ladder for her" replied DeVere.

"Bon, he'll be pleased to hear it, now, what can I do for you?"

"Well, by chance, a very good friend of mine has an almost identical boat to the 'Sea Goddess', and I've been telling him all about your exciting new business……"

"Oh, oui" interrupted Henri as he began to fear what was coming next.

"And my friend, Raymond, would like to offer his services to you as well."

"I see" mused Henri.

"At the moment, his boat, the 'Boulogne Princess', has had her winter overhaul and is ready to go to sea now."

"Bon."

"So Raymond suggested that you and Michel might like to have a look at her and go for a little trip with us tomorrow to see if she's suitable for your tourists."

"That's very considerate of you, I won't be able to come unfortunately as I have a new collection arriving from Paris, but I'm sure Michel would be delighted to meet Raymond and go for a short voyage."

"Bon, that would be good, tell him to come to my office about ten in the morning."

"Oui, ten o'clock at your office, au revoir, Maurice."

Michel looked at Henri and waited.

"Maurice has invited you to go on a short voyage with him and his friend Raymond on the 'Boulogne Princess' tomorrow."

"That's nice."

"I can't go because, as you heard, I'm expecting the new shoes from Paris, why don't you take Josette?"

"Good idea, I'm sure she could do with a bit of a break."

"Couldn't we all" murmured Henri. Michel felt quite excited by the idea of a short sea trip and he hoped that a morning out in the fresh air would improve his relationship with Josette.

Just before midday the cousins appeared in the reception of Monsieur Robardes office and were then shown into the presence of the sombre notaire who waved them to sit.

"Messieurs, I am certain you will be delighted with this contract as I am sure, that, legally speaking, it is absolutely water tight and you may now sleep soundly in the knowledge that the only harm that Madame Christiane can possibly do now is to Monsieur Ronay" he beamed.

"Bon, Charles, we can never thank you enough" said Henri

"Oui, thank you" murmured Michel uncertain of his position.

"Now, if you would both be good enough to sign here" he tapped at the document before him on his untidy desk "I'll get my secretary to witness your signatures and then we're all finished." He rang for the young woman who appeared as Michel signed his name under Henri's. After three copies of the contract had been signed and witnessed, Monsieur Robardes smiled and said "one each for you to read at your leisure, Messieurs, whilst I retain a copy here for safe keeping."

"Bon" said Henri.

"Now Monsieur Ronay, do you wish to make an appointment to discuss your divorce?"

"Oui, Monsieur."

"Then my secretary will arrange a mutually suitable time" smiled the notaire as he fixed his steely gaze at Michel over his glasses. The appointment was made for ten thirty in three days time to discuss the pending divorce and after leaving the office, Michel insisted that he needed a drink. Henri agreed and they made their way to the Bar Americaine clutching their copies of the contract. Seated in the corner by the window the cousins toasted their escape from Sophia's threatened litigation with a large brandy each.

"Thank heavens we had Charles to help us out of that mess" said Henri.

"Oui, I'm grateful" replied Michel.

"And Michel, I hope you won't mind me saying this, but please try and stay away from women until you've sorted out your divorce and we've got the business going" pleaded Henri.

"OK, I'll try" replied Michel in a resigned tone. Henri seemed satisfied at that and then suggested they should have a light lunch in the bar before returning to the salon. Half way through mixed cheese baguettes, Henri decided that as he would be very involved with customers after the Paris collection samples arrived, he should take a break from the salon this afternoon and suggested that they take a leisurely ride out into the countryside.

"What for?" asked Michel with a mouthful of baguette.

"After my meeting with Monsieur Ricard the other day I started thinking that for a few very select customers who didn't want to go on a coach trip......."

"Those with plenty of money you mean" interrupted Michel.

"Precisely."

"We'd arrange something special" said Michel.

"Oui."

"What for instance?"

"For an appropriate fee, we could drive them around to places of local interest in your taxi."

"We?"

"I mean you, Michel."

"I'm not sure about that" replied Michel.

"Think of the money we'd make" smiled Henri.

"Tourists are not going to pay too much for a trip out in a taxi" replied Michel.

"Not a taxi ride, Michel, but a guided tour with a running commentary" smiled Henri.

"And who's going to give that?"

"You, Michel."

"I can't do that."

"Of course you can, it's easy and you've got the gift of the gab."

"Non."

"Michel, you can charm the birds out of the trees, you'll be a great success."

"I can only speak French" said Michel, certain that that revelation would stop Henri's proposal dead in its tracks.

"No problem at all, we'll just get Naomi to act as interpreter."

"Naomi?"

"Oui, she's Roger's daughter, she speaks English and German perfectly and a little Italian too" he said with pride.

"Your cousin, Roger?"

"Oui."

"Bon."

"And she's a very pretty young woman, so keep your mind on the driving" said Henri.

"So she's Maria's grand daughter then?" queried Michel.

"Oui" replied Henri.

"How nice, keeping it all in the family" said Michel with a smile.

"It's a good idea, Michel."

"I'm all for good ideas, so let's do it." They ordered more brandy and discussed some finer details of the planned 'executive service' before returning to the salon to inform Elaine that they would be away on business for the rest of the afternoon. She followed them upstairs to the office before announcing that Madame Christiane had telephoned and wanted to speak to Michel privately. Henri raised his eyes to heaven and sighed whilst Michel dialled Sophia's number.

"Ma chérie, thank you for calling me back" she said.

"That's OK" he replied.

"I know I've been difficult over the business and things and I am really sorry……"

"Don't worry about it" interrupted Michel.

"Well I do worry and I don't want anything to come between us."

"Nothing will, I promise you" he replied gently.

"Charles has left for a meeting in London, so please come and see me tonight."

"I can't………"

"Oh, chérie, don't say 'no', I need to see you, even just for a short while" she pleaded.

"A short while only" Michel insisted.

"OK" she whispered.

"Well, alright then."

"Come about eight as usual, chérie and I'll have a brandy ready for you" she said brightly.

"I can't stay long."

"I understand, chérie."

"I'll see you later then, au revoir." As he replaced the receiver Henri said "Michel, you're a fool if you have anything more to do with that woman."

"Henri, please leave her to me will you?"

"With pleasure!"

It was mid afternoon when the cousins set off in Henri's car to tour the local area. Michel had a pen and pad to make notes on the route and places of interest. The sun was still shining and there were very few clouds in the sky that were likely to spoil the brightness of the winter day. Both men felt comfortable and relaxed as Henri drove down the Avenue du General de Gaulle, passed Sophia's villa, and out towards the airport. He then swung onto the N39 towards Montreuil Sur Mer, the picturesque medieval town overlooking the Canche Valley.

"We'll start at Montreuil, it's a quaint old place and the tourists will just love it" said Henri as they headed inland.

"Bon" replied Michel as he made a note on his pad.

"After we've had a look around the town, we'll head south to Abbeville" said Henri.

They soon arrived at Montreuil and Henri drove into the centre ville with its narrow cobbled streets whilst giving Michel a vague outline of the town's history.

"Of course we'll have to get a lot more information from the tourist office for our commentary" said Henri.

"Oui" replied Michel slightly overcome by all the facts as he tried to make notes as the car rattled over the cobbles.

"I think it would be a good idea for our executive clients to have an hour or so here, to give them a chance to explore" said Henri.

"Oui, just park up and let them wander around" replied Michel.

"Absolutely."

"It certainly is the place for tourists" said Michel suitably impressed by the narrow cobbled streets and medieval buildings. After several circuits of the ancient town the cousins headed south to Abbeville and as they reached the outskirts, Michel suggested that they stop for a coffee as he was feeling a touch sleepy after the brandy lunch.

"Good idea, I must admit I could do with one as well" replied Henri.

They stopped outside a small bar called 'Bonne Chance' decided that it looked reasonable and were able to park in an empty bay a few metres along. It was warm and cosy inside the bar and although quite busy they found a small table by the window. Black coffee was ordered and the cousins settled back to relax.

"I'm glad I've taken the afternoon off" said Henri.

"I'm sure."

"It'll be a madhouse there tomorrow when the Paris collection arrives" said Henri.

"I'll bet."

"Once one of my customers gets wind of a new selection the word goes round faster than a rifle bullet" said Henri and Michel laughed.

"Women and shoes" he said.

"Oui, they can never have too many" said Henri.

"It's good business, Henri."

"I know, but I'm tired of it and I need a change" he replied.

"Well our business will give you the new life that you want" said Michel as the coffee's arrived.

"And how I'm looking forward to it" replied Henri with glee.

"Bon." They remained silent as they sipped their coffee and relaxed.

"You know, Michel, there's a lot I haven't told you."

"Really?"

"Oui, and I think I ought to let you in on some of my plans for the future."

"As you wish."

"Well I don't want any of it to be too much of a shock and if you already know what I have planned, it shouldn't upset the smooth running of the business."

"Right" said Michel now quite intrigued by Henri's secrets.

"Now promise me that you'll keep everything I'm going to tell you to yourself."

"I promise" replied Michel solemnly.

"First of all, I'm going to give Elaine a good raise and a small share in the profits."

"She deserves it" nodded Michel.

"And I'm going to let her run the salon and I'll only go in one day a week to check that everything is alright."

"Makes sense" agreed Michel.

"Now, I've rented an apartment on the Boulevard de la Canche, overlooking the sea" said Henri with a smile and Michel guessed what was coming next.

"Go on."

"And that's where I'm going to live when I leave Jackie."

"Your absolutely sure about that?" queried Michel.

"Oh, oui, I've had enough of her, her mother, her stupid

relations, all of them and I'm getting out!" exclaimed Henri before he took a sip of coffee whilst watching Michel's expression.

"If that's what you want."

"It is, Michel, it is and when I'm settled into my flat I'm going to have Elaine as my mistress."

"I'm not surprised, she's a very attractive lady" replied Michel.

"Oui, she's divorced and lives alone" said Henri with a smile.

"Good luck to you then" said Michel.

"Oui and that's not all."

"There's more?"

"Oui, you may have noticed one of my young assistants, Theresa, very pretty, black hair and blue eyes."

"I know her."

"Well she has a very soft spot for me, so I'm going to have her as my second mistress."

"My word, you have been planning in depth" replied Michel.

"I have indeed" smiled Henri.

"What if Elaine finds out about Theresa?" enquired Michel.

"She won't, I've got it all sorted out" said Henri.

"Ah, at last I've met a man who can guess a woman's next move, how do you do it, Henri?"

"It's easy, I'll tell you later."

"I look forward to it" replied Michel as he took another sip of coffee.

"Now whilst I was in Boulogne the other day, after I had seen Monsieur Ricard, I popped into the Mercedes dealership and, guess what?"

"Stun me."

"I've ordered a new two seater SLR sports coupe."

"Mon Dieu!" exclaimed Michel, impressed by the size of Henri's apparent financial position.

"Oui, its got red metallic paint, cream leather upholstery and a black hood."

"Bon."

"So, what d'you think?"

"It sounds like you've got it all sewn up, Henri."

"Oui, I think so too."

"As long as Jackie, Elaine and Theresa don't catch you out, you've nothing to worry about" said Michel.

“Of course” smiled Henri.

“Let me warn you, I promise you that it is a dangerous game you play and I know from bitter experience, take Madame Christiane as an example.”

“Elaine and Theresa are not like that bitch” replied Henri.

“Well for your sake, I hope not, but believe me, women can turn pretty nasty if they think they’re being two timed by a man.”

“I can handle it.”

“Bon, shall we have another coffee?”

“Oui.” Michel signalled the bar man as Henri gazed out of the window at the passers by, feeling relieved that he had shared his future plans with his cousin.

“And I’m joining the casino club” said Henri when he had regained Michel’s full attention.

“You must be made of money” replied Michel.

“The salon has been very profitable and I’ve been saving for years for this moment” Henri smiled.

“All I can say is, good luck to you because I think you’ll need it.”

Henri laughed and replied “I now realise that life is for living.”

“I agree, but it’s sensible to take things slowly, especially when you’re in unfamiliar territory with no experience” said Michel as he was becoming concerned that Henri was running off the rails too quickly.

“Never mind that, tell me how you managed to get that woman of yours in Marseille to dress up before you had her.”

“Ah, oui, you mean Evette” replied Michel.

“Oui, that’s the one, she worked in a bank.”

“Oui, a lovely, sensual woman.”

“Tell me how you did it, Michel, because I think I might get Theresa to dress up for me if I handle her right.”

“I’m sure you will” smiled Michel.

“Well, what’s the secret?” demanded Henri.

“The secret is the woman” replied Michel.

“What d’you mean?”

“There’s no way of telling what a woman is thinking and they’re all different.”

“I realise that.”

“They have wild fantasies, just as we do.”

"Really?" asked a surprised Henri.

"Of course, they have imagination and they use it to enhance their sexual pleasure."

"I never guessed" replied Henri.

"Most men don't" said Michel.

"So, Evette used to dress up for her pleasure as much as yours?"

"Oui, she's a lovely exhibitionist and it turns her on knowing that dressing up turns me on."

"Wonderful" gasped Henri.

"Oui, during the day at work in the Bank I'm sure she's a quiet, un-provocative, professional woman who's getting randier by the minute as she mentally plans her outfit for my pleasure in the evening."

"Mon Dieu" said Henri as he sweated slightly at the thought of Evette becoming sexually hot at work and he wondered if Elaine or Theresa were doing the same at the salon.

"And if you want to encourage Theresa to dress up for you, then you have to gently unlock the door to her imagination by telling her how beautiful she is and telling her that she becomes a lovely woman of mystery if she is wearing an outfit that hides her charms from you" explained Michel.

"I can hardly wait" said Henri as he finished his coffee and waved to the bar man for two more.

"But, take my advice and don't rush it, some women need time to build their confidence in a lover, others are such exhibitionists that they can't wait and will do anything to turn a man on quickly so that they have complete control over him."

"Oh, oui" smiled Henri.

"Then, when they've got control, they take their pleasure."

"Mon Dieu."

"Take my friend, Sophia, the nude artist in Grambois" said Michel, now enjoying seeing Henri become ensnared in his own imagination of expected sexual pleasures.

"Oui."

"She's direct in every way."

"Really?"

"Oui, she's always naked except for a head band or a pair of shoes, and she demands sex immediately I arrive at her flat."

"Michel, you're so lucky."

"Although, I think Sophia is just plain desperate these days."
"Never mind, you're giving her satisfaction" said Henri.
"Oui, she's an artist and does have needs that must be met."
"Of course" replied Henri as two more coffee's arrived.
"But they're all different, take Eleanor, she owns the store in Grambois with her husband, Jean."
"Oui, I've seen her, she's quite a well built woman isn't she" commented Henri.
"Oui, now she likes it on the table in the store room."
"Go on" said Henri with eyes wide open in anticipation.
"And I know that she loves the danger of being caught."
"Who by?"
"Her husband."
"Mon Dieu!"
"She goes into ecstasy if she thinks we've only minutes to finish before he arrives back from the bar."
"I can't believe it" said Henri.
"It's true, and she gets so worked up if she sees me coming towards the shop if Jean is out and is expected back at any moment."
"How do you do it, Michel?"
"I can't resist her, she's so soft, wet and comfortable that I slide into her effortlessly" he replied and on hearing that, Henri's eyes crossed slightly.
"Go on" Henri whispered.
"Well, we've nearly been caught several times and I'm sure Jean suspects, but it just makes Eleanor all the more randy for the next time."
"What a life you lead" said Henri as he sipped his coffee to steady his nerves.
"Now I hope you understand how easy it is to get involved with a woman like Sophia Christiane" said Michel firmly.
"Well, oui, oui........"
"She's a superb exhibitionist with a body and panache to match, I promise you" interrupted Michel.
"I can imagine."
"A gentleman doesn't normally disclose such details, but I can tell you that when she took off her bra, her breasts didn't drop at all" whispered Michel.

"Mon Dieu."

"And I'm sure that no man on this earth could resist her if she's made up her mind to get him."

"I believe you…….."

"So please understand how my involvement all came about" said Michel.

"Oui, what you've told me does put it all in a different light" replied Henri meekly.

"You Henri are about to experience the same pleasures and entrapment that I've enjoyed and suffered over the years" said Michel with an air of authority.

"Oui" replied Henri quietly.

"It's a good job you've got a flat to go and hide in as well as a fast sports car to escape from Le Touquet when necessary!" Michel laughed but Henri looked a little serious and only managed a nervous half smile back.

"Oui, I'm looking forward to it all" stammered Henri.

"Keep it all under control and don't let your personal life affect the business" said Michel firmly.

"Of course not" replied Henri.

"Although you will find it hard sometimes, as I have" said Michel.

"I have noticed" replied Henri.

"Oui, but we have now overcome the problem of Madame Christiane" said Michel.

"With the help of Charles Robardes" added Henri.

"Oui."

"And you're going to see her again tonight" said Henri.

"I am indeed" replied Michel as he drank his coffee. Henri then looked at his watch, it was just past five o'clock.

"I think we'd better be getting back" he said.

"OK, I suppose we've seen enough this afternoon" replied Michel.

During the drive back from Abbeville to the salon they discussed plans for the business and did not once mention Henri's proposed complete change of his life's direction. Michel, however, gave it all a lot of thought as he chatted amiably to his cousin in the car. Once back in Le Touquet Michel promised Henri that he would call into the salon tomorrow afternoon after his sea trip with Josette on the 'Boulogne Princess'. They parted and Michel went home to face an unhappy fiancé.

"He's fixed the wiring in the kitchen, thank heavens" she said with menace.

"Bon" replied Michel.

"But somehow he's done something that's cocked it up in the dining room and our bedroom!" she exclaimed.

"Mon Dieu!"

"So, you can't use your 'office' tonight, ma petite and we'll have to go to bed with a candle" she said.

"That'll be romantic" replied Michel with a smile.

"I don't feel romantic at the moment, ma petite" said Josette

"Nothing new there then" replied Michel.

"Listen, I've had just about enough of all this nonsense and it's getting me down!"

"OK, OK, chérie" replied Michel calmly.

"You try staying here and dealing with it all on your own" she said angrily.

"Alright, chérie, now cheer up and tell me what's for dinner?"

"Soup and chicken salad" she replied.

"Very nice, chérie."

"Glad you think so."

"Now, I've a little surprise for you" he said.

"Really?"

"Oui, a short sea trip from Boulogne tomorrow in a boat like the 'Sea Goddess'" he smiled.

"Oh. Mon Dieu!" she exclaimed.

"It'll be fun" he said.

"I hope so, Michel."

"It will be, I promise."

"And talking of disasters, you better go and see where they left your desk after Pascal had finished giving them their instructions" she said.

"Oh, non."

"Oh, oui, I told you to put it upstairs" she retorted as Michel left the kitchen and hurried to the gloomy dining room. The desk was placed at an angle across the far corner of the room and it was so close to both walls that Michel just managed to squeeze past to sit in the large black leather chair placed behind the desk.

"Mon Dieu" he mumbled as he attempted to push the desk away from him, but to no avail. He returned to the kitchen where Josette was dishing up the soup and said "I should never have left them alone."

"Quite so" replied Josette. Michel decided to leave the unpalatable news that he was going out again for a short while until they had finished the meal.

"I shan't be long, chérie" he said before kissing her. Josette was unhappy but thought that his proposed meeting was obviously casual and low key as he left the house in the clothes he'd been wearing all day and he had not washed and looked a little unkempt. He arrived at Sophia's villa and was greeted by a smiling Evette who showed him into the lounge, poured him a brandy before telling him that Madame would be down in a moment. Michel was suspicious and waited anxiously for Sophia to make her entrance. Suddenly the door opened and she swept in looking fabulous.

"Ma chérie" she chortled as he stood up to kiss her.

"Sophia, you look wonderful" he said as he took her in his arms.

"Merci, chérie" she replied and kissed him passionately.

"Let me look at you" he said as he stepped back a pace and she did a twirl for him. Her blonde hair was swept up into a French roll and was as perfect as her makeup. Her diamond ear rings were matched by a diamond studded blue choker that was the same colour as her satin dress, which had a plunging neckline and was gathered tightly at her waist. Blue Italian shoes finished the ensemble and it all quite took Michel's breath away.

"Do you always dress like this for a quick drink?" Michel asked.

"Change of plan" she smiled.

"Oh, oui" replied Michel slowly in a suspicious tone.

"I've booked a table at Flavio's for dinner before we go to the casino" she said pertly.

"Oh, non!"

"Oh, oui, chérie, you're my lucky charm and I'm going to win back the money I lost the other night before Charles finds out!"

"Mon Dieu!"

"I'm sure we'll have a lovely evening."

"But I'm not dressed for all that, just look at me" he replied plaintively.

"Soon sort you out with one of Charles' dinner suits, you're about the same size or close enough for jazz" she said.

"Sophia, I can't……."

"Follow me, chérie, and hurry up otherwise we'll be late for dinner!" She turned and led the way upstairs whilst commanding him to have a quick wash while she sorted out a shirt, tie and suit for him. Unfortunately the trousers were too tight and Evette was called to help in expanding the waist band which she did expertly. Half an hour later they were on the way to Flavio's in her Mercedes with Michel feeling distinctly uncomfortable in a suit that was still a little tight around the waist and under the arms.

"As I know you're under cover now, I promise I'll act normally, but do point out any crime boss that you see at Flavio's or in the casino" she said in a half whisper.

"OK, but if I do, you must, for your own safety, take no notice."

"Oh, I won't, it's so exciting though" she replied and Michel raised his eyes to heaven.

As they entered the restaurant they were met by Guy who showed them to a romantic candle lit table for two in a discreet part of the dining room. Presented with menus and wine list the lovers settled down to peruse the cuisine on offer with Michel once again suffering the problems of two dinners in the evening.

"I'll have something light, I think" he said.

"You're not hungry, chérie?"

"Non, I've had a busy day with Henri……"

"And possibly something to eat before you came out tonight" she interrupted. Michel just smiled and replied "I'll start with crevettes."

"I'll join you" she said.

"Then I'll try the coq au vin" said Michel staying with chicken for the evening.

"I think I need something substantial tonight, so, I'll have the Tournedos Rossini" she smiled. The attentive waiter took their order and Michel chose St. Emillion, a dry, red claret, to drink.

"So, what have you and Henri been up to?" she asked when

they were alone.

"Do you really want to know or are you just being polite?"

"Chérie, I really want to know" she replied.

"I wonder."

"You're so cruel" she smiled.

"But you like it" he replied with a grin.

"I like everything about you, chérie" she said slowly and with intent.

"I worry about that" he replied.

"Why?"

"I just sometimes wonder where I actually fit in your life" he said.

"Right at the top" she replied.

"Just underneath your husband?"

"He doesn't count."

"Oh?"

"He's only interested in money."

"Well we all are to some degree" replied Michel.

"Oui, but not to the exclusion of everything else." Michel began to worry that his involvement with Sophia was going to be very deep as well as difficult and would probably end in tears. The waiter arrived with the crevettes and then produced a bottle of the St. Emillion which he opened and then poured for the lovers. They toasted each other and then ate in silence, each thinking about the situation they were in and Michel becoming increasingly concerned with the ever tightening waist band of Charles' trousers.

When Sophia had finished her crevettes she took a lingering sip of her wine and then, still holding the glass by the side of her face, she looked into Michel's eyes and whispered "you know I've fallen deeply in love with you." Michel did not reply immediately but looked down into his wine glass before taking a sip in order to give himself time to think as his brain became over loaded with the ramifications of what Sophia had just said.

"I've known for some while, chérie" he replied in a whisper.

"And?"

"I think I've fallen in love with you too" he said gently.

"You only think you have?" she demanded.

"Non, I know I have" he replied quickly in order to placate her.

"Bon, I just believe, truly believe, that we we're made for each other" she half whispered. Michel felt a knot of cold fear tighten in his stomach which seemed to relieve the pressure on Charles' waist band. He knew for certain that Sophia would play him like a helpless fish caught on an angler's hook and that there was little chance of escape. The waiter arrived and cleared the dishes before serving their main course giving Michel more time to think. When they were alone again, he looked into her blue eyes and said "what do we do now, chérie?"

"What do you mean?"

"Well, I'm engaged to one woman, but still married to another and you have a husband" he replied.

"They can not stand between us, our love will overcome anything they try and put in our way" she whispered passionately.

"Bon, let's eat up before it gets cold" he replied.

"Oh, Michel you're so unromantic!"

"I'm not" he replied.

"Say something romantic then."

"The Paris collection arrives at the salon tomorrow" he smiled. At that her eyes sparkled as brightly as the diamonds she wore.

"Oh, bon, I'll be there first thing" she smiled.

"Who's unromantic now?" he asked and she laughed.

"You're so wonderfully unpredictable, chérie."

"Non, just wonderful and predictably in love with you" he whispered.

"Chérie, I know we are going to be so happy together" she smiled.

"I'm sure." They took their time over the meal whilst exchanging meaningful glances and gentle smiles punctuated with half whispered words of love. Michel felt that he was in a dream of ecstasy with this lovely captivating woman and only the tightness of her husband's trousers brought him back to reality. They finished with glacé and coffee as Sophia insisted that she would win handsomely at the tables tonight and they both should leave room for the celebration champagne. Sophia put the bill on her husband's account and after Guy had extended his charming courtesy to his very regular customers on their departure, the lovers left the restaurant and drove to the casino.

On arrival the immaculate Paul welcomed them and after complimenting Sophia on her elegance, always a good ploy to use on a regular client who lost heavily, he ushered the couple directly into the gaming room and into the hands of Monsieur DeVaux, the manager.

"Bonsoir Madame Christiane and Monsieur Michel" beamed DeVaux.

"Bonsoir" they chorused.

"We are delighted to welcome you again, Madame."

"Merci, and I warn you, I'm feeling very lucky tonight" she smiled.

"Bon, Madame, we look forward to your good fortune" he replied as he gave a little bow.

"But before we start, we'll go to the bar" she smiled.

"Of course, Madame" he smiled. Michel gave a little bow to DeVaux before he followed Sophia to the bar where she hoisted her elegant behind onto the only vacant stool.

"Bonsoir, Madame and Monsieur, what can I get you?" enquired Rafael with a broad smile.

"Champagne, Rafael."

"Oui, Madame."

"Môet Chandon, s'il vous plait" demanded Sophia.

"Oui, Madame" replied the bar man as some of the regulars nearby acknowledged her.

"Wish me luck, chérie" she whispered to Michel.

"Oui, chérie, I do."

"Bon, and hold my hand every time I put the chips down" she said.

"I will."

"I just know if you're with me I'll be lucky tonight."

"Oui." Rafael popped the cork and poured the champagne into two elegant flutes and placed them before the lovers.

"Here's to us forever" she said.

"Forever" replied Michel as they touched glasses and drank. They were quite relaxed and a touch giggly when they eventually made their way to Sophia's favourite table where Pierré was the croupier. After greeting the couple and accepting Sophia's five thousand Francs in exchange for chips Pierré called "Madames and Messieurs, place your bets, s'il vous plait." Sophia gripped Michel's hand under the table and placed a thousand Francs on seven and twenty three. They waited for Pierré to spin the roulette wheel still holding hands tightly. The ball clattered and came to rest on rouge seven.

"Oui! Oui!" exclaimed Sophia as Pierré called the winning number. Her pile of winning chips were then deposited in front of her by a smiling Pierré.

"There, chérie, I told you that you brought me luck" she said as she held Michel's hand once again and he just nodded.

"Madames and Messieurs, place your bets, s'il vous plait" commanded Pierré. Sophia put a thousand Francs each on eleven and twenty one. Pierré spun the roulette wheel and when the clatter stopped the ball rested on number nineteen.

"Oh, mon Dieu" whispered Sophia.

"Better luck next time, chérie" whispered Michel.

"Oui" she replied anxiously. Sophia then doubled her investment and placed two thousand Francs on both six and eighteen. The wheel spun for what seemed an age with the lovers holding hands and at last the clatter stopped with Pierré announcing "eighteen, noir!"

"Mon Dieu! Mon Dieu!" exclaimed Sophia as she gripped Michel's hand even tighter with excitement. He was too amazed to speak as Pierré slid a huge pile of chips in front of Sophia.

"Stop now, chérie" whispered Michel in an anxious tone.

"Non, I'm on a winning streak!" she exclaimed.

"Believe me, chérie, stop now and I'll take you home" said Michel firmly.

"Non" she replied as she placed two thousand Francs on both seven and thirty. Pierré spun the wheel and when the ball came to rest it lay on number seven.

"Oh, mon Dieu" she half whispered as she placed her hands over her mouth and then waved them, fanning the air in front of her. Michel was speechless as Pierré piled up the chips in front of Sophia with the other gamblers looking on in envy.

"We have to go" said Michel firmly.

"Non, chérie" she replied.

"Let's have a drink at the bar and take a few moments rest" he suggested.

"Alright" she replied.

"Pierré, look after my chips, s'il vous plait."

"Oui, Madame."

As they walked to the bar Michel asked her if she realised how much she had won. Sophia was unsure so he said “on my calculations at thirty six to one, you’ve won a hundred and eighty thousand Francs!”

“Mon Dieu!”

“So I suggest that we call it a night and go home to celebrate” he whispered.

“Non, Michel, we’ll go home later, much later.” Michel then decided to save this foolish woman from gambling her winnings away by whispering to her “you know you wanted me to point out certain people to you?”

“Oui” she replied.

“There’s one at the bar, the fat guy with grey hair smoking a cigar” he whispered.

“Oh, non, how exciting” she whispered.

“Act natural and don’t look at him” said Michel under his breath so she did look at the man who caught her glance and smiled at her.

“We’ll finish the champagne, cash in your winnings and go” said Michel firmly as Rafael poured the Môet Chandon.

“Alright, chérie, if you say so.”

“I do, it’s important, believe me.” It was while they were finishing the champagne that Monsieur DeVaux, after Sophia’s request to Rafael, came to the bar and presented an envelope enclosing the cheque for her winnings.

“A very satisfactory evening for you Madame” he smiled.

“Oui, Monsieur, I told you I felt lucky tonight.”

“Indeed you did, Madame, and we look forward to seeing you again soon” he replied anxious to have the chance to recover the house losses.

Once they were in her car Sophia asked “who was that man at the bar?”

“I shouldn’t really tell you” Michel replied.

“Why not?”

“It could be dangerous.”

“How exciting” she whispered.

“You must understand, chérie, that in this business you’re dancing with shadows” he said mysteriously.

“Mon Dieu.”

“Dangerous shadows” he said with emphasis. They did not speak again until they were at home and sitting comfortably in the lounge drinking brandy.

“What a wonderful evening” she said.

“Oui, and I hope you’ve recovered all your losses of the other night.”

“Oh, I have, with some to spare” she replied.

“Bon.”

“I feel so relaxed and just ready for love” she mused.

“That’s a pity.”

“Why?”

“Because I have to leave you, chérie” he replied.

“Why?”

“I’ve a very busy day tomorrow, starting with a sea trip from Boulogne” he replied.

“Surely you’ve time for a ‘quickie’?”

“Non, chérie, I must not get too tired and if I stay with you I know that I’ll be exhausted by the morning” he smiled.

“Well stay the night and you can take me on the boat trip tomorrow” she said brightly.

“Non, I’m sorry, it’s strictly business, chérie” he replied.

“OK then, meet me for lunch at Le Café and you can make it up to me after” she smiled.

“I may not be back in time.”

“Ring me as soon as you can then” she replied.

“I will, I promise.” He then finished his drink and kissed her passionately before leaving with many ‘au revoirs’ and promises exchanged between them.

Michel arrived home to find Josette sitting up in bed reading in a brightly lit bedroom. He had hoped that she would be asleep so that he could slip into bed un-noticed.

“Chérie, I didn’t expect you to be awake at this time” he said gently as she looked up from her book.

“Michel, you’re late and where did you get that suit?” Her question hit him like a sledge hammer and he struggled for an answer.

“A business acquaintance kindly loaned it to me as I………”

“Michel, you must think I’m a complete idiot!”

"Chérie……"
"I've warned you before and believe me this is the last time!"
"Chérie……"
"Get undressed and come to bed now!"
"Oui, chérie."
"And don't touch me!"

CHAPTER 10

Michel and Josette had glum expressions on their faces as they started their breakfast of coffee and croissants whilst awaiting the arrival of Pascal. The house electrics were still 'not quite right' according to the Boulogne handy man and Michel was getting to the stage where he did not really care anymore. The optimism that he had for the new and exciting life in Le Touquet was beginning to fade in certain areas and he wondered if it would ever be as he wanted. He felt guilty about letting Josette down and he began to regret his involvement with Sophia, not to mention Maria, but they were both so irresistible. Then he remembered that he was due to have dinner with Maria and her friend Louis this very evening. He was angry over his stupidity with Charles' suit and planned to return the ill fitting clothing to the villa as soon as possible. There was a knock at the front door and Josette said "that'll be Pascal." Michel nodded and went to let the old man in.

"Bonjour, mes enfants" chortled Pascal breezily as he made his way to the kitchen. They both greeted him and Josette then offered him a coffee which he accepted as he joined them at the kitchen table.

"A nice day for your boat trip" said Pascal as he sipped his coffee.

"Oui" replied Michel.

"You don't sound very enthusiastic, Michel."

"Bit of a late night" replied Michel.

"Not too much of the grape, I hope" smiled Pascal.

"We'll never know" said Josette sharply.

"Hangovers and sea trips don't go well together" said Pascal helpfully.

"I'll remember that in future" replied Michel.

"Have you got any sea sick pills?" enquired the old man.

"Non, we don't need them" said Michel.

"Well, I can assure you that the Channel can be pretty choppy this time of year" said Pascal with authority.

"Thanks for that, Pascal" replied Michel and he looked at Josette who looked even more glum and half whispered "another disaster". They remained silent and listened to Pascal chatting on about his friend with the paint shop and learned almost the whole history of his private life before deciding it was time to go and meet Maurice at his office in Boulogne. They left Pascal to his electrical problems and set off with a small hamper of food for the voyage. They hardly spoke on the journey and Michel realised that he would have to make some real effort to win Josette back to how she used to be in Marseille.

Michel pulled up right outside Maurice's office in the Boulevard Diderot just before ten and was immediately greeted by a beaming Maurice, his son, Jacques, a tall, dark young man who was Raymond and a well built girl in a thick jumper who was introduced as Dominique, fiancé of Raymond. After all the greetings and introductions were completed the party set off in two cars to the hard standing where they could park safely and board the boat, which was moored close by.

Michel was impressed by the 'Boulogne Princes' and her smart, fresh white painted appearance gave him confidence in the trip ahead. They boarded the boat and were given a quick tour by Raymond aided by Maurice, who was definitely over selling the whole operation to Michel.

"I assure you, Michel, that no expense has been spared in bringing the 'Princess' up to scratch" said Maurice.

"I can see" replied Michel.

"Oui, Raymond has had everything inspected and carefully overhauled" explained Maurice.

"Bon."

"Nothing has been left to chance, mon ami" persisted Maurice and Michel began to think that possibly the 'Sea Goddess' might be some time on the hard standing before her overhaul was complete and the 'Princess' would be her stand in. He guessed suitable sub contract fees had been arranged between the two owners.

When they had all assembled on the bridge Raymond started number one diesel engine. There was a clatter followed by a plume of black smoke from the exhaust.

"Listen to that engine, Michel" said Maurice.

"Oui."

"It's perfect."

"Bon" replied Michel as Raymond started number two engine which made as much noise and smoke as the first one. The boat was vibrating and Raymond opened the throttles to bring some smoothness and harmony to the engines thumping and vibrating below the deck.

"We'll soon be ready to go" said Maurice enthusiastically.

"Bon" replied Michel as he looked at Josette, who appeared apprehensive.

"I'll just let the engine temperatures come up and then we can cast off" said Raymond.

Michel nodded and Maurice said to Raymond "Jacques and I will do that."

"Bon, off you go then" replied the captain. Maurice and his son went out on deck and whilst Maurice went forward, Jacques went to the stern and prepared to cast off the ropes holding the 'Boulogne Princess' captive against the quay. Raymond studied the temperature gauges before him as Michel smiled at Josette and Dominique, hoping to give some encouragement to the women. Dominique looked comfortable but Josette still looked concerned.

"OK" shouted Raymond and he waved to Maurice who untied the ropes in the bow and then waved to Jacques who did the same at the stern. The captain engaged the propeller drive before increasing the engine revolutions and then swung the wheel hard over as the 'Boulogne Princess' began inching her way forward and out from the quay. Maurice and Jacques rejoined them on the bridge, their faces wreathed in smiles of anticipation at the voyage ahead. They slowly passed the myriad of craft bobbing at their moorings in the Bassin Napoleon before increasing speed and heading out into the grey green Channel.

"We'll head south to Le Touquet, that'll keep us clear of the cross Channel ferries" said Raymond as he gradually opened the throttles. The engine noise and vibration increased as the 'Boulogne Princess' made her way out into the open sea where the white topped waves became more of an obstacle to the boats smooth progress. The steady 'thump' 'thump' of the waves hitting the bow came in perfect timing with the pitching of the boat and Michel began to feel a little unwell. He glanced at Josette who was holding on tightly to their little food hamper with one hand whilst gripping a rail with the other. She managed a half smile at her fiancé before looking out to sea.

"It's a bit choppy here, but as we swing south, it'll be a lot smoother" said Raymond.

"Bon" murmured Michel.

"Oui, during the summer, your clients will find the sea trips are normally quite smooth" said Maurice with a confidence as he watched Michel becoming paler by the minute.

"Bon" replied Michel in a half whisper, wishing he had never agreed to this out of season jaunt and wondering why anybody would want to spend money on a boat trip.

"I think I'll go out on deck" said Michel.

"Good idea, you'll enjoy the sea air" smiled Maurice. Josette followed Michel out on deck and they made their way, pale faced, to the stern well away from the enthusiastic boat owners. The 'Boulogne Princess' continued to ride the waves in a spirited manner with her twin diesel engines roaring with pulsating power as the twenty metre boat ploughed into the unyielding sea.

"Mon Dieu, I can't stand much more of this" shouted Michel above the roar of the engines, wind and sea.

"Neither can I" replied a very pale faced Josette.

"I think I'll tell them we've had enough" said Michel.

"OK."

At that moment the pitching and roaring began to subside as the boat changed course to a more southerly direction and Michel began to feel a little more comfortable.

"That's a bit better" he said and Josette nodded.

"I still want to go back" she said.

"Alright, chérie, we'll just give it a few more minutes and I'll tell Raymond."

"OK."

Then Dominique appeared, a concerned expression on her face.

"Are you both alright?" she enquired.

"Oui, we're fine, just not used to it, that's all" replied Michel.

"I understand, but now we're staying close to the coast we'll be sheltered and Raymond has reduced speed so it will all be a lot smoother" she said.

"Bon, we'll be alright then" replied Michel with a grin.

Maurice joined them and with a beaming smile he asked "enjoying the trip?"

“Well, oui, now that we’ve slowed down a little” replied Michel as both engines shuddered to a momentary halt before running on for a few moments and then stopping dead.

“Mon Dieu!” exclaimed Maurice before he returned to the bridge in a hurry. The ‘Boulogne Princess’ slowed in the water and then began to roll hideously from side to side as she lost forward momentum.

“This is all we need” said Michel as he heard the starter motors on the engines whirring in a futile attempt to bring the engines back to life. He watched Maurice and Raymond gesticulating at each other as Raymond tried again to coax the engines to start. It was all to no avail and both Michel and Josette began to feel unwell as the boat continued to roll in the Channel swell.

“Another bloody disaster” said Josette.

“Raymond will soon fix it” said Dominique with a smile.

“Bon” replied Josette.

“I’ll go and see if he needs my help” said Dominique before she wandered off towards the bridge.

“How the hell do we end up in these nightmares?” demanded Josette.

“I don’t know, ma chérie” replied Michel.

“It all seems a long way from our life together in Marseille” she said gloomily.

“Oui.”

“I don’t think boats and us go together” she said.

“Non.”

“I’ll never go on a small one like this again.”

“Neither will I” he replied whilst watching the owners leave the bridge and make their way to the engine hatch in the main cabin. Michel decided to investigate further and leaving Josette holding onto the rail, he staggered in time with the roll of the boat towards the cabin.

“I think there’s a fuel line blockage” said Raymond.

“Oui, it often happens after an overhaul” agreed Maurice, anxious to placate any fears that Michel might have about reliability.

“Can you fix it easily?” Michel enquired as he peered down at the hot, smelly engines below.

“Oui, no problem” replied Raymond.

"Bon."

"I'll just disconnect the fuel unions and give them a quick clean out" said Raymond.

"Bon, I'll leave you to it then" said Michel believing he would be more appreciated if he remained out of the way. He staggered back to Josette and gave her the news.

"I hope they can fix it quickly because I can't stand much more of this rolling about" she said.

"It won't take long" Michel assured her as the 'Boulogne Princess' appeared to increase her roll rate as the wind gusted and the sea began to rise. Michel could see Maurice waving his arms about and looking down at Raymond in the engine bay. Jacques and Dominique were standing by Maurice and had concerned faces as it was obvious that the two men were arguing.

"I bet they wish they hadn't come on this trip either" said Michel as he nodded at the group in the passenger cabin.

"Possibly" replied Josette as Maurice turned and waved at Jacques, who nodded and then hurried out of the cabin. He had just come on deck when the boat rolled quite heavily and as Jacques was on the downside he lost his balance, and then, as graceful as a ballet dancer, he just glided over the side into the sea.

"Mon Dieu! Mon Dieu!" shouted Michel as he rushed to the side of the boat and gazed down at the boy struggling in the water.

"Help! Help!" shouted Jacques and Michel took up the call and hammered on the window of the cabin to attract everyone's attention. They all joined him immediately on deck and Raymond grabbed a lifebelt and threw it towards Jacques struggling in the water. It was an extremely good shot as it hit Jacques squarely on his head and the boy sank like a stone beneath the waves.

"Mon Dieu!" shouted Michel and without a second thought he slipped of his coat and jumped over the side of the boat as the others stood transfixed with their mouths open. Josette screamed "Michel!" just as he hit the water and disappeared beneath the sea. He then surfaced, spluttering and cursing before striking out towards the lifebelt bobbing on the waves. The onlookers could see Jacques just below it and were relieved as Michel dived under to rescue the boy. In moments he had brought him to the surface and with one arm around Jacques neck and the other looped through the lifebelt, Michel kicked out hard and soon reached the

side of the boat where Raymond had lowered a rope ladder. Maurice climbed down and put his hand out to grab his son's arm and pull him up out of the water. Jacques was coughing and between coughs was shouting that he was alright as Raymond lent over and helped Maurice to get the boy on deck.
Michel then climbed up and then flopped down on the deck as Josette bent down and kissed him repeatedly, whispering "oh, ma chérie, my brave chérie, thank heavens you're safe."

"I'm OK, chérie, just cold and very wet" he replied.

"Quick, into the cabin and get those clothes off while I get some blankets" said Raymond. Jacques and his rescuer were hurried into the passenger cabin which was a little warmer than outside and started to undress. Helped by the two women they were both stripped to their underpants as Raymond appeared with only one small blanket.

"This is all I've got, I'm afraid" he said apologetically.

"It'll have to do" replied Michel as Dominique used it as a towel to wipe them both down before wrapping it around Jacques who had started to shiver.

"I've got some coffee in a flask" she said.

"Bon" said Josette as Maurice took off his dark blue jumper and put it on Jacques.

"There, you'll soon warm up" he said to his son with relief. He then turned to Michel and said with a smile "thank you so much for what you did, it was very brave."

"That's OK, Maurice" he replied and then began to shiver as Dominique arrived back with the flask of coffee and poured a cup for Jacques who was now sitting in a passenger seat.

"You can have my jumper, Michel" said Dominique and before he could protest, she had pulled the floppy garment over her head and presented it to him. Michel admired her large breasts encased in a sensible, white, sea going brassiere.

"Merci" he smiled as he slipped it on and pulled it down to below his waist. As Dominique returned to the care of Jacques, Michel whispered to Josette "I'll have to take my pants off, ma petite, they're so uncomfortable."

"You can't do that, Michel, they'll all see your willy."

"I'll have to cover myself up somehow, think of something" he whispered in reply. Josette saw a large piece of oily rag by the engine hatch that originally had been part of a blue shirt and she picked it up.

"This'll do, all we need are a couple of pins to fix it to the bottom of the jumper and we can make you a nappy" she said brightly. Michel grinned and asked Raymond if there were any pins on board.

"Oui, in the first aid box" he replied and pointed to a large green box attached to the cabin wall. Josette found enough safety pins to make Michel a suitable nappy that protected his modesty and to the amusement of all the onlookers he presented himself as suitably dressed for the voyage. Dominique then poured a cup of hot coffee for him and handed it to the hero with an admiring look. Michel thanked her and sat in a passenger seat with Josette to compose himself and get warm. The boat continued to roll as Raymond returned to the business of finding out why both engines had stopped and under Maurice's direction undid the unions on the fuel line. Michel was feeling a lot better and was even getting used to the rhythmic roll of the 'Boulogne Princess'.

"I think they'll want to return as soon as they get the engines started" said Michel.

"I hope so" Josette replied.

"After we get back to Boulogne we'll drive straight home, I'll have a bath and then take you out for a nice lunch before we go to the salon" he smiled.

"Oh, bon, ma petite."

"And the surprise is......" he paused.

"Oui?"

"The new Paris collection arrives today and I'll buy you anything you want!"

"Oh, chérie" she smiled.

It was some time later that the blockage was found and the fuel lines re-connected. Raymond and Maurice went to the bridge and attempted to start both engines. Number one fired up after a few hesitant moments but number two failed to show even a flicker of life so Raymond set off on the return journey to Boulogne on one engine. Progress was slow but once the boat started making way it settled down and the uncomfortable roll diminished and became hardly noticeable.

"I've quite enjoyed this" said Michel as the boat limped into the

Bassin Napoleon. Once they were moored Maurice said to Michel "I've got some work trousers in the office, they're not the best but they'll get you home."

"Merci" replied the hero.

After slipping on Maurice's trousers and returning Dominique's jumper, Michel and Josette said their 'goodbyes' on board the 'Princess' and set off for Le Touquet in a warm glow of companionship forged by the danger they had faced together and survived. Back home, Michel had a quick bath before taking Josette to Le Nemo, a pretty little restaurant on the Boulevard de la Mer.

"This is nice" she smiled as they sat at a table for two in the window.

"Oui, I've not been in here before but Henri said it was quite good" he replied.

The waiter presented the menus and wine list and left them to make their choices.

"Potage aux tomates followed by coq au vin for me" said Michel.

"Oui, I need something hot after our adventures this morning so I'll have the same." she replied. Michel ordered a light Rosé to drink and they settled down to enjoy their meal together. They were unhurried and relaxed and Michel was pleased to see the sparkle returning to Josette's eyes and conversation. Whether it was the anxious moments of the sea drama or the thought of the Parisian shoes that made her happy was un-important, he was just pleased to see his lovely fiancé back to her usual self that made her so special to him.

It was gone three o'clock before the lovers made their way to the salon, which was busier than Michel had ever seen it. The news of the Paris collection had indeed gone round Le Touquet like a rifle bullet and the clients had come out in force.

"Bonjour, Monsieur Michel" smiled Elaine as she rushed passed clutching a box of shoes.

"Bonjour Elaine" he called after her as he noticed Henri on his knees in front of Sophia Christiane.

"Mon Dieu" he whispered under his breath before taking Josette's arm and guiding her towards the stairs to Henri's office.

Henri spotted him at the same moment that Sophia followed Henri's glance and she called "Michel, Michel!"

"Who's that woman with Henri?" demanded Josette with a puzzled expression.

"One of Henri's best customers" replied Michel.

"Why is she calling you then?"

"Well, she's seen me here with Henri."

"She seems a bit too familiar for my liking" replied Josette.

"Ma chérie, you've nothing to worry about" he replied.

Sophia stood up and turning one way and then the another to see the new shoes she was wearing in the floor mirror. She paused for a moment before walking over to the couple.

"Michel, what do you think of these?" she asked.

"Very nice, Madame Christiane" he replied.

"Michel, why so formal?"

"Madame……"

"And who's this?" she interrupted.

"Allow me to introduce my fiancé, Josette, Madame Christiane" replied Michel

"Ah, oui, I saw you at Flavio's recently" Sophia replied.

"How do you do" said Josette firmly.

"Your fiancé has good taste, that's why I always ask for his opinion" said Sophia ignoring Josette's polite greeting.

"Bon" replied Josette.

"I should keep him on a tight leash if I were you" said Sophia.

"I do, and believe me Madame, it's getting tighter by the day" replied Josette as Henri arrived.

"Ah, Michel, Josette, bonjour, er, Michel, just in time, can you assist Elaine for a moment whilst I attend to Madame Christiane?" asked Henri having observed the potential flash point and acting quickly.

"Of course" replied a relieved Michel.

"And if you would like to wait in my office upstairs, Josette, I will be there as soon as I have served Madame" said Henri with a smile.

"Oui, merci" replied Josette as Michel excused himself and went in search of Elaine.

"This way, Madame" said Henri as he led Sophia back to the chair to continue the fitting.

When she had regained her composure and wiggled her toes in the elegant but extravagant dark red Parisian shoes she said "Henri, I want to speak to Michel on a private matter, s'il vous plait."

"Oui, Madame, in just a moment, tell me how do they feel?"

"Comfortable."

"Bon, would you care to walk in them again, Madame?"

"Oui" she replied as she stood up and searched for Michel in the busy salon but he had disappeared with Elaine upstairs into the stockroom. Josette came out of Henri's office next door and said to Michel in an angry tone "who is that bloody woman and who does she think she is?"

"I've told you, ma petite, she's Henri's best customer" he replied.

"And the worst trouble maker" said Elaine with a stern face.

"I can imagine" replied Josette

"Henri will get rid of her in a minute, I promise you, now why don't you have a look at some of these lovely shoes while we're waiting for her to go?"

"OK." Having pacified his fiancé for the moment, he then introduced her to Elaine and was about to leave when Henri came upstairs.

"Michel, she wants a quick word with you" and seeing Josette's face cloud with suspicious anger, added "she just wants your opinion on the shoes she's wearing."

"Oui, of course" replied Michel.

"And Elaine if you could find a black pair in the same style for Madame and bring them down immediately, s'il vous plait."

"Oui, Monsieur Henri."

Michel followed his cousin downstairs to the salon and while Henri made his way to the counter, Michel approached Sophia.

"Oui, Madame?"

"When are you going to bring Charles' clothes back?" she whispered.

"Tonight."

"Bon, he 'phoned me from London and he'll be back in the morning."

"OK, I'll drop them in about six."

"Bon, then where are we going tonight?" she asked.

“Nowhere, I’ve got a meeting in Boulogne I’m afraid” he replied.

“Meet me for lunch at Le Café tomorrow at one then” she said.

“Sophia, I can’t……”

“Is everything to Madame’s satisfaction?” interrupted Henri with his salesman’s smile.

“Oui, Henri, these shoes are divine.”

“Bon.”

“And Michel approves” she smiled.

“I’m so pleased” said Henri insincerely.

“And have you got them in black?”

“Elaine is just looking for you, Madame.”

“Bon.”

“And in the unlikely event that we’ve not got what you require, Madame, I shall personally contact Paris on your behalf and place an order” he beamed.

“Merci, Henri.”

“Now excuse me just for a moment, I’ll be right back” said Henri as he caught a signal of despair from Theresa who was struggling to fit a slim shoe on an overweight woman in a large hat and fur coat.

“Tomorrow at one, then” said Sophia in a half whispered firm tone.

“Alright, alright” replied Michel on edge. Elaine then arrived clutching an open box containing a pair of black shoes and smiled at Sophia.

“I’ll leave you with Elaine, Madame” said Michel and gave a little bow. He then made his way quickly upstairs towards Henri’s office. Josette had found a pair of blue metallic finish shoes that fitted her perfectly and she was walking around the stock room in ecstasy.

“What do you think of these, chérie?” she asked with a beaming smile.

“Oh, they’re perfect, just perfect” he smiled.

“Can I have them then?”

“Of course, chérie.”

“I expect they’re expensive” she said anxiously.

“I don’t care, chérie, I promised you that I’d buy anything you wanted and I will” he replied.

"Oh, Michel, I do love you so."
"I know, and I love you, especially in blue shoes!"
They sat in Henri's office chatting, until the harassed man arrived and slumped down behind his desk.
"Mon Dieu, women and shoes!" he exclaimed shaking his head.
"It's good business, Henri" replied Michel.
"I know, I know."
"And Josette has chosen these " said Michel and his fiancé stood up and paraded for Henri.
"Bon, Josette, they look very smart but are they comfortable?"
"Oh, oui, Henri, they're perfect."
"Bon, you may have them with my compliments."
"What?" Michel asked in amazement.
"Oh, merci, Henri, merci, but Michel will pay for them….."
"Non, I insist, now then, how did you get on this morning cruising with Monsieur DeVere and his friend?"
"I fell overboard" replied Michel.
"What!" exclaimed Henri in shock. Then amidst a lot of laughter Michel and Josette recounted the adventure and Henri was almost hysterical when they told him about Michel's oily nappy.

It was nearly six when they made their way home in a happy and relaxed mood. Josette was clutching the bag with her new shoes and it was easy for Michel to tell her that he had to go out tonight to meet Monsieur Louis Montarde in Boulogne. As he did not expect to be too late he asked her to wait up for him so he could see her promenade in her blue shoes and nothing else. She laughed and promised him that she would take care of his every need. He managed to retrieve Charles' clothes whilst Josette was busy in the kitchen and take them to the car. After many kisses and 'au revoirs' he set off for Sophia's villa.
"Bonsoir, Monsieur Michel" said Evette with a smile.
"Bonsoir, Evette, is Madame at home?"
"She's in the bath, Monsieur, would you like to go up?"
"Er, non, I have to go to Boulogne and I'm already late, so perhaps I could leave these with you?" he said as he handed the clothes over to her.
"Certainly, Monsieur, I'll see Madame gets them."

"Merci, au revoir."

He raced away to Boulogne and pulled up outside Maria's flat in the Boulevard Voltaire just after seven.

"You're a little late, chérie, and I was beginning to worry" she said as she kissed him hard on the lips.

"I'm sorry, but it's been a bit of a day and you'll understand why when I tell you everything" he replied.

"Come and sit down while I get you a brandy, you look as if you need one."

"Certainly do" he replied as he sank down onto the settee. Maria was looking quite spectacular in a short, red dress with a plunging V neckline. Her hair and makeup were just so but her perfume was a touch overpowering. Her high heeled red shoes tipped her forward provocatively and her breasts seemed to jut out more than usual.

"You look good tonight" said Michel as she handed him his brandy.

"I feel good" she replied with a smile as she sat next to him.

"Bodes well for later then."

"Certainly does, chérie."

"Pity that Louis is coming" said Michel.

"He'll leave soon after dinner, I promise, and then you and I can get right down to business" she laughed and touched his glass with hers. Michel smiled and sipped his drink.

"I think you're a bit of a mystery" said Michel.

"Oh, non, I'm an open book for the right man" she replied.

"Really?"

"Oui, my husband taught me so much and now I'm ready to practice all of it" she whispered.

"Bon."

"Are you ready to be practiced on, chérie?" she whispered.

"Oh, oui."

"Bon."

"You'd better tell me about Louis before he arrives" said Michel changing the subject.

"Right, now he's a dear friend with some problems" she began.

"Only some?"

"Oui, and I've been thinking about this ever since we first met."

"Go on" said Michel.

"And, as you're very much a man of the world and a kind person........"

"True" interrupted Michel.

"I thought you could really help him" she smiled.

"I will if I can" replied Michel.

"I knew you would."

"What's his problem?"

"Well, he needs to be appreciated."

"We all want that."

"I know, but he needs someone like you, a nice man to be kind and help him, give him confidence, that sort of thing."

"I'll try."

"Merci, chérie" she whispered and kissed him hard on the lips.

The sonnette rang and Maria said "that'll be him."

When Michel was introduced to Louis he was unsure of what to make of him. He was quite tall and slim with short dark hair, blue eyes and a fair complexion. Michel guessed he was about thirty and was impressed by his youthful good looks. His voice was light and gentle and Michel was unsure whether Louis was gay or not.

"Maria's told me so much about you Michel" said Louis as he sat in an adjacent chair.

"Well I'll try to live it down" replied Michel and Louis smiled.

"So I'm very pleased to meet you at last" said the young man.

"Brandy?" asked Maria.

"Oui, ma petite" Louis replied

They chatted for a while and Louis began to relax in the company of Michel until Maria left them to attend to the preparation of dinner. When they were alone he appeared to become a little anxious.

"Has Maria told you about me?" he asked in a half whisper.

"Not much, she just said that you were a good friend, who she thought I may be able to help" replied Michel.

"Oh, merci."

"And if I can help at all, I certainly will" smiled Michel.

"Maria said you were a kind person and so understanding" said Louis gently.

"I try to be."

"Tonight will be a very important moment for me" said Louis.

"Really?" asked Michel, now becoming curious about this

anxious young man.

"Oui, everything depends on you" he replied as Maria came into the room and announced that dinner was served. They followed her into the dining room and sat at the table set out with glistening cutlery and glassware.

"I hope you enjoy the meal tonight" she said.

"I'm sure we will" replied Michel as Maria served the starter of moules marinieres.

"Bon appetite" she wished them both as she poured a dry white Pouilly-Fume into their glasses before they toasted one another.

"A night to remember" said Louis.

"Oui" replied Maria, whilst Michel remained uncertain about what lay ahead. The mussels were extraordinarily good and the trio became more relaxed and talkative as the wine flowed and a second bottle was hurriedly opened.

Maria had prepared carré d'agneau for the main course and they moved onto a large bottle of Rosé d'Anjou to complement the lamb.

"This is delicious" said Michel and Louis nodded, adding "superb, Maria, as usual."

"You're a lucky man if you often get invited to dinner here" said Michel.

"Don't worry, Michel, you're going to get more than your fair share of invitations" smiled Maria.

"I look forward to it" he replied as he picked up his glass and raised it to the desirable woman sitting opposite him.

"So do I" she half whispered as Louis smiled. They finished the meal with Pear Belle Hélène and coffee. Michel recounted his sea adventures amidst a mixture of laughter and concern before they chatted about relations and Maria insisted on telling them all about her late husband's side of the family until both men were totally sure that they knew everything there was to know. Michel hoped that she would stop talking so that he could find out how he was supposed to help Louis. He was anxious for him to leave so that he could have a quick session with Maria before going home to Josette and her new shoes.

"Now then, it's time for you to relax in the lounge with a brandy whilst Louis comes with me for a few moments" said Maria.

"Bon, then all will be revealed?" asked Michel.

"Oui, so just be patient, chérie" replied Maria as she led the way back to the lounge where she poured Michel a brandy whilst Louis disappeared into her bedroom.

"Shan't be long" she said as she handed him his drink before kissing him passionately.

"Bon." It seemed an age before Maria came back into the lounge and asked "are you ready, chérie?"

"Oui, I'm ready for anything" Michel replied with a grin.

"Then meet Edith!" announced Maria as Louis came through the door dressed as a woman wearing a shoulder length blonde wig and too much makeup.

"Mon Dieu" whispered Michel.

"What do you think?" asked Maria as Edith paraded into the centre of the room and did a twirl.

Michel felt slightly uncomfortable but being kind he replied "wonderful."

"I'm so glad you approve, Michel" said Edith with a big smile.

"Oh, I do, you look lovely and I guess that if you feel like a woman that's how you want to be" said Michel.

"Oh, I do want to be a woman, I really do."

"Bon, now give me another twirl and let me see some more of you" said Michel. Maria had dressed Edith quite well and she was wearing a green satin dress with a high neck line, square cut, with a thigh split, which showed off Edith's very long and shapely legs, matching high heeled shoes completed the ensemble. However, her makeup was too heavy and her perfume was a little overpowering.

"You really do look very nice indeed" said Michel truthfully.

"Bon, now then, would you go out with me?" asked Edith with an anxious look.

"Oui, of course" replied Michel, uncertain in his own mind whether he would or not.

"Oh, wonderful" replied Edith.

"This is Edith's first time dressed as a lady in front of a man" said Maria.

"And this moment means so much to me" said Edith breathlessly.

"Of course and I understand" said Michel gently.

"I have to know if I look like a woman" whispered Edith.

"You do, now come here and let me kiss you" said Michel in the heat of the moment and without thinking.

"Oh, Michel" whispered Edith as she rushed towards the new man in her life as he stood up to embrace this anxious young person. The kiss was not as bad as Michel feared and Edith held him with a man's embrace until they were forced to break for air.

"Wonderful" said Maria as she clapped her hands.

"Oh, Michel, I'm so grateful" whispered Edith.

"No need to be, Edith, you're really lovely and you'll be a wonderful woman" he replied.

"Oui, I do hope so."

"Men will be queuing up to take you out" said Michel.

"Oui, and after I've had the operation I'll be able to make love just like any other woman" Edith said with conviction.

"Oui, you certainly will" replied Michel.

"Now then, Edith and I have been out buying several outfits and we'd like your opinion on them before she goes out shopping on her own" said Maria.

"Of course" replied Michel, now quite fascinated by this situation he was in. At this point Edith kissed him passionately once more and smudged her lipstick all round his lips.

"Shan't be long, chérie" whispered Edith as she released him from her embrace and followed Maria out of the room. Michel poured himself a large brandy and returned to the comfort of the settee whilst bracing himself mentally for the next session.

It was not long before Maria returned with Edith close behind.

"This for elegant day time wear" announced Maria as Edith strode forward and gave a twirl. A neat two piece in apricot over a white blouse with white shoes made her appear elegant and sophisticated. Her lipstick had been fixed and she looked quite good.

"Very nice indeed" said Michel.

"I knew you'd like it, chérie" said Edith and Michel was becoming more alarmed at the familiarity.

"I do" he said and then added "ideal for shopping in town."

"Precisely" agreed Maria.

"Now kiss me again" said Edith with a smile.

"Certainly" replied Michel.

"I want a kiss for every outfit I wear tonight to bring me good luck" said Edith as she grabbed Michel and kissed him passionately once more. When they broke for air she led the way out and Maria stopped for a moment to say "this means so much to her and I'm very grateful that you're being so kind and helpful."

"My pleasure" he replied and when he was alone he poured himself another large brandy hoping the alcohol would help deaden his senses. Edith arrived for the last time in a one piece red bathing costume and white shoes.

"Now then, chérie, this is the tricky bit, tell me honestly, can you see my little willy?" she asked. Michel had never actually had to answer such a question before and for the moment he was stumped.

"Give me a twirl" he replied, playing for time, "then just stand sideways so that I can get a good look."

"Oui, chérie." Edith did as she was asked and Michel squinted and then closed one eye as if he was sighting some important monument.

"Well?" Edith demanded.

"There's a small bulge……."

"Luckily, that's because I've only got a small willy" Edith interrupted.

"I think it'll be noticed if she goes on the beach" said Maria.

"Possibly" replied Michel.

"If I can tuck it between my legs, do you think that would be alright?" asked Edith.

"You could give it a try" replied Michel and before he had finished speaking, Edith had undone the halter straps around her neck and had pulled the costume to her knees. She did have a small willy that protruded from a little mound of black pubic hair. Helped by Maria she tucked the offending penis between her legs and pulled up the costume as Michel sat stunned on the settee.

"Now what do you think?" asked Edith.

"Much better" stammered Michel.

"Bon, then that's what I'll do."

"Oui, but to be safe you'd better tie you willy up with a bandage or something otherwise it'll come forward when you walk" said Maria.

"Oui, I know, I'll be glad when I've had it cut off" she replied and Michel winced at that.

"Now, kiss me chérie" demanded Edith and Michel obliged a little unsteadily. Edith and Maria left the room chatting about the problems of beach wear and when they returned Edith was wearing her apricot outfit and announced that she was going to go for a short walk for the very first time. Michel had hoped that she would just go home but he guessed that Maria had been keeping her clothes safely at the flat, so she was bound to return. All he wanted was just a sharp 'quickie' with Maria before going home to Josette.

Edith was nervously poised at the front door of the flat gathering her courage to go out when someone knocked at the door.

"Who's that I wonder?" said Maria as she opened the door to a young woman. A moment of silence followed.

"Louis!" screamed the woman.

"Gabrielle!" moaned Edith as she backed up into the lounge where Michel was holding his head.

"You poor, sick, bastard!" exclaimed Gabrielle as she followed Edith.

"Mon Dieu!" moaned Michel.

"Who are you?" demanded Maria.

"I'm Gabrielle Montarde, his wife!" she shouted as she pointed at Edith who collapsed onto the settee next to Michel and began to cry.

"Oh, Mon Dieu!" exclaimed Maria.

"Oh, non, not tears as well" moaned Michel as he glanced at Edith.

"And you're covered in lipstick!" exclaimed Gabrielle looking hard at Michel who nodded.

"So what's been going on? As if I didn't know" shouted Gabrielle.

"If you must shout, please do it quietly" said Michel.

"Well?" demanded Gabrielle.

"How did you find me?" wailed Edith.

"I knew you were up to something, so I had you followed" replied Gabrielle.

"I'm so unhappy, I just wish I was dead" moaned Edith.

"Any more games like this, Louis, and you will be" replied Gabrielle.

“Mon Dieu” whispered Edith.

“Now get out of those clothes and get dressed properly” said Gabrielle firmly.

“I don’t want to” replied Edith between sobs.

“Louis, were going home and I promise you that you’re not going out dressed like that!”

“Michel, help me please” pleaded Edith.

“I can’t.”

“Why not?”

“Because I’m totally useless at persuading angry women to change their mind or do anything they don’t want to” he replied.

“Oh, Michel” sobbed Edith.

“I think the best advice that I can give is that you go home with your wife now and have a long talk tomorrow” said Michel. Edith shook her head in despair.

“You heard the man, now get changed” demanded Gabrielle.

“I don’t want to” sobbed Edith.

“Louis!”

“Alright, but I want you to know, you’ve just ruined my life, Gabrielle” said Edith.

“If this is your idea of life then I’m glad I’ve ruined it, now hurry up” replied his wife.

Edith struggled back to Maria’s bedroom followed by Gabrielle and the pair emerged a short time later with Edith dressed in his original clothes. She came into the lounge and said “thank you Maria and you Michel, you both made me feel like a real woman tonight……...”

“Shut up, you bloody fool and get on home” interrupted his wife.

“We only tried to help him” said Maria in a plaintiff voice.

They left without another word and Maria closed the front door behind them, joining Michel in the lounge and sitting beside him on the settee where they remained silent for a few moments.

“Well, that went well” said Michel and Maria had to laugh.

“Oh, mon Dieu, we were only trying to help the poor boy” said Maria.

“I know chérie, and we can say that we did our best” replied Michel.

“You were very kind to him” said Maria.

"It wasn't difficult."

"I feel very sorry for him, it must be awful if you're a man and want to be a woman" she said with sympathy.

"Oui" Michel nodded in agreement.

"They're bound to split up" said Maria sadly.

"Of course, now, what about us?"

"I'm ready for bed now, are you?" she smiled.

"Certainly am" he replied.

In a very short while they were both naked and in bed with Michel kissing Maria passionately. They did not spend too much time on the preliminaries and he found her moist and receptive to his rigid penis. He entered her with ease and moved gently and purposefully to a relaxed climax which was all he could manage after all the alcohol he had consumed. They fell asleep in each others arms blissfully unaware of the time. Michel awoke busting to go to the bathroom and after he had finished there he glanced at his watch and was horrified to see that the time was almost four o'clock.

"Mon Dieu!" he mumbled and hurried back to the bedroom to get dressed. After many kisses and 'au revoirs' he left Maria with a promise that he would telephone her later and make a date when they could explore the pleasures of love at their leisure.

He drove the Mercedes quickly through the empty streets of Boulogne and out onto the road to Le Touquet. He arrived home and let himself in as quietly as he could, hoping not to disturb Josette. In the darkness of their bedroom she suddenly said "Michel, I give up with you."

"Ma chérie……."

"And so does everybody else" she interrupted.

"Really?"

"Oui, Monsieur Gerrard 'phoned tonight and wanted to know where you were and why you hadn't called him, as you promised."

"Mon Dieu!"

"I told him I didn't know anything as usual."

"I forgot all about………"

"So bonsoir, Michel."

"Chérie……."

"Now come to bed and don't touch me."

CHAPTER 11

The lovers started the day over another glum breakfast with Michel wishing that he did not have to join Monsieur Ricard's coach trip at nine o'clock. His head felt heavy and his mouth was as dry and gritty as the bottom of a parrot's cage.

"I'll be back after lunch" said Michel as he gazed watery eyed at Josette across the table.

"I don't care when you come back" she replied.

"Chérie….."

"Or even if you ever come back."

"Ma petite………"

"Hurry up or you'll be late for your trip" she interrupted.

"Chérie…."

"Michel, please don't bother me with any more excuses, I'm not in the mood."

He sighed and finished his coffee thinking 'the least said the better'. Pascal arrived, cheerful as ever, and Michel hardly spoke to him before he set off for Boulogne.

"Another bad night?" enquired the old man after Michel had left.

"I'm afraid so" replied Josette as she poured a cup of coffee for Pascal.

"It must be difficult for you" he said.

"It is and I'm not putting up with it for much longer" she replied firmly.

Michel arrived at Monsieur Ricard's coach station in the Boulevard Chanzy, which is at the beginning of the commercial area in Boulogne, just after nine and parked the car. He made his way towards a very bright blue coach that had a number of smart, casually dressed people milling around it and he guessed that these were the Dutch tourist agents. As Michel approached the group, a man in a dark blue blazer broke away from the others and smiled before saying "you must be Michel Ronay."

"Oui, Monsieur."

"I'm Jean Ricard."

"Bon, I'm pleased to meet you, Monsieur Ricard" Michel

smiled as he shook hands with the dapper little man.

"Call me Jean, please."

"Merci, and I'm Michel."

"Bon, now come and meet our interpreter, Naomi, she's Roger's daughter."

"Oui, I know."

"And then I'll introduce you to our Dutch friends."

"Certainly."

"It's the first time we've had any Dutch agents come to us for tours and I'm keen to impress them" said Jean his eyes twinkling with anticipation.

"Any new business must be good" replied Michel as a young attractive woman came up to Jean.

"Ah, Naomi, this is Monsieur Ronay……"

"Michel, please" he interrupted as he took her delicate hand and shook it gently.

"Pleased to meet you, you're Uncle Henri's cousin from Marseille" she smiled.

"Oui, Naomi."

"I've heard a lot about you" she smiled again.

"Shame" replied Michel and she laughed.

"Bon, now come and meet our Dutch friends" said Jean as he guided Michel towards the agents. Jean Ricard was a precise man who obviously planned everything in advance as every agent wore a smart blue badge that matched the colour of the coach, and declared their Christian name in gold. Michel shook hands with them and was glad when he had been introduced to all twenty. At the end, Naomi pinned his badge on and smiled as he said "at last I know who I am." They boarded the coach and when they were all seated Jean stood up at the front with a microphone.

"Mesdames and Messieurs, let me officially welcome you aboard one of Tour Ricard's luxury coaches, today our interpreter is Naomi, although I know that you all speak French….." At that there was some laughter "and our driver is Pierré, a man with a lot of experience and panache." There was a muted chorus of 'bon' at that.

"Also joining us is Monsieur Michel Ronay, a prominent local business man, who besides running a very successful operation on the Cote d'Azure, from Marseille to Monte Carlo, is expanding his business empire to include this region and Normandy." Michel beamed as he approved of Jean's style, so similar to his own and a chorus of 'oh's' in approval met this statement and Michel nodded in all directions.

"So you see, Tour Ricard is very much under the microscope today and we will do our very best to ensure that you all enjoy the trip this morning and are impressed by what we have to offer. When we arrive back here at midday you will be the guests of Tour Ricard for a buffet lunch and we will be joined by the Mayor of Boulogne, Monsieur Pierré Laureons." There was a gasp of approval at that and Michel was suitably impressed and rather regretted the fact that he had agreed to meet Sophia at Le Café des Arts.

"So, without further ado, I'll ask Pierré to move off on our trip around the local area" said Jean as the agents gave him a round of applause "and either Naomi or myself will be giving you a running commentary en route." He sat down, next to Naomi at the front to further applause as Pierré, resplendent in matching light blue blazer, eased the coach forward and out of the Tour Ricard station. Michel was sitting at the rear of the coach, next to a plump middle aged woman who had the name 'Anna' pinned to her heaving bosom.

"So, Michel, you're from Monte Carlo?" she enquired with a smile.

"Well Monaco is included in my operations" replied Michel.

"How exciting, I expect you meet a lot of rich and influential people" she said coyly.

"Quite a few."

"Anyone I should know?"

"I'm afraid that I can't divulge any names, I have to maintain my professional integrity at all times" he replied.

"I do understand, but can't you give me a hint?"

"Only if you promise to keep it absolutely confidential" he whispered.

"Oh, I will, I will, I promise" she whispered back.

"Bon, then I'll………"

"Now we're just leaving the south of the town and heading on the coast road to Le Touquet, and for those of you that haven't been there before, I promise that you will be impressed by this chic, extension of Paris and everything French" interrupted Jean with his microphone. A muted chorus of 'oh's' greeted that and before Jean sat down he handed the microphone to Naomi.

"Now on your left you'll see one of the remnants of the second world war, it's a pill box built by the Germans as they expected the Allies to launch the invasion both here and at Calais." There was murmuring at that and when it had died down, Naomi continued " luckily, Le Touquet missed any serious damage during the conflict and you will see many older buildings still intact."

"So tell me about someone famous" whispered Anna as Naomi paused for a moment.

"Well, there's a very well known politician, he has direct links with the President you understand, who I see on a regular basis……."

"And on our right is the memorial to the Free French who fought alongside the Allies after the Normandy landings" said Naomi with fervour.

"Go on, Michel" pleaded Anna.

"Look, this might be a bit difficult, so why don't we wait for a moment when we can talk quietly together?"

"Alright, Michel, but I can hardly wait, I'm just dying to know" she whispered. A woman's curiosity knows no limits and is a complete mystery to all men who struggle with that often heard statement 'I want to know' and when questioned 'why?' reply with one word, 'because….'

Pierré eased the swishing blue coach along the coast road to Le Touquet before driving past the busy airport and into the Avenue du General de Gaulle. As it passed Sophia's villa Michel was surprised to see Evette and a man loading two suitcases into the boot of a car parked on the driveway. The coach was passed the scene in a flash but Michel was concerned by what he had witnessed. The running commentary continued as Pierré navigated the coach around Le Touquet before heading off towards Montreuil Sur Mer. Jean regaled the Dutch agents with the long history of the town from the ninth century onwards and commenting on famous people, like Victor Hugo, who was inspired to write Les Miserables after staying there. The agents were suitably impressed and a chorus of 'oh's' punctuated Jean's flowery descriptions of the medieval town. The coach shook on the cobbled streets and Michel, suffering with the hangover from last nights activities, was glad when the quick tour of Montreuil was over and they were back on a tarmac road heading for Abbeville where they were scheduled to stop for coffee. Everything had been arranged to the last detail and when Pierré brought the coach to a halt right outside McArthur's Bar, the agents followed Jean into the warm interior whilst Naomi and Michel remained at the rear to ensure that no one was left un-escorted.

"Come and sit with me" smiled Anna as she waited by the door of the bar for Michel.

"Oui, certainly, Anna" he replied and followed her to a table in the corner. As they sat down two more agents joined them, Jan and Pieter, much to Anna's disappointment. After introductions Pieter asked " so, how's business in Monaco?"

"Very good" replied Michel.

"Michel's been telling me all about the influential people he does business with" Anna exaggerated.

"Really?" said Jan as the barman brought coffee for them on a tray.

"Oui" replied Michel and continued " but I can't say too much in here, you understand."

"Of course" nodded Pieter.

"But what might be of interest to you is my special service to important clients" Michel half whispered and on hearing that their eyes lit up and they leaned forward to catch his every word.

"Go on" said Pieter.

"My organisation can offer exclusive boat trips on elegant, twenty metre boats, fully equipped for special activities at sea" said Michel as he spooned sugar into his black coffee.

"How many clients can you take at a time?" asked Jan.

"No more than ten we want to keep it very select" replied Michel to which they all nodded and said 'ah'.

"Then there is our night time activities."

"We all want to hear about those" said Pieter as the other two nodded.

"We can arrange an expensive dinner for a very small number followed by an evening in the Casino at Le Touquet, where I am a frequent guest and acknowledged to be a very lucky person at the tables" said Michel with a smile.

"I like the sound of this" said Anna.

"Oui, and of course I would accompany select parties myself to ensure that everything went smoothly as well as being their lucky mascot."

"How lucky are you?" asked Pieter.

"The other night my client won just over a hundred and eighty thousand Francs" Michel replied before sipping his coffee.

"Wow!" exclaimed Pieter as the others opened their mouths in awe.

"How can we get our customers onto your client list?" asked Jan.

"If you'll give me your business cards, I'll contact you after this little jaunt is over" replied Michel. They each scrabbled for a card which they handed to him.

"Give us firm prices, Michel" said Pieter.

"Of course, and I suggest that all of you come on a select trip with me to see if it interests you" he smiled.

"You can be sure of that" said Anna.

"You'd come as the guests of my organisation, of course."

"That's very generous, Michel" said Jan.

"Not at all, my pleasure" he replied.

"Anything else we'd be interested in?" enquired Anna.

"Possibly."

"Well?"

"Part of my organisation owns a very select shoe salon in Le Touquet with the latest fashions from Paris and Milan……."

"Oh, my God, is there no end to this?" interrupted Anna.

"And for clients on our executive tours we are able to offer substantial reductions on the prices" Michel smiled as Anna took a deep breath. They all sat quietly and drank their coffee, seemingly quite overawed by Michel's organisation.

"I must find the ladies" said Anna as she stood up before wandering off.

"Michel" whispered Jan as soon as Anna was out of earshot.

"Oui."

"Some of our clients like to come on their own, without their wives, to enjoy the local amenities" Jan continued.

"Oui, I can understand that" replied Michel knowing what was coming next.

"Can your organisation arrange escorts for the evening?" Jan asked, his eyes glinting.

"Naturally, we have the contacts that can provide discreet ladies who will be pleased to offer their services as required" Michel replied.

"Wonderful" murmured Pieter.

"Have you got yourself a deal" said Jan as Jean then attracted the party's attention, informing them that the coach would be leaving in five minutes.

Pierré followed the coast road back toward Boulogne stopping for a while at Berck-Plage for the agents to stretch their legs and admire the quaint village on the coast whilst gazing out at the Channel. Anna stayed close to Michel who noticed Jan and Pieter circulating amongst the others and talking excitedly in Dutch. He was aware that soon all the agents were looking at him and Jean also realised something was going on. They boarded the sleek coach and made their way back to Tour Ricard's station where, after they had disembarked, each agent came up to Michel, handed him a card and said "call me."

Michel made his excuses to Jean Ricard, promising to contact him after he had discussed the morning's trip with Henri. Jean did not look too pleased and gave Michel a suspicious glance as he said 'au revoir' before escorting the Dutch into their buffet lunch with the mayor.

Michel drove as quickly as he could back to Le Café des Arts to meet Sophia, knowing that he was late and she would be waiting impatiently. He had to park some way past the restaurant in the Rue de Paris and hurried back to meet his lover. She was seated at her favourite table in the alcove looking very chic in a dark blue two piece costume over a cream blouse. She looked radiant as usual and a little angry.

"Here you are at last, chérie" she grumbled.

"I'm sorry, ma petite, but I had to go on one of Henri's organised trips" he said.

"You poor thing."

"Oui, and you'll say that again when I tell you all about the boat trip I had yesterday" he replied as the waiter arrived with the menus.

"Never mind about that, I've had a terrible morning, absolutely terrible" she said grimly.

"Oh, ma chérie, what's gone wrong?"

"I was expecting Charles this morning but he 'phoned from London and said he wouldn't be back 'til this afternoon and I wanted us to be together on the beach" she said as she dabbed her handkerchief at one tearful eye.

"Never mind."

"And then when I got home from shopping just now, there was a note from Evette, telling me that she was leaving right away, the little bitch!"

"Mon Dieu!"

"She's just gone, heaven knows where, what am I to do, chérie?"

"I don't know for the moment" he replied.

"I mean, I really can't manage without her."

"I understand."

"Help me, chérie" she wailed as the waiter arrived to take their order and Michel politely told him that they were not ready yet.

"Let's eat while I think about it" said Michel calmly as he perused the extensive menu.

He chose bouillabaisse followed by boeuf en daube and as Sophia was too upset to make her mind up she ordered the same. Michel decided on a bottle of St. Emillion to accompany the meal and when they were alone, he said "I saw Evette this morning."

"Where?"

"Outside your villa with a man and they were putting suitcases into a car."

"Mon Dieu, what time was this?"

"About half past ten, I can't be sure."

"What were you doing there?"

"I was going past on Henri's coach trip with a load of Dutch travel agents."

"Oh."

"And I wondered what she was doing."

"Obviously leaving me!"

The waiter arrived with the soup and provided a welcome distraction.

"You'll feel better when you've eaten" said Michel gently as he started on the bouillabaisse. They did not speak again until they had finished the soup and had tasted the claret.

"Here's to us" he said and she managed a half smile when they touched glasses.

The boeuf was very tender and they finished the main course quite quickly and then ordered coffee as Michel sensed that she wanted to leave the Café as soon as possible.

"Let's go to our spot on the beach to talk" she said impatiently and Michel nodded and called for l'addition.

They went in her car and they hardly spoke until she pulled up in the little car park by the dunes.

"I just wanted a nice afternoon with you and my bloody husband and my silly maid have contrived to cock it all up for me" she said angrily.

"What time is Charles due back from London?"

"Oh, he said about three, but that means nothing, he's often late" she replied.

"Do you have to be at home when he arrives?"

"He's says he wants to talk to me about something or other, I don't know what I'm sure" she replied.

"You'd better be there then."

"I suppose so, but I wanted to spend some time with you, and what am I going to do without Evette?"

"Get another maid as soon as possible" said Michel.

"Mon Dieu, what a performance that is!"

"Go to an agency."

"That's hopeless, the little tarts they send you are either foreigners, thieves or drunks."

"Surely not."

"I promise you."

"OK, well advertise for one then" said Michel hopefully.

"In Le Touquet?"

"Oui."

"Finding a maid with references around here is impossible, there's too much money sloshing about so they can be bloody fussy who they work for" she replied.

"It seems you're stuck then" said Michel and at that she began to cry.

"I'm so unhappy, Michel, nothing ever goes right."

"You won a lot of money at the Casino the other night, so it's not all bad" he replied.

"That only replaced what I lost before." Michel gulped at that and said "look, why don't you go home and wait for your husband to arrive, I'm sure he'll have an answer for you." She nodded and dried her tears. Michel then kissed her and smiled.

"Come on, cheer up, things can only get better" he said positively.

They drove back to the Rue de Paris and with kisses and 'au revoirs', parted company, Sophia to her villa and Michel to the salon to brief Henri on the trip with Jean Ricard.

Michel bounded up the stairs to Henri's office and with a flourish tossed all the Dutch business cards on the desk in front of his cousin.

"And what are these?"

"Business, Henri, very lucrative business."

"So you had a successful morning then."

"Certainly did" replied Michel as he slumped into his chair.

"Tell me more."

"All of them, Henri, want to send clients, and I insisted on wealthy ones only, on our executive boat trips, restaurant and Casino evenings."

"Bravo, Michel, but we haven't arranged anything with local restaurants or the Casino" said Henri.

"Not yet, but we will do pretty quickly" replied Michel.

"And they've all agreed to do business with us?" asked Henri as he looked at several of the cards before him.

"Oui, when we're ready, I've just got to 'phone them with available dates and firm prices and they'll do the rest."

"Michel, that's brilliant!"

"I thought you'd be pleased."

"I am."

"On top of all that" he lowered his voice at this point "we've been asked to provide discreet lady escorts for some very important clients to help relieve the stress of big business."

"I'll leave that to you, Michel."

"Suits me."

There was a knock at the door and Elaine entered.

"Sorry to interrupt, Monsieur Henri, but Madame Giennois is asking for you, she wants your opinion on a larger fitting on several pairs of shoes."

"I'll be down in a moment, Elaine."

"Oui, Monsieur Henri." When they were alone, Henri said "I'm sure that some of these women just want me to feel their feet."

"Well I'm sure you have a soft touch" replied Michel with a grin.

"They're funny creatures."

"And so unpredictable" replied Michel as his cousin left the office to attend to Madame Giennois. Michel sat in Henri's chair and looked through the business cards until he found Anna's, he then made a note of her telephone number. He sat quietly gazing out of the picture window whilst contemplating the events of the day. He hoped that Sophia would not cause any more problems for him and he was uncertain what to do about her. Maria then entered his thoughts and without hesitation he picked up the 'phone and dialled her number.

"Hello" said Maria brightly.

"Bonjour, ma petite."

"Ah, Michel, ça va?"

"Oui."

"Bon."

"Have you recovered completely from last night?" he asked.

"Almost, and you?"

"Not quite."

"I can understand."

"I'm sorry we didn't have more time to relax together" he said.

"So am I."

"And next time you want me to help one of your friends, ask them to lunch so we can get rid of them before dinner." She laughed at that and replied in a sensuous whisper "oui, chérie, I'd like a nice long session with you, without any interruption, so we could explore each others fantasy's and go really deep."

"Oh, oui, I want to go very deep with you" he replied.

"And dirty."

"Oui, deep and dirty" he whispered.

"Stop now, chérie, I'm getting hot, wet and randy."

"Change the subject then, have you heard from Edith?"

"Non, but I know she'll 'phone, probably tonight."
"Give her my love, poor thing."
"I will, now, when are you coming to see me?"
"Tomorrow."
"Bon, come to dinner at about seven" she said.
"I will, ma chérie."
"Then we can deeply explore so much together" she said.
"Oh, so deeply, au revoir."
"Au revoir, chérie." As Michel replaced the 'phone he heard a noise coming from the stockroom and he went to investigate. The door was slightly ajar and he heard a muffled murmur before he peered in to see Henri and Elaine in a close embrace kissing passionately. Madame Giennois was either totally satisfied or waiting for more shoes downstairs, so Michel decided to leave them to it and return to Henri's office where he sat in his own chair. He had been there for only a moment when the telephone rang and Henri rushed in looking flushed.
"You could have answered it" he said.
"Didn't like to" replied Michel as Henri snatched up the receiver.
"Hello, bonjour, Monsieur Henri's salon." Michel heard a woman's voice on the other end before Henri thrust the 'phone at him and said "it's Madame Christiane for you!"
"Oh, merci, sorry to have disturbed you next door" replied Michel as Henri's face went blood red before he returned to Elaine in the stockroom.
"Hello, chérie" said Michel.
"Oh, Michel, something terrible has happened" she wailed.
"What is it?"
"Charles has left me."
"What?"
"He's left me, he says he's going to get a divorce!"
"I'm so sorry, ma petite."
"Oui, you'd better come and see me."
"I can't, chérie, I'm in the middle of a business meeting with……."
"He's naming you……."
"What?"
"He's naming you as my lover and getting a divorce on the

grounds of adultery!"

"I'll be right there" replied Michel with cold fear gripping his heart.

"And hurry, chérie."

"I will, and er, is Charles there now?"

"Non, he's left for Paris but he'll be back tomorrow."

"Bon, that'll give us time to think."

"Oui."

"I'll be with you soon, chérie."

"Just hurry, Michel."

"I will." Michel replaced the receiver and felt a cold chill run up and down his spine.

"Henri" he called "I have to go now, I'll catch you tomorrow some time."

"OK, Michel" replied Henri from the stockroom as Michel descended the stairs to the busy salon.

Arriving at the villa, Michel found Sophia in floods of tears and he poured them both a large brandy before he sat down on the settee with his mistress, who looked old and somewhat bedraggled.

"Can you believe it, chérie?" she whispered.

"Non, I can't."

"First Evette and then Charles, I feel like a sinking ship" she moaned.

"Courage, ma chérie."

"What am I to do?"

"I don't know yet, but we'll think of something" he replied.

"What?"

"We'll get some legal advice, I'm seeing Monsieur Robardes tomorrow about my divorce, and I'll ask him" said Michel firmly.

"Would you?"

"Oui, there must be a way out of this mess" replied Michel with courage before he took a large gulp of brandy to support his bravado.

"I hope so, chérie" she said as tears rolled down her cheeks once again.

"There's always an answer to everything" he said positively.

"I'm glad you think so."

"I do." They remained silent for a while, both deep in fearful thought.

"Tell me now, exactly what did Charles say to you?" asked Michel when he had finished his brandy.

"He said he wanted a divorce because he knew that you and I had been seeing one another and we'd started an affair."

"How could he know that?"

"Someone must have told him."

"Who?"

"Well, I think it was Evette" replied Sophia.

"Mon Dieu! The bitch!" exclaimed Michel.

"I know."

"Are you certain it was Evette?"

"Oui."

"How can you be so sure?"

"Charles said that you'd borrowed his dinner suit and only Evette knew that" replied Sophia as her tears began again.

"The little bitch!"

"And obviously that's why she left in a hurry today" whispered Sophia.

"Of course."

"I expect Charles paid her well for all the dirt and I wonder what else she may have told him about us" she said sorrowfully.

"I wonder."

"I'm desperately worried about money" she whispered.

"Why?"

"I know Charles and he's a hard bastard, he'll cut me off without a penny if he can" she whimpered.

"He can't do that legally."

"Oh, non, you wait and see what his Parisian lawyer friends can manage" she replied.

"Look, cheer up, it can't all be bad" said Michel.

"Oh, oui, it can, I've saved the worst bit 'til last" she replied.

"Go on" said Michel with his heart in his mouth.

"I don't know whether it's true or not, or whether he's just trying to hurt me terribly, but......" she paused and dabbed her eyes "he said he's fallen in love with an English woman at the Bank in London, I mean can you imagine that? A bloody English woman! I ask you!"

"Mon Dieu, he must be mad."

"She's a secretary or something, called Dierdre."

"It's not true, he's lying, a man like your husband would never get involved with an English woman called Dierdre" said Michel with conviction.

"Really?" she asked in a hopeful tone.

"I'm certain, chérie" he replied and she smiled.

"But if it is true, how could he be unfaithful to me?"

"I can't imagine" said Michel, somewhat surprised at Sophia's double standards.

"I've been a good wife, never refused him anything, even tolerated his kinky sex games and never complained" she whimpered.

"Really?" asked Michel, his curiosity aroused somewhat.

"Oui, I just can't believe he's done this to me."

"It's a tragedy" whispered Michel.

"If he divorces me, can we get married right away?" she asked bleary eyed. Michel's mind went into free fall as he tried to stabilise his thoughts and give a coherent answer to his mistress.

"Well, it's early days yet and…….."

"I have to have a husband, Michel, I just can't be on my own, I just can't" she interrupted.

"I understand ma chérie……"

"And I do love you, Michel."

"I know….."

"But do you love me?"

"Of course I do" he replied with little pangs of guilt stabbing at his conscience.

"I'm so glad that you love me too" she whispered and then kissed him passionately.

"I'm always here for you" he said

"I know I can always rely on you, chérie."

"Always."

"Bon, we'll be so happy after we're married" she replied as she snuggled up to him.

"I think I need another brandy" he said nervously.

"I'll join you, chérie." As he poured the drinks he wondered how he was ever going to get out of this ever deepening quagmire of involvement.

"You can't be alone tonight with all this upset so………"

"It's alright, Michel, I 'phoned my sister, Hélène, and I'm going to stay with her tonight" she interrupted and relief flooded over him.

"Bon, does she live far away?"

"Non, at Deauville."

"How long will it take you to get there?"

"About an hour or so" she replied.

"Better go soon then, before it gets too dark."

"Oui, good idea."

"You'll feel a lot better after you've seen Hélène" said Michel with a smile.

"Oui, but I feel happy now I know that what ever happens I've got you with me for ever" she said brightly.

"Oui" he mumbled.

"And I'll tell Hélène all about us" she smiled.

"Oui, and give her my love."

"I will, and when I get back tomorrow I'll tell you everything she says over lunch at Le Café."

"Ma chérie, I'm seeing Monsieur Robardes in the morning and I may not……"

"About one, as usual, and you can tell me all about Monsieur Robardes then" she interrupted.

"Chérie……"

"Michel, please don't upset me, I've had enough today, I promise you!"

"OK, Le Café at one, then."

"Bon" she smiled and kissed him passionately.

Michel left the villa with a heavy heart and drove home to find Josette in the lounge clutching a large glass of wine.

"Hello, ma chérie" he ventured.

"I hope you're going out tonight" she said with a sullen face.

"Oui, I am."

"What time?"

"About eight" he replied.

"You're not certain exactly when?"

"Non, because I don't know how long you'll take to get ready" he replied with a smile.

"Me?"

"Oui."
"Where are we going?"
"To Flavio's for a celebration dinner" he replied.
"What are we celebrating?"
"A huge business deal with all the Dutch agents that I met this morning" he smiled.
"Bon, I'm glad it's all going so well for you."
"For us, chérie" he corrected.
"Don't think so, Michel."
"Why?"
"What have you and Henri been up to?"
"Nothing, ma chérie, why?"
"Do you know about Henri's new apartment in the Boulevard de la Canche?"
"I think he mentioned it" replied Michel casually.
"Well, someone who lives there told Jackie he's rented a place and I've had her, Josephine and Pascal on at me all afternoon about it!"
"Oh, mon Dieu" whispered Michel.
"And I don't know how you're involved but believe me, Henri's in for a real tongue lashing from Jackie and her mother when he gets home tonight!"
"Mon Dieu."
"So, don't deny anything, please, because I don't want to know, I really don't" she said with conviction.
"I promise you, I've had nothing to do……."
"Michel, don't promise me anything, I don't want to know!"
"OK, OK, let's just get dressed and go to dinner then" he said with a sigh.
"And, by the way, Pascal says the house needs to be rewired and we've no electricity upstairs again" she said firmly.

It was well after eight that Guy welcomed them to Flavio's and showed them to a romantic candle lit table for two at the very back of the dining room. Michel knew that he had to work hard to win back his fiancé and certain sacrifices would have to be made. Josette looked very lovely in a red dress with a high neck line and as usual her hair and make up were impeccable. Michel wondered what ever was in his mind that made him neglect and deceive this lovely young woman whom he truly loved.

"I'll have the foie gras truffe to start" she said bringing him back to reality.

"Bon."

"And Châteaubriant to follow" she smiled.

"Good choice, I'll have the moules marinieres and join you with the Châteaubriant" said Michel before he perused the wine list.

"It's very nice here and good to be alone" she smiled.

"Oui, and it is my great pleasure to be with you, ma chérie" he whispered.

"Is it really?"

"Oui."

"Wouldn't you rather be out somewhere doing business or whatever you call it?"

"Non, I wouldn't" he replied with conviction and Josette believed him as her eyes shone with love. Guy appeared at that moment and took their order and complemented Michel on his choice of Burgundy to accompany the meal. When they were alone, she asked "what's going to become of us in this place?"

"I don't know, chérie, some of the business opportunities look good, but there seems to be so many problems."

"I agree" she nodded.

"And I don't know whether Henri's a hundred per cent behind it all."

"What makes you think that?"

"Well, his salon is very profitable and he's obviously very involved with it and although he says he wants to step away from it, I'm not sure he can."

"So you'll end up having to do it all on your own?"

"Oui, I expect so."

"And he'll get half the profit?"

"Oui."

"That's not fair."

"Non." The starters arrived and they spoke little until they had finished and sampled the Burgundy.

"So, do you really want to stay here and struggle on in hope?" she asked her eyes glinting in the candle light.

"I'd like to give it a good try" he replied.

"Well, if that's what you really want, then I'll help you all I can, chérie" she smiled.

"I love you so much, Josette."

"I love you too, chérie, although I sometimes wonder why."

They talked of happy times past in Marseille and Michel was as charming and gentle as he could possibly be, entertaining the love of his life whilst enjoying the very best cuisine.

When they eventually arrived home and wandered up to bed with candles to light their way, they were both happy and relaxed. They made love gently but passionately for a long while before they eventually fell asleep entwined in each others arms.

CHAPTER 12

Josette was bright as a button over breakfast and Michel was relieved to see her so.

"Is Pascal coming today to fix the wiring upstairs?" he asked as he sipped his coffee.

"Non, he said he's done as much as he can and we really need the whole place rewired by someone who knows what they're doing" she replied.

"Well, Henri told me not to let him touch anything" said Michel with a sigh.

"I think he was right, I've noticed that the paint is beginning to peel in the hall and in the bathroom" she said calmly.

"Oh, bloody good" said Michel.

"Never mind, it doesn't matter" she smiled and Michel felt comfortable and re-assured by her gentle reply.

"I'm seeing Monsieur Robardes at ten thirty to arrange the divorce" he said.

"Oh, Michel, I'll be so happy when you're free to marry me" she replied.

"I will be as well, I promise you" he smiled.

"I know that once we're together, everything will be alright."

"I'm sure that's true" and he lent across the table and kissed her quickly on the lips.

Michel was uneasy when he pulled up in the car park at the salon and wondered how his cousin had fared last night with Jackie and her mother. He found Henri in his office drinking black coffee with Elaine in attendance..

"Bonjour, Monsieur Michel" she said as she nodded at Henri and left the two men.

"Are you alright, Henri?"

"Non, Michel, I'm not, I'm really not."

"Mon Dieu."

"Do you know what's happened?"

"Josette said that Jackie and her mother found out about your apartment."

"Oui, some bloody nosey, busy body at the apartments saw me

there, made enquiries and then 'phoned Jackie and said 'you and Henri will like living here, the sea view is so good'."

"Innocently done" said Michel.

"Innocent! Bollocks, I tell you, Michel, it was deliberate, there's a lot of people around here who are jealous of me and the salon."

"I'm sure that's true."

"And my wife and her bloody awful mother gave me hell last night" said Henri as he took another gulp of coffee.

"So what's going to happen now?" Michel asked.

"I don't know what to do, Elaine's telling me to leave Jackie so that we can be together….."

"If you do that then you'll have to forget Theresa" interrupted Michel.

"I realise that."

"So one way or another it's out of the frying pan and into the fire, eh?" grinned Michel

"I don't know why you find it so amusing" said Henri angrily.

"Because, dear Henri, you're beginning to realise the hard way exactly how easy it is to find yourself in a mess with women!"

"Oui, I suppose so."

"And I have more sympathy with you than you do with me" said Michel firmly.

"True."

"Well, I'm here to help and advise you, a shoulder to cry on if you need one."

"Merci, Michel."

"Now, I suggest you have another coffee, talk to Elaine about your future together while I pop along to Monsieur Robardes to arrange my divorce."

"Oui, bonne chance, Michel."

"I'll see you later."

As Michel descended the stairs he saw Elaine at the counter and caught her eye, he smiled as he approached her through the busy salon.

"Elaine."

"Oui, Monsieur Michel?"

"Henri's told me everything, and I think it would be a good idea if you went up to him now and talked to him."

“Oui, Monsieur” she smiled.

“He needs you.”

“Oh, oui, Monsieur Michel” she half whispered as only a woman can when she’s needed by the man she loves.

Michel arrived at Monsieur Robardes establishment on time and was kept waiting for only a few minutes before being shown into the notaire’s untidy office. After polite greetings Michel was waved to a seat and the interview began.

“So, Monsieur Ronay, I trust that you’re having no more problems with Madame Christiane?” That went in like a cold knife into his back and brought Sophia into the forefront of Michel’s thoughts.

“As a matter of fact…….” he paused as Monsieur Robardes smile vanished from his face and he looked over the top of his glasses at him.

“Do go on, Monsieur” said the notaire slowly and in a curious tone.

“Madame Christiane is now having a slight domestic problem with her husband.”

“What sort of problem may I ask?”

“He wants a divorce.”

“Really?”

“Oui, he has a new woman in his life, she’s English and called Dierdre.”

“And how does this unfortunate set of circumstances involve you, Monsieur?”

“He’s naming me as the other man.”

“Other man, Monsieur?”

“Oui, he’s getting a divorce because Madame Christiane is involved with me.”

“But the business contract has put that matter to rest, Monsieur.”

“It’s not the business that Monsieur Christiane is concerned about” replied Michel slowly.

“Oh, I see” replied the notaire as realisation dawned upon him.

“Oui, I’ve been seeing Madame Christiane socially” said Michel.

“And it has become very ‘close’ socially?”

“Precisely.”

“And her husband found out?”

“He was told by the maid.”

“How very indiscreet.”

“Oui” replied Michel.

“And may I ask, Monsieur, does you fiancé or present wife know of this matter?”

“Non.”

“I suggest we try and keep it that way.”

“Indeed, so, have you any advice for me?”

“Oui, you can either face the costly litigation that will surround a case brought by a wealthy man, such as Monsieur Christiane, or run away back to your home in Grambois and hide!”

“Mon Dieu!”

“Those are the options, Monsieur” smiled the notaire.

“And what about my divorce?”

“In the circumstances, unless you have something that we can present to the court, proving the breakdown of your marriage, I suggest you forget it for the time being.”

“Oh.”

“Have you anything we can present, Monsieur?”

“I can’t think at the moment” Michel replied.

“Then I would advise you to return home with your fiancé and think carefully about your next move before consulting legal opinion in Marseille.”

“You think so?”

“Monsieur, you need time to organise your very complicated personal life into a more manageable state before taking any action” smiled Monsieur Robardes.

“I see.”

“I hope you do.”

Michel left the office somewhat taken aback by what the notaire had said and headed straight for the Bar Americaine to reflect over a large brandy. From his seat in the corner he watched the passers by as they wandered along in the bright sunlight. He was confused and angry at himself and wished he could walk away from the situation that he was in and join the carefree people outside as they proceeded along the Rue de Londres, seemingly free from worry. It was the first time for a long while that he had been unsure what to do next when suddenly Antone's concerned face appeared in his mind, repeating the words 'it will be a catastrophe in Le Touquet.' He finished his drink and made his way back to the salon to see how his cousin was coping with the problems and difficult decisions that now faced him. Elaine was still with Henri and offered to make some more coffee for them both as Michel arrived in the office.

"Merci, Elaine" said Henri as she discreetly left them to talk.

"How did you get on then?" asked Henri as Michel slumped down on a chair.

"Not too good, and you?"

"Elaine's being really wonderful and I don't know what I'd do without her" replied Henri as he relaxed back in his executive chair and put his hands on his head.

"It helps if you can make decisions with someone you can trust by your side" said Michel.

"True."

"And you can trust Elaine."

"Oui."

"You have to ask yourself 'do I love her enough to leave Jackie?'" Henri remained silent whilst he gazed up at the ceiling, deep in thought.

"Oui, I do" replied Henri slowly.

"Then leave Jackie and move into your new apartment with Elaine and get a divorce."

"You think I should do that?"

"Oui, I do, otherwise you'll end up in the same, bloody awful mess I'm in!" Henri smiled at that and nodded.

"You're right."

"Keep your love life simple, that's the answer, I promise you." Elaine then arrived with the coffee and was followed un-noticed into the office by Charles Christiane. Henri saw him first and stood up as he recognised his angry countenance.

"Bonjour, Monsieur Christiane" stammered Henri as Michel leapt to his feet like a scalded cat and Elaine wobbled backwards into a filing cabinet, still clutching the tray of coffees.

"Is it, Monsieur?" queried Sophia's husband in a menacing tone.

"Oui, I think so" replied Henri.

"Possibly for some here but not a good day for everybody" he said as he glared at Michel.

"Mon Dieu" whispered Michel.

"I recognise you, Monsieur, from when I caught you at my home with my wife!" exclaimed Sophia's husband loudly as he pointed at Michel. Elaine put down the tray, gave a little nod and rushed out of the office.

"Oui, Monsieur Christiane, but as you know, I was only………" began Michel.

"You were only what, Monsieur?" interrupted the angry husband.

"I was only……."

"Having an affair with my wife, you greasy shit of a Marseille taxi driver!"

"Monsieur" pleaded Henri.

"And you can shut up, you bloody pathetic little shop keeper!"

"Mon Dieu!" exclaimed Henri before he snapped. Everything had obviously become too much for him in the last twenty four hours so he leaned across his desk and with one sharp jab he punched Monsieur Christiane on his nose.

"You've hit me, you bastard!" yelled Sophia's husband as he clutched his bleeding nose with one hand whilst attempting to punch Henri with the other. Michel grabbed at him in order to stop the flailing fist but only managed to unbalance the distraught husband and they both fell to the floor in a flurry of arms and legs.

"I'll have you both guillotined for this!" screamed Monsieur Christiane from the deep pile carpet.

"I don't think so, Monsieur" replied Michel as he struggled to his feet before helping the injured husband to his.

"My lawyers in Paris will destroy you both, by the time they've finished, you won't have enough money for the 'bus fare to get to the recruiting office of the French Foreign Legion!"

"It won't be a problem, I've many friends who are taxi drivers and they'll take us for free!" retorted Michel.

"I promise you that you won't be so cocky when I've finished with you!" shouted Charles.

"Monsieur, please sit down and let us get you something to drink" said Michel calmly.

"A good idea, I think we could all do with one" said Henri as he slumped back into his chair and called Elaine. Charles Christiane sat down and fumbled for a handkerchief in his pocket before holding it to his swollen nose.

"My manageress will get something from the first aid box and attend to you" said Henri calmly.

"Merci" replied the injured husband. Elaine arrived, looking concerned and nodded when Henri ordered three coffees and a bandage.

"So, where were we?" asked Henri calmly much to Michel's surprise.

"I came here peacefully to inform this man........" began Charles.

"Peacefully?" queried Henri.

"I don't think so, Monsieur" added Michel.

"Peacefully, to inform him that I intend to name him as co-respondent in my wife's adultery" said Charles with conviction.

"Go on" said Henri.

"And sue him for a substantial sum for destroying my marriage" concluded Charles.

"Bonne chance" replied Henri.

"I assure you, Monsieur......"

"Let me tell you about your wife" interrupted Henri and Charles was stunned into silence.

"She is a very lovely, elegant, sophisticated woman" and Charles smiled and nodded at the compliment, "but on the other hand, she's a two timing, spoilt, lazy, foul mouthed bitch that has caused Michel and me no end of trouble!" Charles mouth fell open at that and before anything else could be said Elaine arrived with three coffees, a cold compress and sticking plasters.

When Elaine had finished applying the cold compress followed by numerous plasters, Charles looked like a cross between a circus clown and Cyrano de Bergerac.

"I'm sorry about your nose, Monsieur" said Henri trying not to laugh as the irate husband attempted to sip his coffee without disturbing Elaine's handiwork.

"I shall sue you for assault, of course" replied Charles.

"Naturally" replied Henri in an unconcerned tone.

"And I assure you both that I am going ahead with a divorce and......" Charles began.

"Is that so you can marry Dierdre?" interrupted Michel. Charles mouth dropped and for a moment he was lost for words.

"How do you know about her?" enquired the bandaged husband.

"Who's Diedre?" asked Henri.

"His little bit of English on the side" replied Michel.

"Mon Dieu, you're all at it!" exclaimed Henri.

"You too, Henri" said Michel and Henri blushed.

"Are you having an affair with my wife as well?" asked Charles angrily.

"Non, Monsieur, I'm not" replied Henri.

"Thank heavens" whispered Charles.

"But by all accounts, most of Le Touquet is" said Henri.

"Oh, mon Dieu, the disgrace of it all" murmured Charles.

"You'll get over it" said Michel.

"Will I?"

"Oui, in time, because what you don't get over you die of" replied Michel with a smile.

"True."

"And you'll get over this and when you're safely married to Diedre and she's spending any money you've got left after the divorce settlement, you'll look back and laugh at it all" said Michel cheerfully.

"Mon Dieu! All this could ruin me" wailed Charles.

"Oui, I should think very carefully before you make a move to do anything" advised Michel.

"I don't take advice from Marseille taxi drivers" said Charles angrily.

"Pity, because he's not usually wrong about these things" said Henri.

"What d'you mean, Monsieur?" asked Charles.

"What I say, Michel has a world of experience of life and affairs of the heart......."

"I bloody bet he has, and soon his 'experiences' are going to come to a very abrupt end when my lawyers get......."

"Oui, oui, we know all about your powerful lawyer friends in Paris" interrupted Henri.

"Oh, really?"

"Oui, your wife threatens us regularly with them and I'm

assuming their the same friends that you know or is she involved with another lot?" queried Henri and Charles looked absolutely amazed at what Henri had just put to him.

"Well, I, er, er, I'll……" stammered Charles.

"Take Michel's advice and discuss the whole thing very carefully with your wife before coming to a hasty decision that you may regret for the rest of your life" said Henri calmly.

"Oui, and find out who are the lawyers your wife knows, just in case they're not your lot" said Michel.

"Oui, could be a tricky situation that could cost a lot in legal fees" nodded Henri.

"Oh, oui, those Parisian boys know how to charge" added Michel helpfully.

"Mon Dieu! You say my wife has threatened legal action against you?"

"Both of us and our business" replied Henri.

"Well, I never knew……"

"How could you, you're never at home" interrupted Michel.

"What has she been up to?"

"Our legal team have instructed us not to discuss the matter with anyone" replied Henri.

"Your legal team?"

"Oui" replied Henri.

"So if you want to find out, you'll have to ask your wife or your maid!" said Michel.

"Mon Dieu! What on earth has been going on" murmured Charles to himself.

"I'm sure you'll find out in due course" said Henri.

"Meanwhile, I suggest we all have another coffee to steady our nerves" said Michel.

"Good idea, you certainly look as if you need one before you go, Monsieur Christiane" replied Henri as he rang down for Elaine once more.

It was almost one o'clock when Charles Christiane left the salon to drive home to his empty villa, shaken and touching his bruised nose. His wife was already at Le Café des Arts waiting for Michel, who arrived soon after the allotted time, delayed by a conversation with Henri.

Michel joined Sophia in the alcove and smiled as he sat down.

“I’m sorry I’m a bit late, chérie, but Charles came to the salon…….”

“Mon Dieu!” she exclaimed.

“It’s alright, he’s not going to divorce you.”

“He said that?” she asked hopefully.

“Not in so many words, but he got the message loud and clear from Henri and me.”

“Oh, Michel, you’re wonderful, just wonderful…….”

“I know, I know” he replied as the waiter arrived with the menus and wine list.

“And how did you persuade him to………”

“I’m starving, so let’s eat first and then we can go to the beach and talk” he interrupted.

“Oh, oui, let’s do that” she smiled and perused the menu. For a change they hurried their meal as they were both anxious to get to the beach on the sunny afternoon to enjoy unbridled open air sex on the sand. Michel wanted to satisfy his mistress before returning to Josette to discuss their future together. They took Sophia’s car as usual and once they were on their way she bombarded him with questions about Charles. Michel told her everything that had happened in Henri’s office and when Sophia asked about Diedre, Michel embroidered his answer.

“She means nothing to him, I promise you” he said with conviction.

“Bon, I didn’t think there was anything in it” she replied confidently.

“Nothing at all.”

“I mean, how could some silly English secretary be of any interest to Charles when he’s got me?”

“Exactly what I thought” replied Michel.

“Oh, chérie, you’ve made me so happy today” she said with a smile.

“Bon, and soon I’ll make you a lot happier” he grinned.

“I know and am I ready for you” she half whispered.

After they had parked in the usual place they made their way along the beach to their lovers spot in the dunes where she spread the blanket and opened the case containing the brandy.

“This is nice” she said as she poured two large tots for them.

“It is and the sun is quite warm for this time of year, so, we won't be cold when we're 'au natural' in a minute" he smiled. She laughed and handed him his brandy, they touched glasses and declared their love and happy future together.

"Now, tell, me Monsieur, what are you going to do to me today?" she whispered.

"Anything you want me too" he replied.

"Oh, that sounds very naughty."

"Good."

"I think I'll stand with my legs open facing the sea……." she began.

"I like that pose" he interrupted.

"Then when my body has soaked up enough of the sea air, I'll lay face down on the blanket whilst you gently massage my back."

"I'll do that" he replied.

"And then you can kiss my bottom and carry on all over until I tell you to stop."

"The pleasure's all mine" he whispered.

"When I'm ready you can have me from the back, slowly, and in time with the sea" she said.

"Bon."

"I like it like that" she whispered.

"So do I" he replied.

"So don't hurry, I want a long, slow session."

"Of course" Michel smiled and took a sip of brandy. She finished her drink and stood up, looked around the deserted beach and undid her cream blouse before discarding it. Her white lace brassiere followed and Michel marvelled at her pointed breasts that hardly dropped when they were released from the confines of the scanty garment. She undid her black skirt and let it fall, revealing that she was naked except for stockings held up with cream garters.

"Do you approve?" she asked as she stood facing him with her hands on her hips.

"Oh, oui, I certainly do."

"Bon" and with that she turned towards the sea and opened her legs. Michel just gazed at her exquisite form and sipped his brandy as she lifted her arms up above her head.

"This is wonderful" she said.

"It certainly is" he replied. She stood for quite a while,

occasionally moving her arms to form a circle above her head, whilst he just descended into deep thought about Josette and the future.

"I'm ready, ma chérie" she said as she turned to face him.

"Bon." She sank down elegantly onto the blanket and rolled over onto her stomach and faced the sea. Michel moved to her side and placed his hands gently in the middle of her back, then he slid them forward up to her shoulders in a slow but smooth rhythm.

"Oh, that's so good" she murmured as he carried on, increasing the pressure very slightly. Touching her body in this way made him even more aroused and he had to undo his trousers to release his rigid penis.

"I want this to go on for ever" she whispered as she turned her head to one side and he bent forward to kiss her cheek.

"Oh, Michel, I do love you so."

"I know, chérie, and I love you."

"If Charles had divorced me, would you have married me?"

"Of course, chérie" he replied with a heavy heart and she smiled at that.

"I think we're made for each other, don't you?"

"Oui, we are" he replied and added a little more pressure to her back.

"Mon Dieu, that's good." He then moved further down and began massaging her from her legs up over her bottom and then up to her shoulders. She moaned gently in ecstasy as he started to kiss the cheeks of her bottom between the long strokes.

"Chérie, would you like me to have my nipples pierced?" she asked.

"If you like" he replied.

"Then I could wear gold rings in them and you could pull me down with them."

"I'd like that."

"I'd have to do anything you wanted" she whispered.

"This is true" he replied applying more pressure between bottom kisses.

"And suppose we had some ankle chains made so that you could fix them round the bed posts to keep my legs open whilst you had me" she said between gentle gasps.

"A good idea" he replied, encouraging her fantasy.

"Oh, Michel, I'm ready for you now" she whispered. He slipped off his trousers and pants before gently lowering himself onto her. She opened her legs and arched up so that he could enter her with ease. She was moist, warm and very soft as he slowly penetrated her.

"Chérie, this is too good" she murmured as he began a slow rhythm in time with the waves breaking on the shore. He determined to keep going as long as possible and so he turned his thoughts away from Sophia to Ricky's bar in Marseille and all his friends who frequented its welcoming interior. He remembered the happy relaxed evenings with Antone, Jacques and René not to mention Cyril Gerrard, the silly Gendarme, who plagued his life with criminal involvements. His mind wandered to Grambois as he kept up the smooth, relentless rhythm in time with the waves breaking on the deserted beach. Suddenly he became aware of Sophia gasping and whispering "oh, Michel, Michel……."

"Ma chérie" he whispered in her ear.

"Now, Michel, now! Mon Dieu! Mon Dieu!" she called and arched her body up to get every inch of him deep inside. He was caught out for a moment and then speeding up rapidly he rammed himself into her compliant body as she screamed out "Mon Dieu!" He remained hard inside her as he waited for their joint ecstasy to subside.

"Oh, chérie, that was so good" she gasped as he kissed the back of her neck.

"It was wonderful" he replied.

"I'm so happy that we will be able to be together always, now that Charles is not going to divorce me."

"So am I" he said, feeling relieved at the thought of her marriage remaining intact.

"We have all the summer to look forward to" she said.

"Oui."

"We can meet for lunch at the Café and then come here for our afternoon sessions of love" she smiled.

"Oui."

"And I know that when we go to the Casino together we'll be very lucky."

"Bon" replied Michel as he realised that Sophia was planning both their lives for the foreseeable future using Charles' money and there was little chance of escape.

"It's been wonderful this afternoon, chérie, but I have to go, business you understand" he said gently.

"Of course, ma petite" she replied. He released himself from her lovely body and began to get dressed.

"Will I see you tonight?" she asked.

"Er, perhaps later" he replied.

"OK."

"I'll call you when I'm free" he smiled.

"Bon."

When they were dressed they made their way back along the beach to the car holding hands with Sophia discussing more of her future plans for them both. They drove back to Le Touquet and parted outside the Café des Arts with kisses, smiles and 'au revoirs' before Michel went home.

"Ma chérie" he said as he kissed Josette.

"I didn't expect you back this early" she replied.

"Well here I am" he smiled.

"How did you get on with Monsieur Robardes?" she asked.

"Very well and I'll tell you all about it later."

"Later?"

"Oui, I'm taking you out right now to have a drink and a long talk" he smiled.

"What now?"

"Oui, right now."

"What about dinner tonight?"

"We'll be eating out, ma chérie" he replied.

"Bon."

"So get yourself ready."

Half an hour later Michel and Josette entered the Bar Americaine and sat at the empty corner table by the window. Michel ordered coffee for them both before he took her hand and looking deep into her lovely eyes said "I love you very much, chérie."

"I love you too" she replied quietly.

"And I know that you've been more than unhappy here in Le Touquet" he said.

"Well, it has been a bit of a shaky start but……."

"You've been very patient with me and I appreciate that."

"Oh, bon, chérie."

"I also know that you want the business to be a success........"

"I do, chérie" she interrupted.

"But I think it's not going to work" he said with conviction.

"Why?" she asked wide eyed in amazement.

"There are so many outside influences that are going to cause problems and cost money."

"Like what?" she asked as their coffee's arrived.

"Henri and his marriage for a start" he replied.

"Oui, Jackie was going mad when she found out about his apartment" she said with a smile.

"Oui, I bet and of course he plans to have Elaine live with him."

"I wondered about her."

"I caught them in the stock room......"

"Not doing it amongst the shoes?" she queried indignantly.

"Only kissing."

"Thank heavens for that" she replied in a slightly relieved tone.

"I think its being going on for some time" said Michel with confidence.

"Well I can't blame him, Jackie is a bit of a bitch and her mother is worse."

"And you know that all women turn into their mothers one day."

"In that case the best thing he can do is leave her" she replied.

"Oui, I agree, but can you imagine the problems that that is going to cause?"

"Oui."

"On top of that, Henri's salon is a very profitable business and I don't think he's going to let it go, despite what he says."

"I'm sure you're right, chérie."

"I think I am" replied Michel.

"So, what are you telling me?" Michel paused and took a sip of coffee before he answered.

"I think we should go back to Marseille" he said slowly and in a positive tone.

"Oh, Michel, I'm so pleased to hear you say that, I really am" she said with a broad smile and twinkling eyes.

"I thought you would be" he said as tears began rolling down her cheeks.

"Oh, Michel….."
"Please don't cry, ma chérie, please."
"I can't help it, I've been so unhappy here."
"I realised that."
"I only wanted it to be a great success for you but……."
"I know, I'm sure if we stay it'll be a catastrophe" he replied and she nodded.
"So, dry your eyes, drink your coffee and then we'll go home and pack!"
They were soon back in number 19 filling up their suitcases as quickly as possible.
"I'm going to the salon to tell Henri it's all over and while I'm gone you finish the packing and then 'phone the agents in Marseille to see if our flat is still vacant" he smiled.
"Oh, oui, Michel" she replied excitedly.
"When I get back, you can give Eloise a call in Macon and see if we can stay with her tomorrow night on our way back."
"Oh, oui, oui" she replied.
"I'll be back soon" he said as he kissed his joyful fiancé.
Henri was still in his office when Michel arrived.
"I'm glad Monsieur Christiane went home without another fight" said Michel as Henri looked up from his desk.
"Oui, but it's not all over yet" replied Henri.
"What makes you say that?"
"He 'phoned and asked for you, I told him you were out and then he complained that his wife was missing" said Henri.
"Oh."
"I guess you were somewhere or other with her" grinned Henri.
"Oui, I was."
"She'll have a difficult time with him when she gets home" said Henri.
"Shame."
"Still, I expect she can hold her own."
"I'm sure she can" replied Michel.
"I think he'll sue me for assault first before he gets started on a divorce" said Henri.
"Possibly, but I bet he'll think twice about the divorce" replied Michel.
"Why?"

"Money dear Henri, money."

"Oui, she'll take him to the cleaners…….."

"And back."

"Oui" nodded Henri.

"The wealthy are very touchy about money."

"Mon Dieu, imagine being married to Sophia Christiane" mused Henri.

"Can we talk about the business?" asked Michel anxious to change the subject.

"Of course."

"This is difficult, Henri, and I'll come to the point" said Michel as Henri's face clouded with concern.

"Go on."

"I think our tourist business is a great idea and could be very profitable……."

"But?" interrupted Henri.

"I don't think it's going to work" replied Michel.

"Why not?"

"Because of all the outside influences that are going to affect it."

"Like what?" asked Henri.

"Our private lives and commitments will cause major problems and……."

"That's nonsense" interrupted Henri.

"Listen to me for a moment and think about it all seriously."

"OK."

"Firstly, you've got a very good business here and no matter what you say, I promise you that your involvement here will take up nearly all of your time."

"I can assure you……"

"And then there's your private life, if you move into your apartment with Elaine you'll spend every free moment fighting Jackie, her mother and Pascal."

"Don't remind me."

"Once it gets out that Elaine is with you, you'll have trouble with Theresa."

"You think so?"

"I know so, because I've seen the way she looks at you and believe me, you're for the guillotine once she finds out about

Elaine."

"I never thought……"

"On top of all that I've got an unhappy fiancé, wife, Gendarme and Madame Christiane to deal with not to mention Maria."

"Aunt Maria?" asked Henri wide eyed.

"Oui."

"You've not…………"

"Oh, oui, Henri, I have."

"Michel!"

"I know, I know, but I couldn't resist her."

"Mon Dieu!"

"Now I never say 'never', so I propose that we put the business plans on hold for a while, I'll go back to Marseille and you sort out your problems here and then we'll get together again, sometime in the future when everything has settled down."

"Michel, I don't know what to say."

"There's nothing to say because it makes perfect sense."

"Does it?"

"Of course, look, how can we start a successful business with all these distractions?"

"I don't know" wailed Henri.

"It would be foolish to say the least."

"Oui, I must admit I am under pressure at the moment."

"You know I'm right."

"The salon's very busy and I've got a new Italian collection coming in from Rome……"

"Henri, you've got a good business here, look after it, sort yourself out with Jackie and we'll start again sometime in the future."

"OK" he nodded slowly.

"It makes sense."

"When are you going back?"

"We're leaving tonight."

"Tonight?"

"Oui, and by the way, Pascal has made a balls up of the wiring in the house, you'd better get someone in who knows what he's doing before the place catches fire!"

"Mon Dieu! That idiot!"

With many wishes of 'bon voyage' and 'bonne chance' the

cousins embraced and parted. Michel was surprised that Henri had not put up more of an argument but he suspected that he was secretly relieved at Michel's intended return to Marseille. His looming marital problems with Jackie and the very busy salon would focus all his attention and the distraction of a new business venture with his womanising cousin would be too much to cope with at present. Michel left the salon after saying goodbye to Elaine and whispering 'he needs you', which brought a smile to her face, and went straight to the Bar Americaine. He ordered a coffee and sat for the last time at the table in the window whilst gathering his thoughts. When he had finished the drink he went to the pay 'phone and rang Sophia.

"Hello."

"Sophia, chérie."

"Michel, bon, where are you taking me tonight?"

"I'm sorry, chérie, but I've got some important business to attend to."

"Are you going under cover?" she whispered.

"Can't tell you on an open line."

"I understand, chérie" she whispered again.

"Bon, now I'm going to be away for a while but I'll contact you soon, OK?"

"OK, but don't leave me alone for too long."

"I won't."

"Charles and I have had an awful row and he's just gone to Paris to see his lawyers" she moaned.

"Oh, dear."

"He says he's going to get a divorce and he's going to name you."

"Never mind, chérie."

"You will marry me won't you Michel?"

"Of course, chérie."

"Oh, Michel, I don't know what I'd do without you."

"I know, chérie, I'll be in touch soon."

"Au revoir, and do be careful."

"I will, au revoir, Sophia."

Michel returned home to find Josette had finished packing, proof if it were ever needed that she was anxious as he was to leave

Le Touquet as soon as possible.

"Well, what did Henri say?"

"He took it surprisingly well and I think he's relieved that its all worked out this way" replied Michel.

"Bon, well everything is packed and I've 'phoned Eloise and she's delighted to have us stay."

"It's all getting better by the minute."

"And I've 'phoned the agents and our flat is still available, so I told the girl we'd move back in!"

"Bon!" The telephone rang and Josette looked at it for a moment before answering it.

"Hello."

"Bonjour, Mademoiselle, it's Monsieur Gerrard here."

"Bonjour, Michel's here."

"Bon." She handed the 'phone to Michel.

"Hello."

"Bonjour, Michel."

"Oh, Cyril……"

"Monsieur Gerrard s'il vous plait, we're on police business.…."

"We're leaving now" Michel interrupted.

"You're returning to Marseille?"

"Oui."

"Bon, I'll find you as soon as you get back!"

"How reassuring, au revoir, Monsieur Gerrard."

As Michel replaced the receiver he said " let's load the car before anyone else calls." It took no time at all to pack all the cases into the spacious Mercedes. They were just having a last look round their cream home with the peeling paint and faulty electrics when the telephone rang again. Michel answered it impatiently.

"Hello!"

"Hello, Michel, it's Monique."

"Mon Dieu!"

"Michel, you must…….."

"I'm coming back!"

"Oh, bon, when?"

"I'm leaving now!"

"Oh, bon, get back as soon as you can, ma petite, because Mama is ill."

"What's the matter with her?"
"They don't know."
"Oh."
"But they're keeping her in hospital."
"Right."
"Michel I'm so glad you're coming home."
"Bon."
"You are really coming aren't you?"
"Oui, as soon as I can get off this bloody 'phone!"
"Bon, au revoir then, ma petite, I'll see you soon."
"Oui."
"And Michel."
"Oui?"
"I do love you."
"Bon, au revoir." He threw the receiver down and said to Josette "let's go now!"
As he swung the Mercedes onto the road south, he leaned across and kissed Josette lightly on the cheek.
"I'm sure if we'd stayed it would have been a catastrophe" he said feeling very relieved at his decision to leave all the problems that he had created for himself.
"Oui, I agree."
"So it's back to Marseille and a new life together" he said as he accelerated the big car towards the autoroute to the south

Follow Michel and Josette back to Marseille and find out what happens next in:

RETURN TO MARSEILLE

Printed in the United Kingdom
by Lightning Source UK Ltd.
116350UKS00001B/49